BREACHED

K.I. LYNN

BREACHED

INTRO

M Y STORY IS NOTHING BUT DEATH AND DESTRUCTION. THE obliteration of everything I was and those I loved most. For years I existed. Every day I wished for my end. What I never even considered was a rise from the ash.

I'm no Phoenix.

There is no happily ever after for me, only pain until my final breath.

I TOOK A DRAG FROM THE CIGARETTE IN MY HAND AND STARED OUT at the dark loft apartment. It was calm and quiet, with the exception of a little bit of noise from the street below. In the bed beside me was a passed-out brunette.

I didn't know her name. It didn't matter anyway—I was never coming back.

Little groans signaled she was waking back up, and that I'd missed my opportunity to leave.

Fuck.

She reached out and found my thigh, running her hand slowly up and then down.

"Mmm, baby, you really know how to pound a pussy."

Baby.

My stomach turned. A small term of endearment that could either be the first step of clingy, or the less likely—she forgot my name.

I would prefer the latter. Makes my never seeing her again easier.

A different woman every few weeks. They were nothing more than a human fleshlight.

A tool to get off.

"I have to go," I said as I snuffed out the cigarette.

Her hand fell from me as I stood so to locate my clothes.

"So soon? Don't you want to go for another round first?"

"No." Any niceties, finesse, and chivalry I had expressed when we met were gone. Exhaustion took over, and after a fuckfest, I no longer had the energy to keep up the façade.

She balked at me, mouth open and eyes wide before her anger and indignation exploded. She got up and turned the light on.

"Seriously? That's it?"

I pulled my shirt over my head, noticing the way her eyes widened at the large scar on my left side, and I slipped my shoes on.

"Yep."

Fuck and run.

Don't get close.

They're always watching.

"Asshole!" Her shrill scream echoed through the room as she lofted the nearest item—a pillow—at me.

A quick check for my wallet, keys, and phone, and then I looked at her.

"What? Did you think we'd run off into the sunset? Get married? All because you let me fuck you?"

She stared at me, her arms crossing over her chest. "Is a date really too much to ask for?"

I stepped around the bed, stopped right in front of her, and leaned down to run my tongue across her lips.

"Yes."

Matter of fact.

Had to be.

Break down any inkling of more, because there could never be more again.

She cocked her hand back, but I was too far away by the time she swung.

The curses aimed at me could still be heard as I shut the door and walked the few feet to the elevator. When the doors opened, I stepped in and leaned against the far wall, her shrieks drifting away as the doors closed.

How many was it now? Who knew. I stopped counting long ago.

As the anxiety, the PTSD, spiraled out of control, so did an insatiable sex drive.

The doors opened, and I exited into the parking garage. Her hand was on my cock when we pulled in, so I couldn't remember where I parked. It took a few minutes and a lot of clicks on my fob before the lights on my sedan blinked.

Climbing in, I pulled out my phone. It was two in the morning, and I had three missed phone calls.

Before driving off, I looked at the call list—my parents. With a sigh, I hit the button for voicemail.

"You have two unheard messages," the automated voice said before playing the first one.

"Nate, it's your dad." I shook my head and let out a small chuckle. He always started out that way, like I wouldn't recognize his voice. *"Just calling to remind you Erin's birthday is Saturday. We really hope to see you. Call me back when you get this. Love you."*

Backing up, I drove out and headed home. I'd call him back in the morning and tell him I'd go, even though I didn't want to.

Family functions sent me into the worst panic attacks.

Maybe I wouldn't go.

"Hi Nate, it's Jack." My heart stopped before picking up

into a furious tempo. My hands began to shake as my second father's voice came through the phone. *"It's been a while. You haven't been replying to my emails."* Because I can't. Because I have nothing to say. *"I want to get together for lunch this week. I have a proposition for you. Call me… We miss you, son."*

Son.

I clenched my hands around the steering wheel to stop the vibrations, to calm myself.

After everything, he still called me son. It stung. A burning sword of guilt to the gut compared to the pride it used to evoke.

I was the man that got his only daughter killed. The man who should have died.

My body held the scars to prove it.

I drove home, contemplating what he could want, and trying to decide when to call him back. It wasn't like my days were filled with activity. Get up, run, eat, smoke, go to the bar, fuck something or somebody, sleep—my daily routine when I could get out of bed.

For a year I'd rented a studio apartment over some stranger's garage. Contact with anyone I knew was a minimum. Family only if I had to.

Trapped in hell.

My wife was dead. My son was dead. And I should have stayed dead with them.

I died on scene, but they revived me. Every single day since I wished they hadn't.

Recovery from having my body torn apart was long and painful. Chronic pain was just another classified issue in my mountain of problems. The scars, the meds, the migraines, the body aches—all added up to a miserable way of being alive.

Parking in the driveway, I climbed the stairs to my tiny abode. It was just as empty as I left it. The bare necessities.

Nothing and no one else they could take away from me.

I flopped down on the bed, cringing as my scar pulled and my knee protested. Reminders that I needed to do my stretching.

And that was how I lived my life. A stark contrast to a decade ago when I had my love beside me and we were trying to make a family.

When I was happy. When I lived.

My being could not be classified as living. More like the walking dead.

Three years of not working, of existing. Of popping pills all day long to combat the symptoms of my existence.

Every day I lived trapped in the memories. Trapped in the crash. Trapped in the aftermath.

Once an ambitious child, I knew I wanted to be a lawyer after watching shows like *Law & Order*. Later I figured out what I wanted to do and the man I wanted to be.

The end result was far off.

I hated the man I'd become. Pathetic. Broken. Angry. Fucked up beyond any and all repair.

I just wanted to close my eyes and never open them again.

The constant drip of the faucet drove me crazy with each distinct and evenly spaced plopping sound, but at the same time, I couldn't be fucked to get my ass out of bed. One arm was slung over my eyes, blocking out the small slivers of light coming through the edges of my blackout curtains, the other ending in a clenched fist at my side.

The drip seemed to be getting louder, making me cringe at the pain searing through my eardrums.

"Fuck!" I cursed as I flung my arm out and opened my eyes to stare at the ceiling.

I'd hoped an hour after taking my medication things would be better, but there was no calming my migraine. Reaching out toward the nightstand, I blindly patted around looking for my pain meds in hopes that they might be able to help. They probably wouldn't, but they might give me the strength to get up. Six bottles sat on what was actually a side table, my fingers knocking them over as I pulled them to me one at a time.

By the fourth bottle, I found the one I was looking for—Vicodin.

"Shit." The bottle was empty, and I had a vague recollection of taking one before I passed out the night before.

It was another empty day, so nothing pushed me to get up, except the damn drip.

The real question was—how much more torture could I take?

Once I refilled my prescription, I was tempted to just take the entire bottle and climb into bed. It would take a few days for someone to find my body, but at least I wouldn't be stuck in my living hell. A nightmare that never ended.

I let out a long, low hiss as I bent my knee in the first step to picking my ass up from the bed. After lying for hours and not doing my morning stretches, it was pretty tight and stiff. I wondered if it would ever not hurt, but considering my knee was no longer constructed of bone but of metal, I doubted it. My muscles weren't all that happy with the foreign material.

As I stood, I pulled my left arm above my head and leaned

to the side, stretching out the second area that caused horrible feelings. Sometimes, I had a ghost feeling like if I went too far, the scar would burst open, spilling my entrails all over the floor. Evisceration was one way to end it all, but not a very pleasant experience.

Then again, the scar didn't go far enough across my abdomen to reach the level of nasty I was envisioning. It traveled down my ribs, side, and then the twist around my hip.

I was tired of being in pain. Tired of living in hell.

Just fucking end it, then.

It was a thought that crossed my mind almost daily, but for some insane reason, I kept going long past when I should have quit.

Only a few more stretches before I couldn't stand the sound of dripping any longer. Having the kitchen only a few feet from my bed was a huge drawback to having a studio apartment. Every sound the appliances made amplified through the small space, bouncing off the walls. The damn sink had been a motherfucking asshole for weeks, needing just the right angle to stop water flow, and I apparently missed it when I got some water earlier. It took a few tries in the dark, but then finally—silence.

Except the fucking birds.

Jesus, nature was never so annoying before.

Yeah, well, before you weren't a fucking disaster.

It was a very valid point.

Just make the fucking call. Day's not going to get any better.

I craned my neck to the side, cracking it, trying to keep the beast inside quiet.

I'd avoided calling Jack for two days, but any longer and they were all going to show up at my door to check on me, and that was too much socialization for me.

Grabbing my phone, I heaved a sigh and pulled up his number.

"Holloway," a voice said from the other end.

"Hey, Jack."

There was a pause. "Nate...I...I wasn't sure you'd call back."

Stepping to the fridge, I pulled out a bottle of vodka that was just about the only thing on my bare shelves. "Yeah, well... I did."

"Could you do one more step and meet me for lunch on Friday?" he asked.

Lunch? He said it so fast, like he was afraid I'd hang up before he got the words out. I wanted to say no. I had pushed my entire family away after what happened to keep them safe. Meeting him, for something as innocent as lunch, had the possibility of putting him in danger.

They were watching.

They were always watching.

"It's just lunch, Nate." His voice was soft but pleading.

I nodded. "Yeah. Okay."

THE DRIVE TO HIS OFFICE WAS EASY, BUT WITH EACH PASSING mile, my anxiety increased. I couldn't remember the last time I'd seen my father-in-law.

Facing any of the Holloways was difficult. They didn't blame me, even though they should have. I baited the monster and paid the highest price. Haunted by memories and a never-ending vendetta complete with a promise—I would never be happy again.

Death was the only way to be free.

I arrived early, because what the fuck else was I going to do with my day? That left me sitting in my car, people watching. A few minutes before noon, my phone pinged with a text—Jack was running late.

There was no way I was going up. There were many people up there that knew who I was and what I was to Jack, and I hated the looks they gave me. The pity in their eyes.

With the temperature in the car heating up and me in need of a smoke, I got out and leaned against the side. I watched people come and go, moving about their day like it was nothing.

Average people that I envied.

I lit a cigarette and took a drag, then blew it out as I stared at the parking lot. Being the lunch hour, there were lots of people coming and going.

It was sunny out, warm, and as I took another pull, I noticed a woman walking through the lot.

There was no particular reason why she caught my eye. She simply did. Maybe the way the sun lit up her blonde hair.

Intrigued, I stared at her. She was unassuming, skittish even.

Something inside me stirred as I stared at her. The beast inside me pulled at the chains that bound him. She called to him from across the sea of asphalt and cars.

She called to me.

Feelings I'd long forgotten awoke with an interest in her.

But why?

Two men walked toward her, and I watched her change. Shoulders drew up, pace slowed, eyes down as her body went rigid as if bracing herself. From what? An attack?

It was subtle. So subtle, most wouldn't even notice.

But I did, and so did the beast.

She was nothing, no one, but she seemed a mystery I wanted to unravel.

But not. Because nothing good came from me having an interest in anything.

As soon as she passed them, her demeanor returned. Another man came by, and she relaxed.

I wanted her.

The beast wanted her. Some unknown girl, if even for just a taste. Just a small, tiny taste.

The chains that held me in check began to loosen, and just

as I was about to launch myself at her, a hand clamped down on my shoulder.

"Sorry to keep you waiting, Nathan," Jack said, breaking me from the siren's song. His brow scrunched as he looked at me. "Are you all right, son?"

I rubbed at my neck as I tried to get a grip, an understanding of what just happened to me. I'd become completely unhinged by a woman in a parking lot who never even met my gaze.

"I'm fine. Just...lost in thought." *And possibly going out of my mind.*

I glanced back at her to find a woman now walking with her, unaware of me or my internal struggle. Unaware of my strange behavior.

I had no clue what came over me, but it was apparent I needed to stay as far from her as I could. Which would be easy. All I had to do was stay away from Jack's office.

"What did you want to talk about?"

Jack gave me a kind smile. "We'll talk about it over lunch, but I'd like you to come work for me."

My eyes widened, my dick twitching at the thought of seeing that strange girl again.

I shook my head. "No."

Jack pursed his lips and sighed. "Come on. I'll convince you over lunch."

I wasn't so sure about that, but what harm could come from listening to his offer?

A short drive in his car and we were at a pub I hadn't been to since I met him for lunch four years prior. The inside was packed, but there was still some outdoor seating. While it was hot, it wasn't too hot.

"How are you feeling?" Jack asked once we were seated, menus in hand.

My right leg bounced in agitation. I hated being out, and even more so with someone I loved. And while Jack's hair may have gone completely white over the last few years, I knew *they* knew what he was to me.

"Like shit." No sense in saying I was fine.

"Migraines still causing you problems?" he asked.

I scoffed at him. "Jack, if it was just migraines, I could deal, but I'm in pain every single moment of the day. A good day for me is for it to be a low hum that I might be able to ignore."

I pulled out a cigarette and lit it, earning a glare from the woman next to me. What the fuck ever.

"I have a proposition for you."

I shook my head and released the smoke. "No."

"You met with me. You might as well hear it."

I shook my head, my jaw tensing as I glanced around. "I shouldn't have come."

"Nate…"

"It's not safe. I can't…I won't be responsible…" A wave of nausea rolled over me as flashes of Grace popped into the fore-front of my mind.

"You're not responsible for what happened to Grace. They are."

I shook my head. "It's my fault, Jack. I should be with them, but instead, I'm fucking walking on this fucking planet like the fucking bionic man, trapped in hell when I should be six feet under. I was dead, and I should have stayed dead."

He pursed his lips, his brow scrunching as he linked his fingers in front of him. Looking up, he steeled his blue eyes to mine. "Then everyone would be safe? Is that why you're saying that?"

My jaw ticked, and I gave a small nod. "It's the truth."

He blew out a sigh and leaned back in his chair. "No, it's your paranoia. Nate, I'm worried about you. This isn't what Grace would want for you."

"Grace would want to not be…" Fuck, I couldn't even say the word with her name. My wife was dead, but Grace… she was still alive, even if it was only in my cold, dead heart.

"My daughter may be dead, but my son is sitting in front of me, and he needs help," Jack said, his hand reaching up to wipe at his eyes. He pulled an envelope out from inside his suit jacket and placed it on the table in front of me. "I have a position that I think would be good for you."

I shook my head. There was no way. I couldn't do it. Leaning forward, I rested my forearms on the table. "Jack, I can't go back into the courtroom. I tried, remember?" It was a fucking disaster. I lasted two weeks after the accident. After that was when I pulled away. I sold our house, all of our things, and did my best to stay away from everyone I loved.

"This isn't litigation."

Not litigation? I quirked a brow at him. "What, you want me to be fucking support?"

"Transactional attorney," he said, confirming my suspicion. "You'll mostly be going through contracts to make sure there are no loopholes and everything is correct. Secluded, only a client here and there as you explain to them what they see as a foreign language."

I took another drag and held it in. It wasn't the position for me, but then again, I was far off from the man I was.

"Sounds like busy work."

"What else are you doing with your time?"

Fuck, he got me there.

The waiter took our order of drinks and food, giving me a buffer of time, but that didn't stop Jack from staring me down.

"My license lapsed, and I haven't done continuing education in years. There's just no way."

Jack held up his hand. "I'm not talking about now. The position is currently filled."

I scrunched my brow and let out a stunted laugh. "Then why are you offering it up?"

"Because I hope that I will have grounds to fire her soon or that she will quit."

"That bad? How long has she been in the position?" I asked.

"Four years, but between the two of them, I'd much rather keep the other woman who's been doing it two years."

"Other woman?" I asked, then paused as the way he worded it clicked. "Wait, it's a partnered position?"

"Don't worry. Delilah works very hard and is very dedicated to her job."

Delilah? What kind of name was that? How old was she? The name alone sounded ancient, especially since she was obviously born before the song that made it a popular name again. Grace once had it on her list of names for girls, along with a hundred others.

Maybe Delilah moved to the position as a transition from the courtroom.

"There's time, but please, think about it, Nate. I really think it would be good for you."

I nodded and agreed to at least do that. As we ate, the idea grew on me, festered under my skin. The idea of working with the law again perked up a forgotten part of me.

After eating and getting updates on the rest of the Holloways, we loaded back into Jack's car and back to his office.

"Mary wants you to come to dinner."

I shook my head.

He glanced over and grimaced. "Yeah, that's what I told her. She misses you. We all do."

All. The Holloways were my second family from the time I was nineteen—brothers, parents, cousins, aunts and uncles.

"Maybe once you've agreed to take the position, I can then convince you to come to a celebratory dinner."

"I don't celebrate anything," I said. Celebrations were nothing but a reminder of what I lost.

Jack nodded. "Right."

"But I might be convinced to come to a regular dinner." For Mary.

His lips twitched up into a small smile. "She'd like that."

After pulling into a parking spot, we exited his car. I stepped around to say goodbye before heading back to the emptiness of my apartment.

I held out my hand, and Jack narrowed his eyes on me before opening up his arms.

"They're not going to kill me over a hug," he said.

Stepping forward, I wrapped my arms around him. Enveloped in the arms of another person was almost foreign, but my body hadn't forgotten how good such a small sign of affection could be.

"Think it over, and I'll give you a call in a few days. Sound good?" Jack asked as he pulled back.

I nodded. "I'll think about it."

He headed back into his office, and as I walked back to

my car, I found my gaze searching for the woman from before—my enigma. It was best she wasn't there anyway. Better to forget I'd even seen her. Then again, taking Jack up on his offer could result in bumping into her.

Part of me was excited for that, my beast, but the rest of me closed the door on any more thoughts of her.

Climbing into my car, I turned it on and rolled all the windows down to let the hot air out. I sat there, thinking more and more about his offer.

Jack had me by the balls—what the fuck else was I going to do with my time? Just fucking sit around and wait to die? Fucking die of boredom, but at least his way I'd be doing something I once loved, or at least something in the same vein.

My whole life was going to have to change, starting from the outside, if I took him up on his offer. Effort would need to be exerted, strength I hadn't called upon in years, and I would need help from my parents.

I stared into the vanity mirror at my tired eyes and dull expression. Could I even put on a front for eight plus hours a day? Every once in a while was fine, but was it possible to do it all day, every day? If I dug deep enough, called upon the person I was before Marconi and the accident, maybe. Back when I had strength, was cocky as fuck, and charismatic.

It was the only way working at Holloway and Holloway was even a possibility.

Grabbing my phone, I swiped at the screen and pulled up a number a good son would call more often. The phone ringing resonated in my ear, and I waited for someone to pick up.

"*Hello?*" the familiar male voice said.

"Hey, Dad."

"*Nathan? How are you?*"

"Another bad day," I said with a sigh.

"Anything I can do to help?"

Yeah, I'd been that much of a shit of a son that my own father was chomping at the bit for any interaction with me.

It's better this way, the beast reminded me.

"Are you free? I'd like to come over."

I didn't really want to, but if I was going to take Jack up on his offer, I needed their help. Starting from scratch wasn't going to be easy.

"I'll be home in ten minutes."

"Thanks, Dad. I'll see you soon."

I hung up the phone and stared out the window for a moment before throwing the car into drive. Maybe I could do it, but maybe I couldn't. Maybe I should talk to Darren.

Either way, I was giving it the most serious consideration of anything since I woke up from the coma. Something that threw me into the world instead of away from it, and that alone was anxiety inducing.

Six months later…

SAT IN MY CAR.

New car. New suit. New home.

New life.

Almost.

The old one still haunted me, lurked around every corner.

It took Jack hours of back and forth to convince me to take his offer, but in the end, I relented, with conditions. No litigation—that was key. I couldn't do litigation again. Checking to make sure the verbiage was correct and there were no loopholes in contracts? That I could do.

It had taken six months of paperwork and Continuing Legal Education courses to get my license reinstated after having dropped off the face of the earth. In that time, the woman Jack had talked about firing up and left them high and dry one day. He was furious, and helped me get things moving faster.

My heart raced, hands shaking as I sat there waiting for the numbers on the clock to change. Every part of me wanted to run away. But what would I be running to? Back to the black hole I'd been living in for years? At least there was a good chance my mind would be pulled away from my hell.

The parking lot was still pretty empty when a sedan pulled up beside me. I glanced over out of habit, and my eyes widened beneath my sunglasses.

It was her.

The blonde woman I'd seen months ago in the same parking lot. The enigma.

I couldn't help but stare, watching as she threw her hair up into a bun. The frown as she noticed something I wasn't able to see. Couldn't look away when she lifted her hips, dragging her skirt up to her waist. Her thumbs hooked into her pantyhose and pushed them down over her fuck-perfect round ass.

Holy fuck.

My cock was as hard as steel in seconds.

Inch by inch, more smooth, pale skin was revealed as she slid the pantyhose down her legs. She was so innocent looking while doing something so provocative.

Her gaze caught mine, and I couldn't stop my lip twitching up into a smirk. My dick strained against my pants as a blush spread over her skin.

I then startled when she flipped me the bird before climbing out and walking away.

My enigma was cheeky.

Fuck.

Fucking fuck.

I was fucking screwed if she was anywhere fucking near me in the building.

Holloway and Holloway had a non-fraternization policy

that I had *no* interest in breaching. It was one of the reasons I agreed to take on the position.

There was no getting close to anyone because there were consequences. Lives that I would not allow to be lost due to me.

After those sobering thoughts, my dick had thankfully gone down and I headed in to find Jack. Part of our arrangement was that no one who knew me was to speak a word about who I was or how Jack and I knew each other.

As fresh of a start as I could get.

The elevator was packed, and when I got off a familiar face smiled at me, then looked around before going into a neutral expression.

"It's all right, Cassie," I said to Jack's secretary.

She gave me a small smile. "Go on in. He's waiting for you."

I nodded to her. Grabbing hold of the handle, I pulled it open, which happened to be just as Jack was pushing it to step out.

"Ah, there you are."

"Am I late?" I asked.

He shook his head. "No, no, of course not. I was hoping you'd be a bit early so that I could introduce you to your partner before the announcement."

I held my arm out. "Lead the way."

We headed to the stairwell, which surprised me. He looked back at me as we ascended the stairs.

"Mary says I need to get more exercise."

My mother-in-law.

It left me wondering if working there with all the reminders was really going to work.

I tried to smile at him. Faked one, then forced it to look natural.

When we reached the landing, I took in a steadying breath and brushed it all away. The accident, my family, Marconi—pushed aside.

New life.

New beginning.

All channeling the old me.

The one that got me just about anything I wanted. The one I channeled every time I went out to the bar in search of a fuck.

I stood behind Jack as he called a woman in a larger office over. The beast perked up as I noticed the way her voice seemed forced, fake. Much like a voice used over the phone.

"I wanted to introduce you to your new roommate before the announcement was made." Jack stepped aside and ushered me in.

Fuck.

Standing before me was none other than my enigma.

Her mouth popped open, strangely beautiful gray-green eyes wide as she stared at me. It was unnerving, because it felt like she was seeing past the façade.

Fuck.

Not her.

Anyone but her.

"This is Nathan Thorne. He'll need your guidance until he's acclimated to how we operate. Please take good care of him."

"Delilah, was it?" I smirked at her, just as I had in the parking lot, hoping for the same reaction.

Not wanting to be rude, I held out my hand. It took a beat

too long for her to slip hers into mine. A stiff, formal shake, neither wanting to give anything away.

Then we parted, Jack and I heading out.

My hands shaking, heart racing, the beast inside drooling.

Fuck.

The cheeky little enigma was my office mate.

I wanted to fuck her.

Fuck her so hard bent over her desk.

Lusting after my off-limits coworker was a shitty way to start a new job. Hopefully the non-fraternization policy would be enough to keep me in check. Maybe I could make sure she stayed away.

Whatever I had to do to keep my distance.

After hours of announcements, meeting people, filling out forms, and a long lunch with Jack, I returned to my new work-space. The one that held *her*.

"Have a good lunch?" I asked as I glanced down at the half-eaten sandwich sitting next to her along with an unopened bag of chips.

She looked up from her screen, a bit surprised, but after months of quiet, I was sure she was in for a change as well.

"Are you here for the rest of the afternoon?" she asked, skipping over any pleasantries.

I nodded and moved over to the bare desk on the other side of hers. They'd taken two U-shaped configurations with hutches and pushed them together, leaving room for a few fil-ing cabinets between the desk and the wall. Add in a fake tree, a small bookshelf, and two chairs for guests, and what once was a good-sized conference room didn't have a lot of room for anything else.

"Yes. Jack said you would help me get set up."

With a heavy sigh, she nodded and saved whatever she was working on. She stood and maneuvered her chair to my side of the room, slipping it next to my own.

It was my perfect opportunity to test her and to find a way to turn her off from me. If she felt even a little attraction to me, things were going to be bad, because after five minutes I was already having trouble keeping my hands off her.

She's fucking ruining this.

Touch her.

Shut up.

I couldn't stop staring at her as she explained Holloway's intranet, the beast going wild with all the positions to fuck her in. Luckily I could pass off my staring as paying attention.

"Okay, so here's the path to the shared drive. All documents have to be saved out on this drive for backup purposes."

She was leaning across me, dangerously close, directing the mouse around the screen.

Jesus-fucking-Christ.

Touch her.

Shut the fuck up! I slammed my hands against the cage in my mind, eyes locked with his. Wide pupils, his irises almost glowing blue.

The fucking lust for her was fucking me up. I couldn't think straight. "You know, you don't have to climb all over me to get my attention. Lifting your skirt works very well."

I smirked at her, made her remember our encounter that morning. The beast waited to see her reaction. First, there was a jaw tick, but no blush of her cheeks.

Instead, her head dropped and she pulled away from me. "Sorry, I didn't realize there were any voyeurs around. Next time, I'll lock myself up in an empty room to spare you."

She rolled her eyes and attempted to move on, but her words made me and the beast stare at her, unable to understand what she meant.

I cocked my brow at her in confusion. "Spare me?" From what, getting hard?

There was no way she knew how much of a temptation she was to me, and the tone of her voice implied something darker.

"Yes. Temptation is the road to Hell, or at least that's what I hear."

Shit. She couldn't have gotten that any more right if she tried. I smirked at her again, my temptress. "You think I'm tempted by you?"

She blinked at me, her neutral expression shifted to anger. "No, but I don't want to *give* you the opportunity to be tempted by me."

"Why so hostile?" I asked, pushing her further. I had to make space between us, take away any interest she might have. Better for the lust pumping through me to be one way. It would dissipate in time, but I didn't need her teasing me while the high wore off.

She sat back and huffed. "Look, Nathan. I'm here to do a job, not to flaunt my breasts around to catch your eye. I like my job, I like doing my job, and I want to keep it. Plus, I know you *are* not, and *will* not be, interested in a woman like me, so why even try? Now, can we get back to your tutorial?"

She was flustered, annoyed with me, but, again, her words took on a darker tone. It made my pulse tick faster as I tried to understand anything she was saying.

"How do you know?" I pressed.

Her jaw ticked before she turned to look directly at me. "Excuse me?"

"You heard me." I dropped the tone in my voice, allowing my own darkness to leak out. "How. Do. You. Know?"

I wanted to tangle my fingers in her hand and shove her mouth down on my hard cock so she'd see that, yes, my body was definitely interested.

Her eyes bounced between mine, and I saw it again. Her façade slipped, her words little more than a whisper. "Just drop it."

"How?" I asked, pressing harder.

"Why would anyone?" she snapped, her lip curling up before she abruptly stood and ran out of the room.

I sat there, staring at the computer screen, and ran my hands over my face. What was that? Fuck. She was a strange woman, a mystery that intrigued me even more every minute.

I needed to get a handle on myself. Maybe it wasn't a good idea to come back to work. My whole body vibrated with volatile energy, and it took every ounce of strength in me to not lash out or fuck the shit out of her.

Though fucking the shit out of her was one thing the beast and I could agree that we both wanted.

After a few deep breaths, I worked to pull myself together and to calm the fuck down. Being on all the time, acting, used more energy than I expected, and it would take a while to get used to.

It took Delilah more time to return than I expected, but it was a break I needed. I quirked my brow at her as she entered and watched her as she moved to sit next to me again.

"Email and contact list. Then we can see if you have access to the programs IT was supposed to set up over the weekend."

She's just going to ignore it? How odd.

"You're very peculiar, Delilah."

She blinked at me for a moment, then turned her attention back to the computer. "I'm just a woman, Nathan. Nothing special."

Her response stunned me, and the beast, too.

What have I gotten myself into?

TOOK A LONG DRAG FROM MY CIGARETTE AS I SAT OUT ON THE COLD balcony of my new condo and looked out onto the downtown streets. The wind was chilly with the threat of snow, but it didn't bother me. I took one more long drag before I snuffed the cigarette out on the concrete and walked back in through the sliding glass door.

My first day back to work after years, and some woman made me almost blow it in the first few minutes.

The whole situation pissed me off. I didn't want Delilah, not for more than a quick fuck, but due to our working arrangement, that wasn't going to happen. All I had to do was concentrate on work and ignore the call to fuck her until it faded away and she was just another woman.

The problem was getting my body to get with the program. My dick was under the beast's control, wild and uncontrollable. And he wanted her.

I stood in the living room and surveyed the space. My new place was a huge contrast to the tiny studio garage apartment I'd been renting, but a lot was still the same. While the square footage was quadruple or more, the walls were a very similar bare white. No photos, no artwork. No knickknacks.

It was so bare that it made a model home look like a hoarder's house. Even for a bachelor, it was sparse.

But I didn't need *things*. Or people. Or anything.

The goal was one day at a time, so until something changed, my home would remain as empty as I was. The bare necessities to hold life. The walls, floor, and ceiling were like skin, and the inside held what was needed to function, but was otherwise bare.

Just like me.

I stared into the dark family room with no idea of what to do with myself. There weren't many options, but I felt a beer sounded like the best one along with some mindless television. Like with so many other things, I'd lost any interest in what all the different channels had to offer.

Once again, just me, the silence, and the ghosts that haunted me.

Five days in, I was better acclimated to my new job, but no more adjusted to Delilah.

Fuck.

She had me so fucking worked up that I sometimes didn't make it home before I was working my cock.

Fucking hate her.

The hatred for everything about her was so fucking much it drove me into a delusional state of lust.

A shudder rolled through me as I pumped my fist up and down my dick. A cold shower did nothing to kick the overwhelming depravity of my mind and body. She'd corrupted my senses, hijacked my body, and she had no fucking clue.

No clue that I envisioned her on her knees in front of me, taking my cock between her lips. I wanted to annihilate her with my dick, tear her apart with the hatred that consumed me.

"Fucking bitch," I hissed, my muscles tensing and contracting as the pressure built up.

Her perfectly conservative clothes opened up as I watched my cock disappear into her pussy that was stretched to take me.

"Fuck!"

Come all over her, spray her white over and over until she's covered.

Yes!

The vision of pulling my cock from her and coming all over her skin and those fucking skirts was exactly what I needed. I slammed my fist against the shower wall, my cock firing off in one of the most explosive orgasms I'd had in years. Every muscle contracted, my whole body painfully tight as the pleasure whited everything out.

Panting breaths echoed off the tile walls, along with the spray of water as it rained down over my body. I felt lighter, the pressure released, but that itching feeling still continued to crawl around my skin. That basic, overpowering need to feel her wrapped around my dick.

Jacking off did nothing but flare my aggravation. Nothing was going to change, and the situation would continue to grate on me.

Every day I was stuck stewing in that ever-smaller-growing room made my irritation grow. Her scent filled the space, her presence so large there was no way to ignore her, even when she ignored me.

I needed to fuck her solely to stem the curiosity that thrummed through my veins. To shut down the nerves that buzzed for her touch.

She was fucking ruining everything.

Why I promised my father I'd stop by for lunch after my first week of work was beyond reasoning. All my intentions of staying away were brushed aside by the guilt of all the help he'd given me over the past few months.

If it weren't for my parents, I wouldn't have the condo I lived in or the car I was driving. Not for financial reasons, but it was their names on both. I stayed off the radar as much as possible.

My shower did nothing to calm my mood, and I found myself in the closet, jerking hangers of shirts around. I was down to the end of the rack when something on the floor caught my eye. I'd forgotten it was there, forgotten it was out in the open, which was a bad idea.

I stared down at the small chest sitting at the back of my closet. Stared at it almost like I was waiting for it to do something. Transfixed, like it was the most interesting thing I'd ever seen, but it wasn't because of the outside, but what lay on the inside.

The wooden box was filled with the only surviving remnants of my family. Besides a few articles of clothing, the box contained mostly photos and documents. There were also a few mementos, including my wedding band.

I reached out, my heart hammering against my ribs.

Don't! The Beast rattled against the bars of his cage.

The box had been sealed for years, and I shook with just the thought of opening it. Simply moving it to where it sat in front of me had been a huge burden. It took hours of staring at it just to be able to touch it. Why was I suddenly drawn to look?

Stop! We can't. We can't take it.

The problem was, I couldn't stop. My fingers were on the latch.

Don't look! We can't. We can't. We can't!

The panic finally hit me, and I stopped. The shaking moved up my arm, slithered around my chest, and shut every part of me down.

"Grace," I choked out as I stared down at the lid.

I drew in a ragged breath and looked up at the ceiling, forcing back tears that began to fill my eyes. Even the beast was silent, but he heaved in my mind, like the image of her in my mind caused him to physically break down.

I scooted back on the floor and leaned against the wall. I had no idea how the thought of opening the box was in any way a good plan. It never would be. Always a dive into my daily torture and the physical reminders of a life I destroyed.

The shaking continued as I tried to remember what she looked like. The memory of her soft skin, the sparkle of her blue eyes. We were so young when we met, with big dreams.

"What do I do, Grace?" I asked the box.

I closed my eyes and tried to remember her voice, remember our last conversation.

"A boy," I said reverently as I placed my hand on her stomach. We still had a few months, but I couldn't wait to meet him. "What should we name him?"

"Hmm, I don't know. We've never gotten this far, so I've been afraid to even think about names in case I jinxed it."

"Jinxed it?" I grinned at her and shook my head.

"Hey, if someone said I had to wear the same socks for nine months in order for this to happen, I would have done it." She laced her fingers with mine. "We can look up names tonight. Dust off that baby name book."

We never made it home. I remember finding the book as I was getting rid of everything in the house and how I burned it to ash.

That child wasn't the first, but the sixth. The first miscarriage happened while we were still in college. Getting pregnant wasn't planned by any means, and taught us a very important birth control lesson. We were just getting over the shock and sliding into excitement when the cramps and bleeding started. At the time, we took it as a sign, that it wasn't the right time.

It still hit Grace hard and as soon as we graduated, she wanted to try for real. I still had law school to get through, and the thought of a baby then scared the crap out of me. We waited until I was in L3, my third year, making sure I was going to be done by the time the baby was born.

Again, first trimester. At week eleven I got the call in the middle of a finals cram session. I rushed out and found her on the bathroom floor of our tiny apartment, crying.

It happened about once a year after that until finally we made it into the second trimester.

I stared at the box and what it represented, what I'd lost, and what I would never allow to happen again.

After a few minutes, I heaved a sigh and stood. I glanced down at it again, then grabbed a couple of blankets and set them on top of it, shielding it from my eyes, shielding me from the memories.

Once it was hidden under an entire stack of blankets and sheets, I went back to my task of finding a shirt to put on. I was still a bit shaken but managed to rifle through a stack of T-shirts until I found a long-sleeved Henley and pulled it on.

"Shit," I cursed as I looked down at the time. Almost an hour had passed since I entered the closet.

Each episode was a time suck. What felt like only minutes could be hours to the world and almost days to my body.

Physically drained and emotionally wrecked, I headed out to another trying experience. It was always difficult being around my family.

The hard part was going to be when they asked how my new job was going and explaining that I almost lost it due to a woman. Perhaps I'd leave Delilah out of it. There was no reason for them to know about her.

She was no one, after all.

"We expected you an hour ago," Dad said when I arrived at their house an hour later.

I could only nod. "I know, and I'm sorry."

"Is everything all right?" he asked with more than a hint of concern.

I nodded. "I got lost."

"Lost?" He quirked his brow, knowing there was no way I meant the path to their home.

"Swallowed up," I said in clarification.

He regarded me for a moment, then nodded. "How are you now?"

I let out a sigh. "Exhausted."

I froze at the weight of his hand on my shoulder, loving it while at the same time fearing it. "I know it takes a lot out of you. Thank you for still coming."

I gave a stiff nod, and we headed down the hallway to the kitchen where my mom's voice echoed around the room.

"Oh, come on, you silly thing," she said, trying to get some piece of food to cooperate.

"Hi, Mom." I leaned down and gave her a kiss on the cheek.

"Nathan." Her smile was beaming, igniting the guilt. I was an only child, and I'd abandoned my parents for their own safety.

My decisions and actions created a disease that infected everyone I loved, and many others that I knew. I wasn't fit to be around anyone.

CHAPTER FIVE

TWO FUCKING WEEKS OF FUCKING BEING AROUND DELILAH, AND I was a fucking madman. The beast was uncontrollable, banging on his cage, trying to force his way out and into her. I was reduced to nothing more than a monster ruled by my cock.

Every inch of me wanted to be sucked into her pussy, every drop of come splashing inside her.

I hated her. Absolutely fucking loathed her.

It could have been the situation or just the proximity to a pretty pussy, but every five seconds my dick twitched at the thought of bending her over her desk and fucking the shit out of her.

Annoying as fuck, cock teasing woman.

Every day women practically threw their breasts in my face, but the ones I wanted to titty fuck were always conservatively concealed. Somehow, Delilah made conservative sexy. The four-inch heels she wore every day drove me insane, and her skirts just had me clenching my fists to keep from pushing the hem to her hips.

Fucking hard as steel and unable to do a damn thing about it.

Want, the beast said, his pupils blown, exaggerating the wild look in his eyes as his hips rocked against the bars.

Fucking unbelievable. Even your imaginary self is out of his fucking mind.

"Could you not destroy that paperwork?" Delilah asked, her eyes glancing down toward my hand. "I need it."

I looked down to find a stack of stapled papers crumpled up in my hand. "Why is it on my desk if it's yours?" I snarled at her, my eyes slits as I glared at her.

My anger didn't stun her, but her expression slipped to the blank look. That fucking blank look that said so fucking much and nothing at all. That blank look I wanted to fuck off of her. Watch her mouth part, her expression soften before scrunching up as she clenched down around me.

Fuck!

She didn't say anything, just stayed steady under my glare as she held out her hand. I stared at her small, delicate hand and slender fingers, and wondered if she could fist my cock, or if there would be a gap between her thumb and fingers.

I snapped my wrist, throwing them toward her, and moved my attention back to my screen. I could feel her staring at me, probably wondering what was wrong with me, which was something *I* wanted to know too.

"I'm going to lunch," I said as I logged out of my computer.

I couldn't stand to be in that suffocating space with her any longer.

I woke with a start, my eyes wide, drawing in a large, deep breath. Falling down on my side, I attempted to breathe, to force my lungs to fill with air.

My eyes were open, but all I could see was red. The steering wheel off-center. The door was partially gone, and there was a strip of metal in its place. There was blood pouring from my abdomen, from where the metal sliced through me.

Grace.

As my breath calmed, my vision cleared and I stared at the blank, white wall in front of me. It was just a dream, but there seemed to be truth to it. I could feel the weight of her head on my shoulder, could see the car completely crumpled in on her. I didn't know if the vision was real or a product of my imagination, but it *felt* real. It felt like a genuine memory.

The problem was, I didn't have memories past the semi delivering a hefty blow. The next time my mind recorded memory was when I awoke months later from a coma.

A sterile hospital room, completely alone. I couldn't move, and panic set in, confusion over what the fuck was going on spiking my heart rate and setting off alarms. My mouth was so dry it felt like it was coated in sandpaper. When the nurse came in, eyes wide in surprise, I tried to ask what was going on but was having trouble getting any sound out, let alone forming words. I was able to raise my right hand, tubes strapped to my skin.

"Where's Grace?" I had asked.

"Who?"

"My wife."

The nurse's expression dropped. "I'm so sorry... she didn't make it."

The most damaging four words I'd ever heard.

My dream opened the floodgates and memories pouring in, washing over me, drowning me.

Down for months, I missed everything, including seven surgeries to fix my body, and I would need more in the months to come. The doctor came in, but I only caught some of what he said. Tibia and femur displaced fractures, which accounted for the brace. Apparently, I got a knee replacement as well as plates and screws to hold all the broken pieces of bone in my leg together while they healed. Basically, my leg was fucked, and even they weren't sure if it was going to heal right.

Plates and screws had been placed in my arm. Part of my colon was removed and other sections repaired. There was a nick in my hip bone and my pelvis was out of alignment, but besides needing some chiropractic help, my hips overall were fine. Punctured lung and four broken ribs.

Most of the injuries were reserved for the left side of my body, though my right leg had been dislocated at the hip.

My father told me about the car and how the driver's side was so smashed in they were surprised I survived. But I knew he was hiding something. Inside, I knew I had died, but he didn't want to tell me. It was a fact that still haunted me, stared at me every time I looked in a mirror.

My heart should not have been restarted.

Touted as a miracle by the medical profession. They said it had to be my will to live, but the problem was, I had no will to live. I wanted to die, to join my wife, and instead I was stuck between the living and the dead. A purgatory of my own making.

It was all my fault, and no matter how many times someone tried to tell me differently, it would never change the fact that I was responsible. My actions brought down the anger of a very powerful, very dangerous man.

After a few minutes I was able to sit up on the edge of the bed, my vision clearing while I tried to calm the pounding of my heart. That was when I noticed the overwhelming suffocation of the silence.

The sun had barely crested the horizon, so I doubted there was much activity on the streets below. The condo had also recently been updated with energy-efficient, dual-pane windows, leaving the only sound being the blood that pumped through my veins.

I got up and left my room, heading to the kitchen for a glass of water or maybe some vodka. It was Saturday. Nobody could fault me for wanting to get shit-faced at seven in the morning. The vodka could help drown out the nightmare that still had a hold on me.

In the kitchen, I popped open one of the many prescription bottles lying around, this one for Vicodin, and spilled a couple onto the counter. I pulled open the refrigerator and wrapped my fingers around the vodka. I was more than aware that I shouldn't mix the two, but I didn't give a shit. I wasn't driving or operating heavy machinery. The most I'd do is order takeout maybe and push buttons on the TV remote.

I headed to the living room, bottle in one hand and pills in the other. After unscrewing the lid, I slipped the pills between my lips and bottoms up.

The alcohol burned as it slid down my throat. I was thankful for the feeling as I needed it to cover the oppressive numbness that consumed me. After I screwed the cap back on, I set the bottle on the floor and pulled the blanket off the back of the couch and wrapped it around me.

It was going to be a long fucking weekend that I just wanted to silence it all. Drown out the misery, drown out the attraction to Delilah, and drown out the world.

Maybe later I'd go to the club and see if I couldn't find a girl to help me get off. I needed a pussy. Hopefully that would calm down the craving to bend Delilah over her desk.

The combo of pain pills and vodka did the job, sending me back into a blissful, dreamless state. I awoke around noon and ordered some food. One day I would find the grocery store and maybe make my own food, but ordering it to be delivered to my door was so much more appealing.

I didn't leave the couch and spent hours just staring up at the ceiling. With nothing else to do and nowhere else to go, I sat in the emptiness. In the silence, the numbing minutes and hours, the loneliness sunk in.

I'd been able to keep it at bay for years, but for some reason the craving for the soft caress of physical contact was almost suffocating. That itch was the only thing that drove me to get my ass up. That, and the sun had gone down, the only light that filtered in coming from the streetlights way below.

Somehow, I managed to get in the shower. As the water rained down on me, I wondered if every weekend was going to be filled with the same nothingness. The answer was yes. It'd been the same for years, the only difference being that I was working again. I had a schedule, a routine.

That difference, though, was what created the stark contrast of my day-to-day. Constantly surrounded by people, women, talking, wore me down, but it also enhanced the nothingness that was my life outside the office.

By the time I was dressed, the club would just be picking up. I needed a fuck. A hot, rough, get-all-the-fucking-aggression-out-of-my-system type of fuck. A cleansing, mind-wiping orgasm.

The music was loud, the lights low, and the bar packed. As I looked around, there were lots of beautiful women, some even with their eyes on me as they sucked down whatever their fruity alcohol of choice was.

I ordered a beer and leaned against the bar, surveying the place.

"Hi," a female voice rang out next to my ear.

I turned to find a pretty, petite blonde next to me. She had overdone makeup, over-bleached hair, but her full, dark pink lips were enticing. With a short skirt, a lot of cleavage, and on the curvy side, she was just what the doctor ordered.

All I had to do was smile at her, show some sort of interest, and I could have my dick between her thighs in less than an hour.

"Hey." No smile, no look of interest. She wasn't right. The beast was dispassionate, not even responding when someone pushed her from behind and her hand bumped right into my crotch.

Nothing.

"S-sorry," she stuttered as a blush began to cover her cheeks.

Normally, I would have said something like "Trust me, baby, you're all good. You can touch my cock however you want."

Some bullshit to seduce her, to get her thinking about my dick, so it would be easier to get it in. But instead, all that came out was, "It's okay."

She backed away, returning to her pack of friends, and I looked back out at the crowd.

Fuck.

Something was off. Maybe it was me, maybe not. The drinks weren't doing it, the women weren't catching my attention even when they threw themselves at me, and I couldn't understand why.

When the fuck did it become impossible to pick up a woman?

You know when. You've only had one fuck since you first saw her.

I hated that he was right. The weekend after I first saw her was the last time I had a one-night stand. After that, I was working so hard to change my life that the times I did try to go out, I wasn't in the mood or no women enticed me. I was in the mood to fuck, but I did not feel like putting in the effort to charm my way into a pussy.

Seven months of nothing but my hand, and it looked like that streak would continue.

If my sex life had been reduced to my dick pining for Delilah, the next few months would make the first few weeks a fucking cakewalk. Delilah intrigued me more and more each day, which only served to piss me off. I didn't want the pull to her, the attraction that had me waking up with a hard cock every morning.

"Fucking cock-blocking bitch," I grumbled to myself as I headed out to the parking lot.

My fucking dick went from zero to hard in less than two minutes just thinking about her. As soon as I was in my car, I had my dick out. It was so hard, I contemplated going back in and finding that little blonde, but I had a feeling that I wouldn't be hard anymore.

"Fucking Delilah." I slammed my head back against the headrest and ran my fingers down the underside of my shaft.

I was thankful for the dark tint of my windows along with the low light of the alley as I fisted my cock.

Want her lips.

Yes.

Laid out on the desk, her pussy open for the taking.

The tempo of my strokes picked up.

Spear her, spread that tiny pussy. Watch the shine on our dick grow with each thrust. Make her cream all over it.

The fantasy took on a life of its own as I frantically worked my dick. I wanted to hear her moan, scream my name, fucking come all over my cock, forcing my come to explode out and into her.

"Fuuuccckkkk," I hissed as my muscles tensed, my balls drawn up as a spray of white covered my dark shirt.

My chest expanded with hard, deep breaths as my dick softened and the droplets began to soak into my shirt.

I glanced at the clock and blinked in shock. Thinking of her was so powerful it only took two fucking minutes to come.

It was official—I was fucked.

FUCKING, FUCK, FUCK, FUCKING FUCK.

I clicked the pen in my hand in time with the fucks I was spouting in my head. All attempts to ignore her and turn her against me were failing, thanks to the beast.

Fucking drooling, pent-up hunger mixed with rage. That part of me wanted to fucking find out where she lived and decimate her body, just to get it over with.

Yeeesssssss.

"Do you have to do that?" Delilah asked from beside me. The vein on her forehead was almost twitching, and it was the anger and hatred I needed from her, so I continued on.

"It's my thinking tool."

She glared at me. "Well, your thinking tool has me thinking about all the ways I could harm you with it."

I turned toward her and clicked it again, right in her face. "That time of the month, Palmer?"

"You're an asshole. Get back to work." She huffed and looked back down at the stack in front of her.

Asshole. I was on the right track, now to continue to push the issue. "Which leads me to the question: what have you been doing for the past four months?"

She had one of the best death glares I'd ever seen. It excited me more than it should have. God, how I wanted to fuck it off her. Watch it morph into a perfect O as she clamped down on my—

"Hi, guys!"

Fuck.

My insides rolled with the voice—Kelly. It was bad enough the barrage of women throwing themselves at me every day, but the necklines seemed to drop as each day went by. Not that I was complaining about the view of cleavage. No, the problem was that any time I even glanced in that direction, they took it as a sign of interest.

"Nathan, I was wondering if you could help me with something."

Smile on, mask in place—time to act. "What can I do for you?" I asked. It made me sick. I didn't want anyone close to me, least of all the whore parade.

If I offered, I was sure any one of them would sit on my dick with Delilah next to us and the door open. The idea of Delilah being the one riding me flashed in my mind, and the beast growled in approval.

Out of the corner of my eye, I saw Delilah's fingers flex on her stapler. The reaction was just what I needed—annoyance.

Whatever I had to do to push her away. Even if it meant being overly nice to the intruders. It only took a minute of Kelly's tits in my face for Delilah to let out a sigh, snatch up her coffee cup, and stomp out the door. I couldn't make out what she mumbled as she went, but I was fairly certain she was cussing me out.

"What's her problem?" Kelly asked. "She is so weird."

"Is she?"

"You haven't noticed? Such a frigid bitch." Kelly's lips turned down in disgust. "I always hated having a question because I hated dealing with her." She reached out and stroked her finger up my arm. "It's so nice to have you here now."

Her touch was like acid, and I cleared my throat, directing us back down to the contract and her question. Luckily, she didn't seem put off by my change of topic. As much as I hated it, their attention and being nice to them was better than the alternative.

Once I had Kelly straight, she reluctantly left but made sure to sashay her hips on her way out. Getting back into the contract in front of me was hard. Due to the interruption, I'd lost my place. The second I found it, Delilah returned with a fresh cup of coffee in hand. She glanced around, her frown softening but her scowl of annoyance still firmly in place.

"Which girl do you have your sights set on?" she asked as she sat back down.

"Excuse me?" I asked, both for clarification and because for some reason, I couldn't keep my fucking eyes off her ass.

"Which one? They've all been vying for your attention," she said, obvious disdain or disgust written all over her face. I couldn't tell which emotion it was. "Each wondering which one of them you'll pick to screw first. I'm amazed they're throwing themselves at you, not even caring about their jobs."

I paused and looked at her. "You're talking about the non-fraternization policy."

She nodded. "Holloway is very strict on it now, ever since the Antonio and Karen incident. Lots of drama and problems there as a result. So, now they get rid of one or both parties.

That's why it surprises me so many of them are willing to give up their jobs for your junk."

My junk? I thought as my lips drew into a smirk. "I do have pretty impressive junk."

That we want to show you.

Shut up. I'm not going there.

A snorting sound left her, and she rolled her eyes. *"Please."*

Sounds like a challenge to me.

"Do I need to prove it to you?" I stood up and pulled at the loop of my belt.

Instead of staring, watching, and waiting, she hid her eyes behind her fingers. "Keep it in your pants, Casanova."

Good girl.

"I'm surprised you care about them," I said as I sat back down.

"I don't."

"Then don't worry. One of the reasons I agreed to come here was because of their strict enforcement of no office fraternization." But it hadn't fucking worked. They didn't seem to care. "I thought it would keep them away, but it doesn't seem to be enough." I let out a low sigh and stared at my computer screen. Why couldn't they just leave me alone? All they did was exhaust me in a situation I was already having enough trouble conquering.

"Do you want me to throw you a pity party because women are throwing themselves at you?"

The energy dropped from me—I couldn't keep the act up anymore. I knew my expression was empty by the time I turned toward her.

It was bad. By the simple way her lips parted, I knew there was no hiding the darkness that took over with each breath.

"They should all stay away from me," I managed to hiss out.

I was up and out of my chair, walking through the door without a word. There was no destination. I just had to get away. From them, from her, from every living, breathing person.

Everything was coming undone. With each step, I crumbled.

Grace.

No!

Her smile, her touch.

The stairwell came into view, and I slammed through the door before racing down the steps.

9 flashed by, then 8. Around and around, my leg protesting. 7, then 6. I couldn't stop. Not until I reached the bottom.

When I broke through the door and out into the cold air, I ran around the side of the building, away from anyone who could see. My lungs burned, arm tucked against me and around my stomach. Everything was on fire, a tearing pain. Flashes of the accident, of waking up, of the reality of my loss.

A scream let loose, unable to be contained as I fell against the side of the building.

Pain. Nothing but screaming, searing pain consumed me.

My slip intrigued Delilah more than I wanted, more than I needed. Her attention, as sly as it was, didn't go unnoticed. It forced me to work harder at containing my inner turmoil.

The problem was her. When I did catch her staring and our eyes connected, it was almost like looking into a mirror. Her eyes were blank, empty of emotion and devoid of light.

No. No. No.

Yes. She's just like us. Broken. Empty. Want her.

Stop it.

I'd arrived earlier than normal, the office even more empty than I was used to. Delilah's side was vacant, which was odd as she usually made it in before me.

Standing in the doorway, I stared at her desk, at her chair.

What the hell am I going to do?

Take her.

I can't.

Take her!

"Stop!" I yelled out, slamming my fist against the doorjamb, my chest expanding with labored breaths.

I walked around my desk and grabbed my coffee cup. Calling up all my strength, I took a deep, steadying breath to right myself, an action that almost faltered when I glanced out the window and saw Delilah climb out of her car. I knew it was her simply because she always parked in the same spot, which was right next to my car.

I can't do this.

You know how to make things easier.

You are no fucking help.

If I was helping, you would LET ME OUT!

Banging of metal bars clanged in my mind, making me cringe.

Talking to myself, envisioning a stalking, deranged version of myself locked in a cage in my own mind probably wasn't considered sane, but I'd long ago given up on any notion of sanity.

The beast was a part of me, but was too uncontrollable to be let loose. With tight chains, I bound him. With bars of steel, I contained him. With sheer will, I silenced him.

Two cups of coffee retrieved, and I was able to get back and set them down before she made it up.

"Morning," she said with a yawn. It was obvious the long hours had gotten to her. With Friday, our work week totaled over fifty hours apiece.

I held one of the cups up. "Coffee?"

She quirked her brow and looked from it to me. "Is it poisonous?" she asked.

Poisonous?

Poisonous?

What the fuck? Where the fuck did that come from? Had I done too good of a job of pushing her away?

I chuckled, stunned. "No, Delilah. Fresh brewed."

She cautiously reached for the cup. "Are you buttering me up for something?"

"No." I let out a sigh and shook my head. "I saw you walking in when I was heading to get a cup of my own. With as much as you drink, I figured you'd need one."

"Oh." She took hold of the cup and held it up to her lips. "Sorry… Thank you."

She smiled at me. It was almost real, or at least part of it was. Enough so that I found my lips pulling up in response before clearing my throat and returning to as neutral of an expression as I could muster.

"Don't mention it," I said as I returned my attention back to the never-ending stack of papers on my desk.

That was the moment I realized that she held the power to breach my walls with a simple, real smile.

FLIRTING WASN'T WORKING.

It was a stupid idea. Flirt with all the women but her. Show her I was attracted to them.

Not her.

Never Delilah.

She made my blood fucking boil. Just sitting next to her was a slow torture, but an agony I endured for some unknown reason.

Fuck. I should have told Jack "No." Been more insistent about it.

I needed a fucking drink. A strong one.

Headlights in my rearview mirror caught my attention. Six miles they'd stayed close, and it could have been a coincidence, but maybe not. Four years of looking over my shoulder had honed my awareness of my surroundings. I'd become a paranoid motherfucker, but with good cause.

Killing Grace and leaving me at death's door wasn't enough for Vincent Marconi—it was only the beginning. I was right where he wanted me; locked in a purgatory of my own making.

My wife was dead. My son was dead. I was the living dead.

A few blocks from my building, the car pulled into the right turn lane, and I caught a glimpse of an SUV that looked full of kids before it drove away.

After parking my car in the lot, I started walking instead of going in. I'd seen the neon sign of a bar the other night, and I desperately needed a drink.

A couple blocks down and one over, I found my oasis, and it was within a short walk of my condo. Beer, booze, anything to numb my mind and my body from all the thoughts of the intriguing grayish green eyes that haunted me. Their emptiness that could pierce me and call out to my own emptiness.

The neon lights of the bar welcomed me, drew me in, and sang me the siren song of drinking away my troubles. The problem was the blonde my eyes immediately found sitting at the bar. A shudder moved through her as I stood, staring at her. She shot me a sideways glance, but it wasn't needed because of this damn current that seemed to move through us.

Fucking fuck fuck fuck!

You have to be fucking kidding me!

Why was she everywhere I went?

"Can I get a Dos Equis?" I asked the bartender.

As much as I tried to ignore it, push past it and her, it never got any better.

"Palmer," I said as I slid onto the barstool beside her. I slipped on a smirk, something to deter her from any desire to speak to me.

"*Thorne*," she replied with more than a little annoyance in her tone.

It was exactly what I wanted, but for some reason, it rubbed me wrong.

"What brings you here?" I asked.

She didn't even turn to look at me. "I'm here every Friday. Why are *you* here?"

"I needed a drink. I just spent the last hour trying to lose Kelly. I think she was trying to find out where I live."

She let out a sigh. "And of course you had to land in my bar."

"Does it have your name on it?" I asked, just to be a smart ass.

She glared at me and was about to say something when John interrupted with my drink.

"Here you go," he said as he set the bottle down. "Wanna start a tab?"

I nodded. "Sounds good."

He turned to Delilah. "Lila, you good?"

She tapped her finger on the glass in her hand. "One more."

The name threw me off, and when he left to make her drink, I leaned on the bar, sliding a little closer to her.

"*Lila?*"

"Short for Delilah."

I took a sip of my beer. "I've never heard anyone call you that nickname."

"Only Caroline at the office does. Delilah is more professional, so only my friends call me Lila."

Friends. Where were all her supposed friends? She sat beside me, in a bar, all alone, and from the familiarity between her and the bartender, it was a regular occurrence.

We sat next to each other in silence, my attention trying to stay on the basketball game on the screen in front of me and not on the few inches that separated us. It was a dangerous situation to be in, especially with how obsessed I'd been with her.

I finished off three beers as Delilah sipped her way through her drink. A firm grip on my bottle was all I had to stop me from reacting to the current that moved between us, from dragging her to the back and fucking her like I'd dreamt of for weeks.

"Well, I'm out," she said as she signaled to the bartender for her tab.

I watched her, the loose way her body moved, the drooping of her eyes. She was relaxed, tired, and a prime fucking target the moment she stepped out those doors.

"See you Monday, Thorne," she said, then let out a small giggle. "Thorne…in my side."

It was barely audible, but I heard it. There was no way I was going to let her walk or drive wherever she was going, so I called for my check and quickly followed her out.

By the time I made it outside, she wasn't very far ahead of me, her steps slow and wobbly. I kept my distance, not wanting to tip her off. As we passed by an alleyway, she caught the attention of two men standing in the dark.

MINE!

They stared after her, whispered words I could barely hear, but it was clear they were drunk and up to no good. I glared at them, waiting for them to move toward her so I could beat the shit out of them for even looking her way. When they finally glanced around to probably see if it was clear to go after her, they saw me.

My hands were balled into fists as I stared them down, daring them to move a fucking inch toward her. They backed down, slinking back into the dark, and I continued to follow her.

She was a fucking idiot. Walking down the city streets, in the dark, drunk off her ass. It practically screamed to the world that she was vulnerable and ripe for the picking.

Very ripe, the beast purred.

You're no fucking help.

We would have ripped those guys apart. Then ripped her pants off and spanked her.

After a few blocks, her spine straightened, and she turned to look behind her.

For the first fucking time in a few fucking thousand feet.

"Are you stalking me now, Thorne?" she asked as she walked backward for a few steps, then turned back around, her feet unsteady as she righted herself.

"You wish, Palmer," I lied. "I'm headed home myself, and making sure you get home all right in your drunken state. Last thing I need is to be implicated because your drunk ass was last seen with me before you disappeared or wound up dead."

"I can take care of myself. Don't worry your pretty little head." She stopped in front of a building and grabbed hold of the door.

A very familiar building.

"Well, I'm home, so off you go."

Fuck my life.

It was *my* building.

I followed her in, cursing whatever fate put us so fucking close together. She waved to the night guard, whose name I hadn't gotten yet. I gave him a nod and continued behind her into the awaiting elevator.

If there were erotic nightmares, I was fucking in one. Where you were hard all the damn time and you couldn't fuck the girl, so you were left in an almost constant state of blue balls. That about summed up my life from the day I met Delilah Palmer.

"Seriously, Thorne, you can go home now."

It was so hard not to grab her and pin her against the wall.

Do it.

No.

Her aggravation amused me, and I let out a chuckle as I leaned down to her ear. "I *am* going home."

Smells so good. Taste her. Lick her neck and fucking taste her!

She staggered, and I reached out to steady her. The gasp that passed her lips didn't go unnoticed, especially when it turned into a moan. Neither did the humming that moved between us where I held her. My whole body tightened, even my grip on her.

"Do you really live here?" she asked.

The beast rattled in his cage, unrelenting, angry, and lust filled. It took every fucking ounce of strength I possessed not to give in, to drag her up to my condo and give in to the overpowering force of my dick's will.

"Fourteenth floor."

"You're telling me I can never get away from you?" she asked as she looked up at me, her eyes glassy from the alcohol.

"What, you think because we live in the same building that I'm going to come find you?" I ripped my arm from her. "Dream on, Palmer. You're not that pretty."

The words were to put her off, to get her to respond by slapping me or getting angry. Despise me. Hate me. Anything to make an inch of space between us.

But she flinched instead, stumbling back, head down, as she refused to look at me. "I know that, asshole."

A chuckle bubbled up, but then ice raced through me. "Wait…What? You're agreeing with me?"

There was no way she could be serious, but by the way the beast rattled inside me, I knew she was.

The one person to tempt me in years, to draw me in like no other and make me beg for mercy, my enigma, thought she wasn't pretty? She was beyond pretty. Gorgeous. A broken beauty whose water-filled eyes tore at my chest.

"Of course I am. I'm not stupid," she said, her teeth clenching as her bottom lip quivered. "I know I'm plain, boring and a workaholic…useless."

Her hand flew up, covering her mouth, but the damage was done. Literally. Darkness poured out of her, despair and loneliness radiated. The beast clawed to be closer, to absorb it all.

I wanted to comfort her, but I couldn't. So I stared as she rocked, one arm across her chest like she was holding herself together.

"Lila?"

I started to reach out, but stopped myself, balling my fingers into a fist. It was the space I needed.

She sniffed and attempted to smile, but it was a poor attempt. Even more so if she was actually trying to divert attention away from what she just revealed.

"Sorry, I'm a depressed drunk." Just then, the elevator chimed for her floor, the doors sliding open. "Have a good weekend."

My mouth popped open to respond, but I had no words and the doors closed. All alone and suddenly feeling even worse, the guilt eating at me. Something hurt her, and I had a feeling there was so much more than she was letting on. There was so much pain, so much anguish pouring from her.

I wanted to give her peace, but it wasn't my place. In fact, I had no place. Not in the world and certainly not in her life.

D ELILAH'S IMPROMPTU CONFESSION DID NOTHING TO SWAY MY curiosity. In fact, it flamed the fire of her draw.

I just wanted to make it through the day, just one day, without thinking about her, but she was always fucking there, in my periphery. The smell of her perfume was a constant torture. If we weren't office mates, working together and she was just some girl at the bar, I could fuck her, get her out of my system, and be done.

Instead, I was left ready to explode like a ticking time bomb, just waiting to go off at any moment. Anger and frustration mounted, and the sight of her made me furious.

I resented her, absolutely despised her for making me want her in the first place.

I didn't want the need that churned inside me. I didn't want the crawling hunger to fuck her like she was the last fucking woman on the planet. I didn't want to crave her with her pretty vacant eyes and her plump, perfect all.

I didn't want *her*.

Liar!

Shut up!

Arguing about it with myself wasn't helping either, because the beast vibrated in his cage as wave after wave of agonizing desire rolled through him, leaking into me. I couldn't get a grip, slowly losing my mind to the insanity within. All because I hungered for the taste of one woman.

It was all made infinitely worse because I woke up late and didn't have time to get off before heading to work. Meaning it was a simple equation—me turned on plus Delilah in my vicinity equaled a fucking recipe for a catastrophic explosion if I didn't watch myself.

Turned out it would have been better if I'd been ten minutes late.

Better for my sanity, which was slipping. Bad enough I had Delilah on my mind, but of course she was wearing the skirt that drove me wild. It was a black pencil skirt with a flirty hem that hugged her body perfectly.

It was not the day for a distraction, but all I could think about was catching her, pulling that fucking skirt up and plowing into her. My cock had been between semi and full hardness all day. I could barely concentrate on the case file in front of me, having stared at the same piece of paper for almost an hour. So unfocused that I told Jennifer we'd have an almost unattainable task done in two days.

"Jesus-fucking-Christ, Nathan!" Delilah snapped. "I would like to leave sometime this century."

We'd been at each other's throats all week, annoyances grating and compressing against the four walls that surrounded us. The building was long empty, even from the cleaning crew.

I narrowed my eyes on her. It wasn't all my fault we were there so late. I wanted to go home as well.

"Well, I do believe this is your fucking fault for telling Jack we could have all of these contracts done by Friday morning!"

"Yes, well, it wasn't a fucking problem until you told Jennifer we would have her contracts for the Sampson takeover ready by Thursday!" she snapped back.

Jennifer was the most annoying of my admirers, and the most aggressive. I didn't know if it was her tits fucking staring at me or my cock twitching with each annoyed sigh that passed Delilah's lips, but something distracted me from realizing just what I agreed to.

"If you had informed me of your agreement with Jack, we wouldn't still be here," I hissed, my lip twitching up toward a snarl.

She slammed her fingers on the keyboard in front of her. "If you read your fucking email, you would have known."

Three "fucks" from her beautiful mouth and I was no longer half-cocked.

"You're saying *fuck* a lot tonight, Delilah. Something on your mind?"

She turned to me, that fucking annoyed glare that only set the beast off more.

Tick.

Spank her. Bite her. Shove my cock down her throat. Fuck her.

Tick.

YES! Finally we can have her!

"Get your mind out of the fu—just get moving so we can leave, okay?"

I couldn't stop my mouth from drawing up. First one side, then the other, my tongue slipping out to wet my lips. I watched her cheeks turn pink as she attempted to avoid me.

Each ticking second that passed, I felt the beast's arousal roll through me. Hairs stood up on my arms, a ripple flowed down my spine, my hips shifting.

Sanity was gone. Control obliterated. All that remained was *want*. All movement and thought taken over by desire and a need that was on a cellular level.

"With all the times you've said 'fuck' tonight, I think I know what you really want. What you need, *Lila*."

Me.

She shifted in her chair, her spine straightening, but the way her thighs rubbed together didn't go unnoticed. "What is it that you think I *need*?"

"Cock." No fucking pussyfooting around the issue. "You need a fucking hard cock in your tight little pussy."

My fucking dick shoved all the way in, making you cream all over it.

A shudder rolled through me. All that kept me in place was the death grip I had on the chair. The last bit of reasonable thought I had left in me.

Her demeanor shifted between many things, probably wondering what game I was playing. No game, only a seemingly unquenchable hunger for her.

Her mouth popped open in the most perfect O. Lips that begged to have me rub the tip across them.

"You're an expert on what my pussy needs?"

Fuck.

Fucking fuck. My dick was about to burst through my pants. My veins were overloaded with lust, and I didn't know how much longer I could hold myself back.

"Yes, and it needs a cock to fuck it."

"What makes you think this?" she asked. Her voice was

slow, unsure, her posture shifting. I didn't know if her head bowing was a conscious move or her body responding to the aura my own put off.

"I can tell."

I could. She was responding to me, fucking calling me to her.

She straightened again in a willful attempt to break out of the powerful energy that consumed us.

"Well, fucking finish so I can go home and get off with my B.O.B. He might not be flesh and blood, but he gets the job done."

I imagined her legs spread, one hand on her tit, the other slipping a vibrator across her clit. Her body jumping at the intense pleasure that jolts through her, before slipping the tip of the vibe between her pussy lips, filling her.

My brain short circuited, the vision of her playing with herself the final blow, leaving me defenseless to my own greed.

I was around my desk and pulling her from her chair, slamming her against the wall before I even comprehended it. I had her arms pinned above her head, ready to break her body like she'd broken my will.

MINE! *Mine!*

Her body arched into mine, a desperation flowing from her that fed into my own.

"Does that turn you on?" I asked in a whisper against her ear.

Shuddering breaths left her, a soft cry as she searched out my mouth. Her eyes were heavy, and I was certain they were close to matching my own.

"My, aren't you a naughty girl, panting for it," I taunted her. "Tell me, Delilah, are you a dirty whore that likes to be fucked?"

An open-mouthed gasp, hips searching out the one thing that could help us both calm the madness within.

"Answer me." I pulled her arms above her head with more force than I should have. "Are you a dirty whore that likes to be fucked?"

I heard the words coming from my mouth, but could hardly believe them. They were always there, hiding, but my anger and hatred toward her brought them to life. She was responsible for my descent into a new level of hell. Her call, her scent, and her submission were all elements that set me off.

She sucked in another ragged breath, eyes completely glazed over. "Yes."

Her acceptance gave complete control to the beast.

I had her body pinned as I leaned forward. Soft, supple lips yielded to me. She arched into me, a little moan that made my fingers flex harder into her skin.

Every cell ignited at the contact. If I'd felt desire before, then I had no idea what had a hold of me. I didn't kiss her, I devoured her.

She had a wet, delicious mouth that I couldn't get enough of. Lips, tongue, teeth—all instruments of my consumption.

I didn't remember letting go of her hands, but shock shot through me as she tugged on my hair. A growl moved through me, vibrating from me into her as I gripped her waist.

Stop.

There's no stopping now.

I have to stop before this goes any further.

We're going to have her.

"Harder."

All attempts to rein the beast back in was obliterated by

her breathy request. With a flex of my arms, I lifted her from the ground, her legs immediately wrapping around my waist, pulling my cock right against her pussy.

The feeling was beyond anything I'd ever felt, and I wasn't even inside her.

I grabbed onto her shirt and pulled, the need to see what seemed to be the only fucking pair of tits hidden from me fueling me. Buttons flew in every direction as they tore away from the fabric.

Once again, she surprised me by making a basic, white bra the sexiest piece of clothing I'd ever seen. I grabbed her tits, soft and supple in my hands, making my hips press into her in a slow, rocking motion. Her nipples were hard, and I moved the fabric away, revealing them and their blush color. A shocked gasp came from her as I pinched and twisted them.

"You have beautiful breasts. Fucking perfect, perky tits."

And I needed them in my mouth. I loved the feel of her hardening nipples on my tongue, the stiff peaks as I flicked them. Her reactions, her high-pitched sighs and humming moans, spurred me to use my teeth. To bite and mark her skin. Little nips all over her chest as I pinched her nipples.

Her whole body shook, hips grinding down on my cock, rubbing her clit against me.

"Please, Nathan."

I bit down on her shoulder as my finger dug into her hips. Fuck, I needed her to say that again.

"Please what, Delilah? I don't know what you want if you don't say it."

I smiled at her and stopped all movement. The furrow of her brow and little growl of annoyance let me know she didn't like me stopping, but I wasn't moving until she said it.

"Please, take out that big hard cock that I can feel you hiding, and fuck my pussy with it."

"*That* was fucking sexy," I said before ripping my own shirt open.

There were only a few pieces of fabric that separated us, and their barrier pissed me off. I wanted inside her, and as I wrapped my hand around her panties and pulled, I felt just how ready she was for me. The seconds it took to open my pants was too much, but the feel of her slick pussy against my shaft obliterated the annoyance to get there.

"Is this what you want?" I asked. I loved the desperation I saw in her eyes.

"Yes."

I grabbed onto her hips and moved her above my cock. "Then fucking take it."

It was like my cock knew exactly where to go. No fumbling, just straight fucking in. Her pussy sucked me in like it was starving. Hot and wet and fucking heaven.

So intense, it took me a second to recover before pulling out and shoving right back in so hard the wall rattled.

"So deep!" she cried out.

How right she was. Looking down, I watched the entire length of my cock stretch her pussy open and disappear inside her. My mind was clouded by the sheer level of pleasure, each thrust magnified by her high-pitched moans.

I continued to slam into her. My muscles burned, but nothing could stop me from fucking coming inside her. Relentless hunger slammed me forward, driving me deeper, driving me to the edge that would release my sanity.

She closed her eyes and turned away. It happened at the same time her pussy got tighter, and there was no fucking way

I wasn't going to get to see her come face.

I let go of her leg and grabbed onto her jaw, forcing her gaze back to me. "Open your eyes. Don't you dare look away." I needed to watch her as I made her come.

"Can't...too much."

Her little whimpers only made me harder. "You will. Even when I make you come and you're screaming my name. Or I won't let you."

She tightened again, glassy eyes locked with mine as her whole body tensed, jaw going slack.

"Nathan," she screamed as her whole body shook, her pussy contracting around me.

Yesssss!

It was hard not to close my own eyes as I continued to drive into her. She was so fucking tight around me, and I gave her no pause as I reveled in her warm, wet, fuck tight pussy.

"Good girl. Fuck, that was so fucking hot. You feel so good when you come around my cock."

I leaned forward and pressed my lips to hers, my hips driven by the need to fill her with my come. The need to devour her had me nipping down her jaw and neck, the need to mark her had me sinking my teeth into her neck hard and deep.

High pitched squeaks echoed in my mind, my balls drawing higher as she became wetter.

"So fucking good," I whispered against her skin. My mind was blank as everything in my body tensed, rocking the final strokes as a harsh mixture of pain and pleasure shot through me. I slammed into her, my cock jerking against her walls as the head of my cock jammed against her cervix.

Mine!

I felt her walls pulse around me as the twitching of my cock slowed to a stop. The high began to wear off, and my mind cleared. My mouth was latched onto her shoulder, teeth clamped onto her skin. I released her as my chest expanded in deep, labored breaths.

All strength left me, but I kept hold of her as we slid down to the ground. I leaned forward, pressing my forehead to hers. With each intake of air, my mind cleared, wiping away the haze. My body was wiped, drained of all the turbulent energy. After a minute I reached between us to pull out. Wet droplets, a mix of our come, brushed against my fingers and fell to the floor beneath us.

Fuck.

I focused my eyes on hers, and dread began to seep in.

Fucking fuck. "Shit."

She looked like a fucking rag doll. Her hair was everywhere, clothes torn, body limp, and the look was completed with empty eyes.

A pressing need to get away from her sparked a wave of energy, and I stood. I frantically shoved my dick back in my pants and belted them back up.

"Shit. Shit. Shit."

What the fuck did I do? What the fucking fuck did I do?

What we needed to do. We filled her.

"Shit."

I pulled my suit jacket from the coat rack and pulled it on as I paced the small room.

I fucked everything up.

We made everything right.

No! This wasn't supposed to happen!

I stared down at her, chest heaving, full of anger and

disbelief. She made me lose all control, all ability to contain the beast and my desires.

This is all her fucking fault.

Everything was as it needed to be, and she came along and fucked it all up.

The need for an outlet took hold, and I grabbed the coffee cup sitting on the edge of her desk and hurled it toward the wall with all my strength. It shattered into many pieces.

"Fuck!" I yelled before rushing to the door and flinging it open.

I had to get away. I had to leave.

What have I done?

THE MOMENT I STEPPED THROUGH MY DOOR, I TURNED EVERY lock and leaned against the heavy metal.

Fuck.

Fuck.

Fuck.

What the fuck did I just do?

What we've been dying to do.

I shook my head, then slammed it back against the door.

My dick was still hard, wanting to go another round, ready to fill her again. It didn't understand the gravity of what I'd just done, only the pleasure.

It wasn't like any other time over the past four years. No charisma to charm my way into her panties and leave her soon after. I was out of my mind, overcome with a powerful need.

High strung, out of control, and the next thing I knew I had her pinned to the wall.

I *forced* myself on her.

What the fuck is wrong with me?

We didn't.

Yes, I did.

She wanted it, begged for it, creamed for it.

"Stop!" I screamed out. My arm swung forward to punch the invisible version of myself and crashed through the wall instead.

It took a moment for the shock to settle in, for me to see my fist stuck inside the broken bits of drywall. Then came the pain, my knuckles aching. I relished in it as some sort of penance, even though small, for what I'd done.

It felt like the blood had fallen from my face, strength leaving me as the oppressive guilt covered me. With heavy steps, I made my way to the kitchen and straight for the fridge and my good friend Ketel One.

The first sip burned, the second less so as I walked to the bedroom. I began stripping off my clothes, tossing them on the floor in disgust, the missing buttons from my shirt another sign of my indiscretion.

I sat on the bed and climbed back to lean against the headboard. Another swig and I found myself staring at the wall.

For years I hated my life, but I had never hated myself so much. When did I lose every semblance of the person I once was?

The bigger question—what now?

Now we take her again, the beast said.

"No." I wasn't going to even entertain that thought. My fuck-up was on a monumental scale, and I knew I would have to pay.

Hours later my alarm blared, an annoying beeping sound that echoed off the walls. I reached out and turned it off as I shifted to put my feet on the floor.

In the bathroom, my bloodshot eyes stared back, accentuating the blue. I didn't sleep. At all. Fear gripped me. Regret filled me past the overflow line, drowning me. What was I going to do? How was I going to face her?

It shouldn't have happened. Ever. But it did. I fucking lost it.

I came inside her.

Jesus.

It felt like a snake crawled around my chest and began restricting my heart. Hours of nothingness, and it hadn't hit me. I didn't think it could get worse, and the realization that I'd fucking emptied my balls into her made my anxiety spike as well as my dick.

Marked her. Filled her. Bred her.

"Shut up and go back to fucking sleep," I said and let out a hard sigh.

I started up my stretches and noticed some muscle aches I wasn't accustomed to. It was another bit of proof that the previous night had indeed happened, even though I hadn't forgotten. What I'd done to her, the way I fucked her, was with so much energy and force that I'd overworked some obviously underused muscles.

After a quick shower, I threw on a clean suit before heading out the door. It was still early, the traffic light and the sky dark. When I pulled up the parking lot was mostly empty, but there were cars starting to arrive.

Hers wasn't there, giving me a little time to try and figure out what to say to her, even though I'd had all night for that.

The light to our office was off, and I flicked it on. All the evidence was still around the room, nothing changed from when I'd stormed out. The coffee cup I shattered lay in pieces on the ground. There were buttons everywhere, and flashes of her breasts filled my mind.

I let out a sigh and hung my coat up. Going down on one knee, I picked up the ceramic bits. Luckily, it seemed to crack into mostly larger bits, but each one was still a reminder. I scanned for buttons, not knowing a total, just knowing I needed to pick up as many as I could find. Anything to wipe away the memory.

But that was an impossibility. The simple act of looking at the wall instigated the feel of her in my hands and the taste of her on my tongue.

Thankfully there weren't many people in the office, leaving me a clear path to the breakroom to throw all the scattered bits away. No one to stop me with curious eyes and questions I couldn't answer.

What the fuck am I going to say to her?

That she's ours now.

For the last fucking time, you know that can't happen.

Mine.

The muscles in my neck tightened and I reached back, fingers digging in as I stretched my neck. I'd closed my eyes as I tried to work out the tightness, and when I opened them I could see a figure standing just inside our office.

I stopped right at the door, Delilah just in front of me. My eyes widened as I waited for her reaction. Slap me, hit me, yell at me, threaten me—whatever she needed to do, I would accept.

Instead, she stared back, with none of the emotions I was expecting. There was something there, but it came across as desire, and there was no way after what I did that could be true. I was confused, stunned even, but lost for words.

I moved to my desk, unable to look at her. "Good morning."

I woke my computer, the contract I'd hastily left still up on the screen waiting for me. She remained silent, and I attempted to read over the contract, to find where I'd left off, but the words were just gibberish. When she leaned over, stretching her neck as she looked down, I saw it—an angry-looking purple mark on her neck. It peeked out from the collar of her shirt, and I couldn't stop staring, knowing exactly what it was.

The incident was a blur as much as it was a memory I'd never forget. One thing still on my mind was the taste of her skin and how I wanted to devour her. The mark was from my mouth, and I was certain it wasn't the only one. I'd been rough, manhandled her, took her like I'd fantasized for weeks.

In her hand she held a round, pearly white button, twirling it in her fingers. The blood in my veins froze. It was the moment I'd been dreading, something that would remind her what happened.

She set it down, but continued to look at it as her computer booted up. I stayed still, unmoving, waiting on edge, waiting for her reaction.

"Nathan," she said in a low voice, her attention still on the button. "I like my job. Do you like yours?"

There was no anger or hatred in her eyes. Something more akin to resignation, which I didn't understand. That was all that she would give me, but after a moment it was enough and my shoulders released some of the tension they were holding.

"I do," I said, truly meaning it.

"Good."

I watched as she turned back to her computer screen, ending the conversation.

I sat there, still a little confused by her reaction, still waiting for the ax to drop. Going through what she said, replaying her reactions, I tried to dissect her meaning.

It couldn't be that simple to sweep what I did under the rug, could it?

No, because I couldn't handle that outcome. I needed to atone for my actions, for my breach.

Every day I waited for her to go off on me, to make me pay, but it never happened. My anger and agitation at myself only grew, setting my temper off every time I caught myself staring at her. Sleep eluded me, only exacerbating my mood.

My diet was shit and was mostly alcohol and Chinese. I ran on the treadmill like I was fucking running for my life. Pushing past fatigue all the way to collapse so that maybe I could knock out for a few hours, but my brain refused to let me.

I'd snapped more than once at my admirers, and they'd kept their distance, with the exception of when one of them was in genuine need of my help.

Delilah was aloof. My enigma had my complete attention. No work was getting done.

We sat there, staring at each other. She caught my gaze and held it. Once again, no ill will toward me, just a curiosity and something else I couldn't identify.

The phone on my desk rang, breaking our locked gaze.

"Hello?" I said into the receiver.

"Nathan," Jack's familiar voice said.

Fuck.

"Jack."

Delilah glanced over at the name.

"Can you come up?" he asked.

Everything in me froze. It was what I'd been waiting for, what I'd been expecting.

"Be right there." I hung up the phone and stood, saying nothing to her.

That was it—the moment I was fired and possibly put into jail. For days, I'd been waiting for the call. Being Friday, I should've known that would be the day. They always said Friday was the day for firing people.

Each step of the stairs was pain filled and the drumming beat of my march to the gallows. I gave a heavy sigh before reaching out and knocking on Jack's door.

"Come in," he called from the other side.

I twisted the handle and pushed the door open. Jack sat at the large wooden desk he'd had since I'd known him. He had it specially made, commissioned from local Amish.

There was no smile on Jack's face, and he let out a long, low sigh.

"Nate, have a seat," he said as he stood, then walked around to stand in front of his desk.

My blood ran cold as I looked up at him like he was the executioner.

"Is everything okay?"

I blinked at him in complete confusion, my brow furrowed. "Why?"

"Well, I've overheard some talk of your attitude this week. It seems the atmosphere around you is quite dark."

"My attitude?" *That* was why I'd been called up? Because I was in a bad mood? Fearful of losing my job and my freedom because I fucking lost control of the beast and myself.

"Do you want to talk about it?"

I shook my head. "I'm sorry, Jack. It's a personal matter, and I didn't realize I'd let my mood leak out in such abundance."

"It's been hard on me, too," Jack said.

Hard on him?

Oh, fucking shit cock-sucking bastard.

How could I forget? How did I get so consumed by Delilah and what happened with her that I forgot my wife's birthday? Grace would be thirty-four. Our son would be approaching his fourth birthday.

My jaw locked down and I stared at the floor, my breath becoming labored. Guilt flooded in, but for a different reason than before.

The loss of my family was what had consumed me for years, but I realized that for weeks I'd hardly thought about them. Instead, I'd been filled with a physical need for another woman.

"We're headed to the cemetery this weekend to see her, bring her some birthday flowers," Jack said with a sniff.

I kept my gaze from his eyes and shook my head. "I can't, Jack."

He nodded. "Yes, I know, but I hope one day you'll join us."

Only once had I visited their grave, a few weeks after I'd woken up. The pain of seeing her name etched in granite was too much.

Loving wife and mother, it said.

But she never got to be a mother, our son trapped forever inside her. They were locked in a wooden box buried beneath the earth, and he was never to take a breath.

As I left Jack's office, I detoured to one of the empty conference rooms. My whole body shook as I stood against the window looking out at the street.

I'd fucked up my life, ended it for all intents and purposes, and yet still, in my purgatory, I could still wreak havoc on others. Stuck in limbo, I didn't think things could get worse, yet they had.

It seemed rock bottom had many levels, and I had reached an all-time low.

What the fuck was the purpose of my life other than destruction?

SPENT ALL OF SATURDAY STARING AT MY FRONT DOOR, AT THE couple of holes I'd created. There was nothing but guilt that consumed me as I waited, expectant of some type of retribution. All week I'd waited, and I was somehow convinced the weekend would hold my punishment.

The sun rose on one side of my condo and set on the other, and nothing happened. There was no banging on the door, no phone calls. Nothing.

Silence.

It did nothing to assuage my feelings. Even the beast was silent. Being the unpredictable, emotional, violent side of me, he had begun to feel remorse, too.

Though even with the remorse was the itch. Soft at first, but as the day faded, it became almost unbearable. The notion that one time with her would be enough was obliterated the second I was inside her.

I didn't sleep that night. I'd barely slept all week. By nine in the morning I was showered, dressed for some ungodly known reason in my slacks, shirt, and tie, pacing my condo, probably driving my neighbors on the floor below crazy.

Minutes before the time the clock turned to ten, I nearly had a burn on my neck from rubbing it and was agitated beyond belief. I couldn't take any more.

I flew out the door to the elevator, my thumb pressing the button until the ding signaling its arrival sounded. It was one of the times I wished the stairs weren't emergency only. All of my pent-up energy had no outlet, forced to wait impatiently as the elevator seemed to crawl down the few flights.

As soon as the doors opened I was out in the hall, forced to choose between right or left. Drawing up the memory, she'd headed to the right.

There were only two condos on her floor, creating little room for error that I had the wrong place. I slammed my fist on her door, knocking so loud, in time with the pounding of my chest. Through the thick wood I heard the click of the deadbolt and then the door swung open.

"Why didn't you say anything?" I asked as soon as I saw the smallest piece of her, my hands braced on the door frame for support as well as to keep me in place.

There was no anger, only confusion as she looked up at me. "Nathan?"

"Why?" I asked again.

Why didn't she report me to someone, anyone? I needed to pay for my transgression.

There was a ping somewhere in the background, then her fingers wrapped around my tie, pulling me inside. "Idiot! Do you want the whole building to know?"

I didn't fucking care about that. It was trivial. My pacing began again. "I don't get you. All week long I've been waiting for Jack to pull me into his office and fire me, or the police to come, knocking down my door to take me away, and…nothing."

Her brow scrunched. "Why the police?"

I pulled at my hair as I stared at her in disbelief. Was she that used to abuse? "I practically fucking raped you, Delilah."

Her eyes popped wide. "Is that what you think happened?"

"Yes!" I yelled. She needed to see, to understand, because it was obvious it was lost on her. "I took you against your will against a wall. Fuck!" I glanced at her, my eyes stopping at her exposed neck and shoulder.

I was right that the one mark I'd seen wasn't the only one. Faded patches of discolored skin were like leopard spots across her chest and neck.

Fuck!

Yeesssssss! We did that.

I swallowed hard and tried to ignore the beast who was now at the bars of his cage salivating at the sight of her marked skin.

"Listen, Nathan, I think we need to get some things straightened out because I thought you understood. First off, I asked for everything you gave me."

She couldn't be serious.

"Fuck. You sound like a battered housewife."

Her lip curled up. "Will you shut the fuck up? I'm trying to talk!"

I stopped pacing, stunned by her outburst.

"I'm pretty sure I recall begging you more than once, and I never asked you to stop or said no, did I?"

Begged?

Images of that night flooded to mind. "*Harder,*" she had requested. The way her body moved with mine. Her nails scratching my scalp as she pulled my lips to hers.

"Please, take out that big hard cock that I can feel you hiding, and fuck my pussy with it."

Begged. She begged us to take her, fuck her, mark her.

"No," I said in agreement. I began pacing yet again, despite the guilt that dissipated with each word.

"Second," she continued on, ignoring me and my breakdown, "that was the best sex I've ever had in my life."

Best sex *ever?*

My lip curled up. "Really?" A guy could get an ego with words like that.

Ours. Marked her with our come.

The blood fell from my face at the reminder. "Fuck, I came inside you."

The idea of my own lack of self-control resulting in a child, someone they could take from me, made my hands begin to shake as panic set in.

She tilted her head. "Are you clean?"

I nodded. "Yes." With all the shit out there, I hadn't fucked a woman without a condom since Grace and was tested just in case. I was a mess as I was, no need to add to it.

"Then we're good. I'm on birth control." The way she said it with so much nonchalance concerned me. "Third, if I did do any of those things you said, there would never be the possibility you would ever do them to me again...not that you would."

I stared at her, completely confused. "Okay, I'm intrigued. Why wouldn't I?"

"Because no one wants me, so why would you?"

It was said like it was the most obvious answer, at least to her. She really had no clue how beautiful she was, how many men desired her. Whatever haunted her from her past had created a warped sense of self.

"You have such a fucking low opinion of yourself it pisses me off." The fact that someone was responsible for her way of thinking angered me. Someone treated her like trash, and my guess was that it was for a very long time.

We would worship her.

I can't…

"What?" she asked, clearly stunned.

Anger consumed me, my muscles rippling, the beast growling, taking over. All the guilt and fear was gone, quickly replaced by the need to show her just how desirable she was.

"You are so fucking sexy, Lila, that all I can think of doing right now is bending you over that table and slamming into you again and again. Hard. My cock is like fucking steel at the thought of being inside you again. You need to be punished for making me want you this much."

My chest expanded in labored breaths, the beast grinning, ready to take her. I stepped forward, and her eyes widened as she drew in a ragged breath. By her reaction, the glazed look in her eyes, parted lips, and the growing arch of her back toward me, I knew she wanted it too.

"Fuck!" I stopped in my tracks, inches from touching her, and paced once again. "What the fuck is it about you?"

Why couldn't I stop wanting her? Why did I want her in the first place?

Broken. Empty. Fill her.

Fill her with what? I'm just as fucked up.

Want her.

No.

Want her!

"I. Don't. Want. You." I can't. She cringed, taken aback. Good. "And you really don't want me. No one should want me. I'm not a fucking catch, I'm a fucking…"

I needed an outlet, to center myself. There was a weight on my arm and then I was pushed against the wall. Lila had caught me off guard. I stared down at her, a sideways glance to my right hand that was balled into a fist.

Was I about to punch her wall?

She was so close. So fucking close I felt her breath against my lips.

Kiss her.

I wanted to. So badly.

"You think you forced yourself on me? Well, how about a little payback, then?"

My eyes widened as she dropped to her knees, her fingers pulling my pants open. Before I could even comprehend what was happening, her small fingers were wrapped around my cock, pulling me out.

"Shit!" I slammed my hands against the wall, bracing myself. Legs locked, waiting in starved anticipation of my enigma's lips wrapped around me. All of my attention was on her. There was no looking away.

My mouth fell open as she looked me over, her eyes darkening as she gripped my shaft with her hands stacked down the length. The cockiness I once had wasn't overcompensation for a small dick. I stopped breathing when she leaned forward, taking the head between her lips. Then, I sucked in an unneeded breath as the warmth of her mouth encircled the first few inches.

Blow jobs were nice, but none before compared to the few seconds of being in her mouth. Every place she touched was like fire licking at my skin, burning me.

I reached up and fisted my hair, the feeling almost too much to handle. "Fuck, fuck!"

Inch by inch, she took me in. It felt like I was going crazy, unable to form thought, my mind going blank. She reached as far as she could, leaving an inch or two, and pressed her tongue against my shaft as she pulled back. The feeling was so intense I drew in a ragged breath, my eyes rolling back.

"Shit, that's it, baby. Fuck, you are such a good little cock-sucker." I stared down, watching as she bobbed up and down, my cock disappearing between her luscious lips. "You can't stop yourself from craving my dick, can you? It's all you can think about, isn't it?"

The beast rattled, wanting to grab her head and fuck her fast. I kept him back, but my hips rocked, pushing her deeper. Slowly, he took control, hands in her hair, pushing and pulling, getting all the way down her throat.

"You have such a hot, wet little mouth." I let out a groan and slowed down. The urge to be completely inside her was too much. She choked around me, sending shooting pleasure through me and caused my balls to draw up. Fuck, her mouth was perfection. The way her throat stroked me was almost too much. "Fuck, I'm all the way in…feels so damn good. You love it, don't you? You love sucking me off like a little cock slut."

I was so close to coming, so close to unloading my balls down her throat.

We don't want that. Breed her, mark her as ours.

She let out a surprised squeak when I pulled her off me and wrapped my hands around her arms. I flipped her around, switching our positions. Nothing held me back from pressing my lips to hers, from opening her mouth and sucking on her tongue. I was so far gone.

I needed her.

I wanted her.

I was going to motherfucking take her.

She was all I saw, all I felt, her skin soft and supple beneath my hands.

"I don't think I want you to swallow me. I want to come in that fucking tight cunt of yours."

One hand was still in her hair as I kissed her again, the other having a death grip on her ass.

"How do you taste on my lips?" she asked as we parted for a breath.

The beast growled and pulled her closer, running my cock against her pants.

"Oh, baby, I'm about to ask you the same thing," I whispered. The skin just beneath her ear was the perfect spot for an outlet, and I bit down.

The reaction it incited only increased the thickness of the air around us. Nothing but arousal and need. Each lap of my tongue on her skin only increased my want for more. I stopped and stared down at the bruise on her shoulder, the one that still held the outline from my teeth. The first mark.

Ours. She's ours.

I licked the skin, a reverent show of what it was and what it meant, then clamped my teeth down on the impression, freshening it up.

"That is so fucking sexy." I yanked at her tank top. She wasn't wearing a bra, and her perfect tits bounced into view, nipples hardening. They were in my mouth, between my teeth. I loved her cries as I switched to the other side, then back again before working my way back to her lips and her luscious tongue.

"Now to taste your pussy. I bet you're so fucking sweet." I drew in a deep breath, my dick twitching. "I can smell you from here."

"Fuck!" she cried out.

"Soon. Very fucking soon." I fisted her waistband on both sides and yanked downward as I sank to the floor, exposing all of her to me. She shed her tank top as she stepped out. I couldn't help running my hands across her skin, lost in my reverie for her.

I grabbed onto her leg and put it on my shoulder to give me full access to the pussy I'd been fantasizing about. The one that my cock fit in so well. I bit into her thigh and created a trail of bites all the way until I was up close enough to see the sheen on her pussy lips.

"Baby, you are fucking dripping wet for me." I swiped my finger across her slit and brought it to my mouth. "Mmm, so good. This is what sucking my cock did to you? Dirty girl… So fucking naughty."

I bit down on her thigh just to release some of the need before swiping my tongue across her slit and scraping my teeth against her clit. The sounds coming from her only made my dick harder and the need to eat her until she came all over my face overwhelmed me. I attacked her clit, relishing in the way she jerked, her hands fisting in my hair.

She was close.

I ran my fingers across her slit and pressed two of them inside. A few strokes and she was mashing my face against her mound.

"Oh, shit, Nathan! I…I…"

She rode my mouth and fingers through each pulse until her muscles began to relax and the aftershocks took over.

"You are so fucking hot when you come." I gave her another lick before standing.

Inside her. Now.

I groaned as I flexed my hips, grinding against her.

"Time to fuck that pussy of yours. That's what you want, isn't it? You like being fucked fast and rough, don't you? You want my cock to own your pussy and pound it hard."

It was what I fucking wanted, what my dick was dying for. To be inside her again, to mark her again.

No more walls. I grabbed onto her arm and pulled her down the hall until I spotted the perfect place.

It was the pose I'd fantasized about since the first day I met her, and while it wasn't her desk, her dining table would do. In my frenzy, I pushed her against the table.

"Bend over and hold on," I growled. I scraped my teeth against the other side of her neck while I pushed her over with my body.

The animalistic need was too overpowering, and I gave her no time to grab hold before I slammed into her.

"So fucking good! So wet…tight…shit, Lila."

I pulled out and slammed in even harder, the force of each thrust moving the table beneath her. It forced me to step forward, chasing her ass so I could fully drive into her.

My fantasy was part truth as I held her hips in my hands, watching as she stretched around me, her juices making my cock shine. The table continued to scoot, so I reached up and twisted my hand in her hair.

The new arch of her back as I tugged her head back and pushed down on her back with my other hand kept me at a steady angle. It forced her body to stay in place, letting me decimate her with my dick.

"That's it, take my fucking cock. You love it, don't you?"

All she could do was whimper and moan, and all I could do was thrust my cock in her like it was the last fucking time I would fuck anyone.

"Answer me! You love my cock in you, don't you, little slut?"

She was going to fucking answer me.

"Yes. Yes! Please fuck me with your...ugh...hard cock... shit...p-pound my naughty pussy."

That was it, the shit that pushed me to slam into her harder and faster with each stroke. With each thrust, I took my pain, my frustration and anger, out on her. I couldn't handle the feelings, couldn't deal, and I fucked her like I hated her because it was the only way to expunge my being of all of it.

"Harder. Deeper, oh fuck...so deep inside me. More! Pull me down, take me over...shit. Make me sorry for being so naughty."

Fuck!

Her dirty talk back to me was so unexpected I almost came right then. She wanted it, needed it. The depravity, the torture, the intensity of what we created was too much for me and not enough for her.

"Yes... Punish you. Fuck. I don't want this...don't want you. This." *Slam.* "Is." *Slam.* "All." *Slam.* "Your." *Slam.* "Fault!"

Her pussy locked down around me, my name falling from her lips like she was praying to me. It was the high I needed as I climbed toward the mind-wiping numbness I craved.

"That's it, come on my cock. Shit, your pussy feels so good... Milk my cock, baby. Fuck!"

She shook beneath me, each way pulsing around my shaft, locking down more and more. I stood back up and she fell down to the table. I used her hips to help me get all the way in, skin to skin each time, watching her ass cheeks jiggle with every slam. "That's it. Grip it tight like a vice. That's what you do. It's how you torment me. Fucking cock tease."

Sobs shook her, and I continued on. My hips moved on their own, my brain no longer registering anything, but the fierce pleasure and energy that was boiling inside me until it exploded. I buried my cock all the way in, jerking with each stream.

With the last drop emptied inside her, I fell down onto her back. Our breaths were in time, hard and labored as we came down.

"You should stay away from me, Lila. I'm no good for you," I said. My breath was harsh against her back. I needed her to understand. There was no safety with me. "Run while you can. Run away from me, and don't look back. I'm not worth your life."

When I regained some semblance of strength a few minutes later, I stood up. Lila didn't move, her eyes closed. A panic began to wash over me, but then I watched as her chest rose and fell in a steady rhythm.

Passed out.

Another boost to the ego I didn't need—fuck a woman until she passes out from pleasure.

Pulling out of her was almost torture, and there was come everywhere. Days worth saved up and emptied into her.

Look at that. Our come, sliding out of her freshly fucked pussy.

This is your fault.

You wanted it. Don't lie.

I can't want it. This can't happen again.

Two tastes. There's no stopping. We've never felt this intensity. Ever.

I hated that he was right. The sad fact was that he spoke the truth. I was the one who tried to deny, who forced a separation.

There was no way I was going to leave her like that, so after stuffing my cock back in my pants, I found a washcloth and wet it with warm water before cleaning her up. She was completely out, almost like she hadn't slept in days. Dead weight in my arms as I picked her up. One arm crossed her waist while the other hung down, her head rolling back and forth on my shoulder as I carried her toward the bedrooms, searching for the master.

Bruises had already begun to form on her pale skin, pink dots from my grip. I gently set her on the bed and pulled the covers out from under her, then draped them across her body.

I couldn't help but stare at her face. So innocent looking, so vulnerable. Reaching out, I brushed a few strands of hair aside. There was no makeup on her skin, and none was needed. Her hair was a natural blonde, not dyed. She was a natural beauty.

A sigh left me, and I sat on the edge of the bed, head held in my hands.

What am I going to do?

You know what.

I can't keep doing this.

Yes, we can.

It's not right. It's not good for her. I'm not good for her.

But we want to be.

What I want is irrelevant.

No one else would be hurt because of me. I meant those words. I refused to have more pain upon me. I couldn't handle the weight. Bad enough I was already a crumbled mess that was barely held together.

Standing, I headed back toward her kitchen. She was going to need some water when she woke and, based on the bruises, probably some Aspirin as well.

As I walked through, I noticed how neat her condo was, sterile almost, but it held an unexpected warmth. Much like the feeling I got when my wife and I toured some model homes. There weren't a lot of knickknacks, but it was lightly decorated.

I poured a glass of water and walked back to her bedroom where I took a look around and found much of the same. There was no medicine in the kitchen, so I walked into her master bathroom. Going through drawers, there was some makeup and various toiletries, all in their place. Finally, I found a drawer with a basket full of bottles.

Prescription bottles outweighed the over-the-counter medications. My expression dropped as I read some of the labels. It wasn't just the fact she had some of the same medications I was very familiar with, but also the name that appeared on them—Dr. Darren Morgenson.

"Shit."

How the fuck did I get in such a mess with one of Darren's patients?

I glanced through the open door, my eyes locked on her sleeping form. Every suspicion I'd had about her and a horrible past was confirmed with a single name. Darren's practice was specified. He worked with trauma patients and their families.

Placing the bottles back, I opened the Aspirin and shook out two pills, then put it back with the rest before closing the drawer. I set the tablets next to the water. She was still asleep, peaceful even.

"What happened to you?" I asked in a whisper, the backs of my fingers trailing across her cheek.

M Y HANDS WOULDN'T STOP SHAKING. THEY COULDN'T.

Twice. I'd fucked her twice.

It'd been four years since I touched a woman more than one time, and my wife was the only one for a decade. That was how much Lila had unhinged me.

I never slept with a woman more than once. There was no way I was going to let anyone in, and more than once would imply there was something more. Yet, I'd been inside Lila twice and my dick was hard, dying to be inside her again.

My skin crawled, vibrated with the desire to taste her. To sink my teeth into her skin as my hips flexed my cock deep inside her.

And it fucking pissed me off.

I had to stay away. Never again.

Things I said to her in the chaos, words that would have earned a slap, she reveled in. They weren't definitions I associated with her, but I wanted her to be a whore for my cock. A slut willing to do anything to have me inside her. Me and nobody else.

Mine.

Every cell in me vibrated, more life coursing through me than there had been in years.

Almost three days down without incident. It was like one of those fucking signs, but instead of three days since the last accident, it was three days since the last fucking.

It hadn't been without great effort, and I found myself staring at her a lot, trying to figure out just what it was about her that turned me on so much.

Lila was dedicated to her work. She rarely got frustrated, with the exception of visitors. The interruption messed with her flow, along with the inane chatter of the true sluts annoyingly trying to get into my pants every day.

They truly were the definition of sluts in my opinion. In the moment, my dirty mouth would call Lila that, but I wanted her to be only for me. There had never been a time that word even remotely entered my mind when thinking about her outside of those times.

Probably because I saw her beauty, her frailty. I saw what she kept from everyone. The darkness that was intoxicating. So much that I wanted to drown in it and her.

In no way was that a good idea, but I couldn't stop thinking about her or trying to figure her out.

I looked over and she was frozen, staring down at the contract in front of her, but not moving or blinking.

"Delilah?" I asked, a bit concerned. She'd never done that before.

Her eyes focused again, and she swallowed hard. "Yes?"

"Are you okay? You've been staring at the same contract for the last fifteen minutes, your hands hovering over the keys." I couldn't stop from smiling at her. It amused me, and I wondered if her mind was just as filled with me as mine was of her.

"I just need more coffee."

"Your mind seemed preoccupied, not tired." I pressed her, pushed her, wanting a reaction, to see what she tried so hard to hide.

"Don't worry, Thorne, you weren't starring in my preoccupation."

The way her cheeks turned pink proved me right. She was lying. Whether embarrassment or arousal, I wasn't sure. What I did know was I wasn't the only one struggling, caught in this cage of an office.

A giggle floated in through the door and in walked a set of breasts, followed by Jennifer.

"Nathan, I was hoping you could help me."

Her voice was like nails on a chalkboard, but I plastered a smile on my face anyway.

"I'm going to lunch," Lila said as she stood.

Fuck!

My eyes were wide as I watched her grab her coat and practically run from the room.

Fuck, fuck!

"What can I help you with?" I asked, turning my attention back to Jennifer.

"Good, she's gone," Jennifer said as she blew out a breath.

"What?" I asked, a bit taken back.

"Well, she'd probably be a bitch and snitch on us."

I furrowed my brow. "Excuse me?"

She reached out and ran her hand down my chest. "I was wondering if you'd like to come to dinner at my place tonight."

Oh, that was what she meant.

Kick her out.

Go back to sleep.

They're cock sleeves, nothing more.

I gave her as charismatic of a smile as I could muster. "I'm sorry, I can't do dinner, but I can help you with your problem."

Her smile faltered, but she nodded and showed me the paper in her hand. It was simple, just a misspelling that auto-correct probably switched.

"Maybe we could do dinner some other time?" she asked.

I shook my head. "I can't risk losing this job."

She nodded. "Thanks for your help."

As soon as she was out the door, I reached up and ran my hands over my face. I didn't want her. I didn't want them. Not a single fucking one.

Liar.

I wasn't counting Lila.

It felt like I had barely moved when there was a soft knock on the door. I looked up to find a stock of brunette hair attached to the youngest of my admirers—Kelly.

Jesus-fucking-Christ! Why were they always coming in, nonstop? Did they draw straws to see whose turn it was to try and seduce me, hoping one would succeed? Kelly was nearly half my age and didn't know anything about the law. She was an office clerk, helping out with the little shit nobody had time for. There was no reason for her to come to us, or more specifically, me.

It was an even simpler matter than Jennifer arrived with.

"Oh, my God, you're so right," she said in fake surprise.

"Usually am." I smiled at her.

"I was wondering, I mean, if you're free, I'm having a party at my house this weekend. Consider this your invite."

A party at a nineteen-year-old's house? Yeah, right. I

wasn't going near that. I'd likely be arrested for aiding in the consumption of alcohol by underage teenagers.

"I'll have to take a raincheck," I said.

Seconds later, Lila returned. Immediately she glanced toward Kelly and then glared at me, obviously irritated by Kelly's presence. She wasn't the only one.

"Next time?"

"Maybe," I said with a chuckle. It was never going to happen.

"Kelly, have you set up my appointment with the Sanders yet?" Lila asked, her tone clipped.

"Nope," Kelly replied, completely oblivious to the authority of one of her superiors.

I watched Lila for her response, which was one of the coldest glares I'd ever seen.

"I asked you to set that up three hours ago."

Kelly still hadn't looked at her. "I'll get to it," Kelly said, much like an obstinate teenager she was.

"Well, I'd say if you have time to sit in here and talk, you have time to make the call you should have made three hours ago."

Lila's voice rose, trying to assert herself, but Kelly was exceptionally dense. That or so completely full of herself she thought that the earth revolved around her. As if she deserved my attention and could ignore Lila's request simply because she breathed, because she was alive.

"Fine, I'll go do it now." Kelly finally relented. "I'll be back." She winked at me, and I rolled my eyes the second she was out the door.

"Better not be," Lila said under her breath. I couldn't take my eyes off her. "What? It's your damn fault they're in here all of the time. You could at least *discourage* their advances."

"How is it my fault?" I asked. I knew the answer, but I liked watching her get flustered, liked watching her lose control.

"Your damn pheromones are drawing in the bees, and they're pissing me off. You're the best looking man in this office, and they all want you."

Pheromones? Best looking?

She wants more. So do we.

I've abstained for three days, and I will continue.

Let go, and maybe you'll understand.

"And you don't?" I asked.

I got the response I was looking for. She blinked at me, stunned I'd even eluded to what happened. I watched as her face turned red.

I told you. She wants us.

You think I don't know that? It doesn't matter. I can't.

She fidgeted and, without warning, picked her stapler up and threw it at me. It missed my head, but collided with the wall and burst into half a dozen pieces as well as leaving a dent in the wall.

What the actual fuck?

"Back to work," she mumbled.

Did she really just throw a stapler at me and then blow me off?

My jaw ticked, and I turned to glare at her. "Yes, throw shit, Palmer, that's mature."

I clenched my fist, wishing the office was empty so I could bend her over her desk and spank her, then fuck her.

She let out a hard sigh and turned to glare at me. "Do you really want me to go there, Thorne? Answer me this—do you plan to screw one of them?"

Her question hinted at jealousy.

"No."

"Then why do you flirt with them?" she asked, her jaw jutting forward.

An easy answer. It was the reason I always got what I wanted before.

"Because I've found that being friendly makes people more apt to do what you ask without delay or complaint. You catch more bees with honey, Palmer."

"Oh, that's right. I forgot you're the friendliest person in the world. Oh, wait, no…" she leaned forward and whispered, "You're damaged and hiding behind a fucking mask."

The last words were almost hissed, anger pouring out of her. She was pissed, and the beast liked it. More black to revel in.

I met her rage with my own anger, lip curled back. "You have no idea what the hell you're talking about."

I sat back and returned my attention to the screen. She didn't know anything, and if I had any say, she never would.

I refused to get close to her.

LILA FINISHED JUST BEFORE SIX, AND INSTEAD OF STARTING something new, opted for what was an early night compared to the rest. She didn't say a word, still mulling in her anger from earlier, and just grabbed her coat and jacket and headed to the door. The moment she was out of sight, I saved my work, putting slips of paper with notes for where to pick up in the morning, and followed.

I stalked her ass home, speeding in order to decrease the time it took for me to catch up to her. Seconds after getting out of her car, I pulled into the parking spot next to her.

We had shit to talk about, namely what the fuck got into her at the office. She avoided my stare, tried to act like I wasn't there, and that annoyed the fuck out of me.

Once I was within ten feet of her, something in the air changed. We weren't in the office, bound by rules and watchful eyes.

We entered the elevator and pushed the buttons for our floors. She still refused to acknowledge me, even in the mirrored reflection of the doors.

Confined space with only her was a dangerous pairing. Part of me wanted to hurt her, make her acknowledge her want, be cruel to get it.

"Were you jealous?" I asked, my mouth ghosting her ear.

She drew in a stunted, jagged breath, but it wasn't enough to hide the effect.

"No."

Liar.

Yes, the beast was right.

"You shouldn't be. I don't want them, and I don't want you either." She flinched at what I said, making my chest clench. I couldn't do it, especially knowing she was just as broken as I was. "No." I reached up and moved a lock of her hair, leaning into her, unable to hold back. "That's not true, is it?" My voice broke, unable to lie about that one thing. I did want her. "I don't want to want you, but I do. I fucking crave you, but I can't…I can't give in." There was no stopping me from getting closer, increasing the current that grew ever stronger with each passing second. "Please, Lila, push me away." The plea was barely a broken whisper, my lips running up the column of her neck. "Don't let me take you again."

One more time and there'd be no stopping me, stopping whatever was happening between us. I refused to let it happen, but at the same time, I was so fucking weak for her. I needed her to shove me back, get me in line.

"I can't stop you. I want you too much." She turned, her hand right above my heart. "You've given me a taste, and now I want more. I *need* more."

No! No, please! Don't say that.

Yes! She's ours. Ours!

I stared into her eyes, into the warmth, the affection, the

need that was as much emotional as physical.

"Fuck." I backed up, needing space. "No. Don't say that."

It was me begging, but for release from the hold she had on me.

She pulled at my tie, our lips so close I could feel her breath, then the faint teasing touch.

"You're like a drug, and I'm going through withdrawal." She licked at my lips, and my dick twitched. "I need your help."

I struggled for breath, for control, a fight I was desperately losing with every inch her hand slid down my chest. Her hot hand over my cock, gripping it, rubbing it, was a fight I would never win.

Relent.

No.

Let me out!

My hips rocked into her hand, my mind overpowered with the lust that consumed me.

The ping of the elevator and the sliding of the door jolted me. She stepped away, and I stared at her, confused, my mind still clouded with desire. I needed to stay, to go to my own floor, my own condo, and forget her.

The doors began to slide closed, and I jumped through. She gave me a shy smile, then turned toward her door.

I was consumed, driven by greed for her skin. The door hadn't even slid closed and I was on her, my mouth tasting, biting, marking her while my hips showed her just how much I needed to be inside her.

We stumbled down the hallway, all due to my inability to let her walk thirty fucking feet without every inch of my body attached to hers.

Getting the door unlocked took so much time I was about to say "fuck it," pull her skirt up, and shove my cock in.

I didn't care about neighbors or someone seeing us, nothing except getting my dick inside her again. The beast and I were one, in search of the same end goal, unable to stop.

Nothing could stop me.

The door opened and wasn't even closed when I pinned her against the wall. Her eyes were hooded as her arms drew me closer.

"I want your hands and lips on me. You've kept me waiting long enough, Mr. Thorne."

"Fuck." If she called me Mr. Thorne again, I was going to tear her pussy up. "What about my cock?"

"I want it in my pussy where it fucking belongs."

"I'll fuck you so hard, you won't be able to walk." My voice was low and rough. "You make me so hard; you better be ready to work your ass off for my come."

"More," she begged as she worked on undoing the buttons of my shirt. She was so worked up, her head falling to my chest as her body moved against me.

"Excited, my little whore? Yes, that's what you are, letting me fuck you the way I do. You know that's not good, letting me punish you. My cock wants to be down your throat, inside your pussy, and," I paused, my grip on her ass tightening, "in your ass. You tease me with it every fucking day."

I wanted all of her holes.

A small moaned slipped from her lips before her fingers frantically worked to unbutton my shirt.

Panic coursed through me when she grabbed the hem of my shirt and started to pull it up. I immediately moved her hand to my belt and away from exposing my scars.

A few rushed movements and all thought of my scars vanished from of my mind when her hand wrapped around my cock. Her hand was cool, but I barely noticed because of the heat that raced through me from her touch.

My hips jerked, an involuntary reaction to her tongue hitting the sensitive underside of my cock head. When she took me between her lips, they then began more instinctive movements to get more of my throbbing cock into her hot mouth.

A groan rumbled through my chest as I watched her take more and more until she was so far down I could feel her throat contracting around me. "That's it, take it all. I'll fuck your mouth until I come, and you'll fucking swallow all of it. Do you understand?"

She let out a moan. "Fuck, you have such a filthy mouth."

"You think you own my cock, don't you?" I growled and slapped her cheek with the head of my cock. I repeated that a couple of times before running it along her bottom lip. "You don't, little whore. You don't own it, but you *will* take it."

I shrugged out of my jacket, losing the restrictive fabric so I could get a better grip on her. With one hand I pushed on the back of her head while the other got my tie undone. Once free, I tangled my hands in her hair, taking control of the speed and depth that she took me in. I fucked her face with ferocity. A wild abandon that had her gagging as I pushed her all the way to the base.

Fucking perfection.

"Get your ass up here and let me fuck you the way you love it: hard, fast, and dirty. That's what you want, isn't it?" I taunted her. "It's what I want. To stretch you open and have your pussy suck me back in."

I wanted to be inside her and never leave. Pain seared in my chest, honest with myself for the first time.

I ripped the rest of her clothes off until she was completely naked except for her bra. Small dots cast a shadow on the fabric, and I bit down on one of them before sucking it into my mouth.

"Oh, God!" she cried.

"Not God, baby…*Nathan*. That's the name you'll be screaming when you come."

A flick of her bra, and it was where it belonged—on her floor. I glanced around for the perfect place for her to ride me and ended up pulling her to the living room. I pushed my slacks further down my legs, then sat on the couch, drawing her down with me.

With her legs straddling my own, her pussy was open and inviting.

"You're so fucking wet. Was this from sucking my cock?" I asked as I got my fingers as wet as possible and moved them to press against her ass. My cock wanted in there so badly. "You're so uptight and frigid. I should warm you up, then shove my cock in your ass. Fucking shoot my load up there."

She said nothing, but her hips told me everything, especially the moan that left her each time her clit moved against my cock.

"Maybe I'll paint you white. Fuck. You'd love that, wouldn't you? Have my come all over your body."

"Please. I want everything you want to give me."

Stop stalling and fuck her!

Part of me had never learned patience, but I had learned that teasing only got her hotter.

I slipped my fingers inside her again as I slapped my cock

against her clit. She leaned forward, and I stared at her tits as she began to ride my fingers.

"That's it, baby, you love my cock deep inside you. You need me to fill you."

I needed inside her. Needed to fuck her. I needed the pleasure to wipe out the pain, even for a few minutes. I pressed my middle finger against her ass. "Have you ever had a cock up here?" I asked. She shook her head, but a whimper came out. What kind of answer was that? "Don't lie to me, slut."

"None…j-just a dildo. Now stop teasing me, and fuck me!"

Fuck, yes. A grin spread on my face as victory stared back at me in the form of a woman begging me to fuck her.

"You're a naughty little slut. I'll show you what it feels like to have a cock shoved up there. Soon." As I pulled my fingers out of her, the image of both her holes stuffed entered my mind. I wondered what it would feel like to fuck her while she had a toy in her ass or pussy. Or maybe both holes taken by toys, teasing her while I fucked her face. "That is fucking sexy, the thought of you stuffed everywhere with a vibrator. You love that, don't you?"

"Y–yes."

"My cock likes the sound of that, and," I glanced down between us, "so does your pretty little pussy."

A clear drop of precome slid down from the tip, and I couldn't take it anymore. With my hands on her hips, I drove up as I pulled her down.

"Damn, you feel so fucking good wrapped around me, squeezing me." My grip tightened as I recovered from the shock and lifted her before pulling her back to me again.

"Deeper," she moaned.

"Deeper?" I pulled out, leaving just the tip.

"Fucking tease," she hissed as she let her weight go and sank back down.

Tease? Yes, and she was going to take it without complaint.

"Nobody tells me how to do this shit." I flipped our positions so that she was below me and drilled her into the couch. "Yeah, that's it, squeeze me. Take me all the way in. I'm not going to stop until you're coming while screaming how much you fucking love it."

And she did. All of it. From every time before, the harsh words and the names to the hair pulling and spanking. She fucking loved everything I gave her. And I gave her eight fucking inches all the way to the base.

"That is a fucking spectacular view. I could watch it all fucking day."

The feel of her nails digging into my arm along with her screaming my name spurred me on. She was squeezing me, her walls contracting around me as I continued to pound into her.

I lost the ability to think, words and moans spilling from my mouth, hips driven by the need to empty my balls inside her. She was so fucking beautiful beneath me. A fucking goddess for the way she made me feel.

For the third time I was inside her, and there still was no getting enough. I held the back of her neck in my hand, our bodies chest to chest as I sucked and nipped at her neck. When that wasn't enough, I clamped my teeth down on the meat of her shoulder while I slammed into her. She arched into me, her pussy squeezing me again.

Fuck.

"You're going to come."

I pressed my lips to her and groaned, the sound passing

between us. It wasn't enough. I needed harder, faster. My body begged for the furious tempo.

Grabbing onto her legs, I placed them on my shoulders. It was an even deeper angle, and I loved how it made her even tighter.

"Oh God!" she cried out as I pounded her.

"Yes, that's it, baby. Take it. Flood your pussy and let it flow out onto my dick. You know you want to."

"More."

Fuck, I loved it when she begged for more. "Shit! Fuck, baby, you're…oh, fucking…clenching so tight…so fucking tight!" The words stammered out as the blissful white started to take over, pushing out thought.

"Fuck, Nate. Yes!" she screamed as she clenched around me.

Every muscle vibrated as she milked me. "Yes! Oh, fuck, baby, fucking you… God, so good!"

I pulled my hips back, removing my cock, determined to mark another part of her. A few pumps and time seemed to slow as I watched my come shoot out and land on her skin. The pearly drops reached her breasts on the first shot, the others landing on her stomach.

Fucking perfect work of art.

"Shit, that is the best fucking sight in the world. You look so fucking good covered in me." I moved my cock around her skin, spreading the last few drops that fell, watching as it soaked into her skin.

"That was… God, I can't describe it," she said as she reached up and pushed away a few strands of hair.

I knew exactly what she meant. As much as I hated to admit it, she was my perfect sexual match.

"I know."

I smiled down at her, watching as more of it dried and settled in.

"I don't think I'll be able to walk tomorrow. I want Starbucks in the morning. You're buying."

Demands now?

I let out a chuckle. "How about I tell the other ladies I'm gay? Would that be sufficient payment?"

"I'm not some damn call girl, you know."

I smirked down at her just to tease her more while I stood and pulled my pants back up to my hips. My lack of response only made it sweeter, especially when I headed toward the door.

"Asshole!" she yelled from the couch.

"You mean 'thank you!'" I said with a snort as I made my way out and into the hall.

It was as I waited for the elevator that the high I felt began to wear off, leaving me once again trying to convince myself that it couldn't happen again. The part that bothered me the most was the lie of an agreement I gave myself.

No, it can't happen again. At the same time, *Yes, I want to be inside her and all around her and never fucking stop.*

I wanted to fuck her again and again and again until there was nothing left of both of us. The sad fact was that my reality didn't allow it.

Fucking the same woman more than a few times was a relationship, and that was something I couldn't afford.

STARED UP AT THE CLUB WHERE I'D SPENT MANY NIGHTS TROLLING for sex and picking up women. The neon of the signage lit up the parking lot.

Why did I agree to this?

Because what's ours is in there, with other males.

As she should be. Finding someone who isn't fucked up beyond repair.

The beast rattled at the bars, making me close my eyes and crane my neck, pulling at the tight muscles.

"Nate, how's it hanging, man?" Jerome, the bouncer, asked as I stepped up.

We shook hands, and I smiled. "Good. How's your wife doing?"

"Aw, man." He shook his head and circled his arms out in front of him. "About like this. She's due in six weeks and more than ready for him to come out."

My smile faltered, but I picked it back up, forced it to reach my eyes. "That's awesome! I didn't know she was pregnant."

He smiled and shrugged. "Well, you ain't been around to tell."

I nodded. "It's been a busy time."

"Well, go on. Lots of hotties in there tonight. Go get you some."

I nodded and waved at him. "Have a good night."

"I'll see your ass on the way out."

There was a sense of familiarity as I stepped inside. Looking around, there was a definite difference from six months ago. It felt like every time before, I was in a fogged-over, dream-like haze. Almost like I was seeing things clearly.

Then again, everything about me was blurred. All the way to the point when I met Lila. She was the shift for everything, all I could think about. She was the reason I was chaos incarnate.

The club was dimly lit with colored lights moving across the dance floor. At the bar, Alex was working his smile as he made a crowd of girls some drinks. There were tall tables by the bar and shorter ones on the edge of the dance floor, which was a few feet below the bar. Surrounding the rest of the floor against the walls were about a dozen half-moon booths.

I scanned each space, looking for my coworkers, searching for…

Shit. I am not searching for her.

Of course we are. She's why we came.

Can't you just shut up?

No. Not until you let me out.

You're nothing but trouble.

We can work together, behave, even out.

I froze the second I saw her profile, watched her head tip back as she took a shot. Her tongue swiped across her lips, and the image shot straight to my dick. I couldn't take my eyes off her, watching her from a different vantage point as she socialized—a rarity.

I stepped toward her, my feet acting almost on their own. Her posture straightened and she froze, her gaze locked on the glass in front of her.

"Hey, Nathan, you made it!" Caroline said with a smile.

I didn't miss the glare Lila shot her as they all scooted around to give me some space to sit. She refused to look at me, to acknowledge me, and it pissed me off.

I wasn't someone she could ignore.

My seat was right next to her, and as I sat down, I made sure to crowd her so much that our bodies touched at the shoulder and legs. There were no hands involved, but even that level sent a ripple down my spine. Lust and desire mixed with the anger and frustration.

"Wouldn't have missed it," I said with a smile.

Still no response or reaction from her, so I leaned into her. "Lila."

Being so close, I felt her tense, watched the bob of her throat as she swallowed before she turned to finally look at me.

"Nate."

Holy fuck. How much had she had to drink before I got there? Her cheeks were flushed, eyes glazed, and the smile on her lips had my cock thumping to life. She was pliable, vulnerable, and more alluring than I'd ever seen before.

I drew in a sharp breath, my jaw clenching to shut it down before anyone noticed. It was a test to keep from fucking pulling her out the back door, shoving her chest into the brick wall, and fucking some sense into her. She was a fucking mark for any guy in there.

"I'm surprised to see you out."

"Oh, we used to see him here all the time," Ian said. "Been months, dude. We thought you fell off the face of the earth or something. Finally find yourself a steady girl?"

I let out a laugh. Once upon a time, I'd tried to pick Caroline up. Ian didn't like it, but somehow we created a bar friendship and I'd often sit with them.

"So, you're a manwhore? Should have known," Lila said, clearly, to me, annoyed.

I wanted to correct her. For some reason, I wanted her to understand. I wasn't a manwhore, but just a man. Relationships were out, but I wasn't going to live like some celibate monk for the rest of my life. My fucking PTSD made damn fucking sure of that.

She was ignoring me, giving me the cold shoulder.

I leaned into her again. "It was just sex, Delilah. Fucking."

Her eyes unfocused, face relaxing as her mask slipped.

I glanced around the table, checking to see if anyone was paying attention to us before moving my hand to her leg. First light circles with my thumb, then I added more pressure.

"I don't want them."

Nothing. She was reserved, not melting into my touch, and I fucking hated it. I wanted her breath to pick up, her thighs to relax open. I wanted to know I was getting to her, and she refused to play along.

"I need another drink," she said.

Every muscle froze, my hand tightening on her leg.

"Are you sure that's wise?" I asked as I glanced down to the lineup of empty glasses in front of her. While she had shut me out, she was still vulnerable to others, and more alcohol was only going to increase her allure to every fucker in the room, myself included.

"Are you my fucking father? No, I didn't think so. Let me the fuck up so I can get another drink."

She was defiant, which was a strength I wasn't sure she understood she possessed. Her nails dug into my arm as she pushed, forcing me to move or cause a scene. Since tipping Caroline off was the last thing I wanted to do, I relented, but looked after her as she walked away.

It was hard to take my eyes off her and return my attention to Caroline and Ian.

"No drink?" Ian asked.

I let out a chuckle, my lip twitching up. "You guys distracted me. Be right back."

Ian nodded while Caroline leaned into him.

My trek to the bar was an exercise in recognizing Lila in a crowd of women in a dark room. Getting a drink was the perfect excuse to walk right the fuck up to Lila and crowd her, let any fucking bastard who was watching see that she was owned.

And I fucking owned her.

All I had to do was find her.

I was halfway down the length of the bar when movement at the end of the bar caught my attention. She'd somehow gotten a drink and instead of heading back to the table, was heading to the dance floor.

Watching her walk onto the dance floor and start swaying her hips was torture. She was prey, and as she passed by, more than one predator started toward her. All the men there touching her, thinking that because she was there they had some right to be physical with her.

I was going to kill every fucker who even looked at her.

I kept watch as she danced, the liquid in her cup sloshing.

Not two minutes passed when some drunk fucker stepped up behind her and pulled her to him.

Hell fucking no.

It was the end of my ability to just watch. I pushed my way through the throng of bodies, slipped past couples grinding so hard together I wasn't sure they weren't fucking.

Ten feet away, I saw he was grinding against her and her eyes were closed as he mauled her with his hands.

"Can I cut in?" I managed to say through clenched teeth and the red haze that had taken over.

She opened her eyes and fucking smiled as she bit her lower lip.

"Wait your turn," the guy said.

Bad idea, because the anger pumped through my veins like a poison, and my patience was gone.

"I'm not asking."

He must have seen the violence vibrating within me emanating out, because he relented.

"Okay, man, shit, take her," he said as he shoved her into me.

She gripped my shirt and leaned in, lips parted before pushing off.

"What the fuck was that about?" she asked.

My last fuse was blown. I grabbed onto her arm and dragged her from the dance floor. There was an empty table near the bar, and I stopped.

"You're letting strange men put their hands all fucking over you!" I said with a snarl.

Every muscle was tight, ready for a fight, and caused my fingers to dig into her arm.

"What the hell do you care, Thorne? Huh?"

Was she fucking kidding me?

"Because you are mi—"

"This guy bothering you, Lila?"

Mine.

Mine.

MINE!

I instantly hated the familiarity to her in the words of whoever interrupted us. The tone was sharp, and he made sure to raise his voice over the music. Average build, above average height, topped off with average looks, and he was taking a stance against me, an unfamiliar male, trying to scare me off.

"Andrew?"

Again, an instantaneous hatred filled me. There was surprise in her voice and the way she looked at him was far too intimate than I was going to allow.

Andrew stared at me, his gaze moving down to Lila's arm which I clutched harder as our eyes locked. If the blond fucker thought he was going to intimidate me, he was dead fucking wrong. He was a toothpick, and I had nothing to lose so there would be no stopping me from smashing his face into the concrete floors and breaking him.

"Let go of the lady." His fists clenched at his side.

I glanced at Lila, then back to the fucker. Who the fuck was he to tell me to do anything? Instead, I pulled her closer.

The douchebag reached for me, and I let go of Lila, ready to lay him out. He was half a second from getting my fist in his fucking face when Lila stepped between us.

"Enough! Jesus, knock it off." She pressed her hands against our chests while attempting to glare. "Nathan, you can let go now. Drew, back off."

His eyes never left mine, refusing to back down. "He was grabbing your arm, Lila. *Hard*."

And I fuck her even harder.

"Yes, after saving me from some drunk sleaze on the dance floor," she explained. "Then he proceeded to lecture my drunk ass about watching out for myself."

Andrew's glare wavered and relaxed, his jaw flopping open like a fish before closing and looking between us.

"Really?" he asked.

I didn't relax at all, the adrenaline flowing freely, my body geared up.

"What's going on?" Caroline asked as she looked us over.

Lila rolled her eyes. "Just a misunderstanding and too much testosterone."

Testosterone she was going to be fucking filled with on the dance floor if Andrew kept looking at her. I was caught between wanting to fight every guy in the building and fucking her right there.

"Okay, then," Caroline said, looking between all of us. "We ordered another round of drinks back at the table. Join us, Drew?"

Fuck. I didn't want the tool anywhere near me or her, so I hoped he declined.

"Sounds great, Carrie." He smiled and held his arm out. "After you, Lila."

I allowed no gap between us, forcing him to step behind me. When Lila wobbled, it was my hands that steadied her.

I forced a neutral look and a fake smile to keep attention off what just happened. It was a series of fucking slips, and I realized being out in public with her was not a good thing. All logic left, possession taking its place.

When we got back to the booth, I made sure to sit next to her, but Andrew secured the other side. I wasted no time placing my hand on her thigh again.

"Okay, so who's this newbie?" Andrew asked.

The whole table laughed, so I remained silent, reigning the gut reactions in. My attempt to keep the peace was going to leave bruises on Lila's leg.

I listened as they talked about Vivian, the woman whose position I filled, trying not to laugh when Caroline gave her surprised reaction that she just left. The truth and the rumors created an interesting dichotomy.

Jack had already given me Vivian's job long before she left. She'd received enough warnings to suspect her end was near and just wanted to screw the company and Lila over by quitting without notice.

A waitress arrived with half a dozen drinks and set them down. Ian pushed a bottle of Dos Equis toward me.

"Thanks, man."

"You don't need that," Andrew said.

Douche fucker says what? I looked over to find Andrew trying to push Lila's Long Island from her. What fucking say did he have in what she did?

I smirked at the death glare she threw at him, almost laughing as she tipped the glass back and chugged the contents.

"Don't mess with my drink, Drew," she said, the glass half empty. "I need it."

"No, you don't," he argued.

"It's the only way I can sleep, okay?" Her voice cracked as she spoke, almost like she was to the point of tears. Even her body language mimicked it in the way her bottom lip trembled and she rubbed at her eyes. "I just want to get some fucking sleep. I can't fucking drink every night, so let me sleep tonight. I can get more than a couple hours in and my brain will shut down."

My brow scrunched as I looked at her. What the fuck was she talking about?

"Her insomnia's back," Caroline said.

Insomnia? More things about my enigma suddenly made sense. The way she passed out, not rousing as I moved her around, a result of pure exhaustion.

I also remembered the bottle from her drawer—Triazolam and Sonata. Not one, but two different options. Probably because of the dependency issues with the Triazolam, but I knew for a fact how it could help with night terrors, which I suspected she suffered from as well.

"All right, off topic Lila. I'm not interesting enough. Next topic," she said, waving her hands in front of her, almost like she was trying to wipe away the conversation.

Andrew snorted. "I see you still love to be the center of attention."

"Yeah, yeah. Drunk, depressed, center-of-attention-hating, stupid, ugly…"

There it was again. The self-deprecation painting an image of how warped she was inside. Evidence of how someone fucked with her, maybe even abused her.

By the look on Andrew's face, I had a feeling I was on the right track.

"Okay, enough," Andrew said as he took the glass from her. "I think it's time to get your drunken ass home."

She let out a whimper that shot right through my cock. "I drove."

"You definitely aren't driving. I can take you," Andrew said.

My grip on Lila's leg tightened at his words. There was no way I was letting him anywhere near her, especially in her current state. It was obvious he had feelings toward her, and not all in the past tense.

It was there in the way he looked at her, the way he tried to protect her.

He was her knight in shining fucking armor, and I was the conductor of the darkness.

"I can take her home."

Everyone's attention diverted to me. Four sets of eyes stared at me before Lila began laughing.

"Oh, Caroline, I forgot to tell you. The asshole lives in my building!"

The asshole? Apparently they'd talked about me a bit.

"You know I can hear you, right, drunkie?" I swept my fingers against the inside of her thigh, keeping her attention on me and not the idiot on the other side of her.

She stared at me, her glassy eyes moving in and out of focus. "Do I look like I care?"

"Don't hold back on me now, Palmer. Let it out."

"I was going to go into great detail on where to stick it, but thought it might be a little too rough for our party here."

Rough? Oh, she was going to know rough soon enough.

Ian laughed. "Oooh, Lila's getting surly."

"Surly wench. That's my name."

The bleeding edges of her mask showed. Darkness leaking out and licking against me.

"I'm going to call you that from now on," I teased.

"Bite me, Thorne."

One more comment and she was leaving with my teeth marks all over her neck.

"You are so fucking asking for it," I whispered against her ear as I slid my hand up her leg and under her skirt. I'd fucking make her come in front of the asshole, in front of them all.

"Alrighty!" She jumped, drawing everyone's attention. "I need…home. Who's taking me?"

"I can, babe," Andrew said, smiling at her.

This fucker.

Rip his head off.

I narrowed my eyes at Andrew. "I live in the same building. Why waste the gas when we're going to the same place?"

"Asshole has a good point," Lila said.

I jerked my head to the side, teeth mashed together as I resisted showing her just how much she was going to regret the last hour in front of everyone.

"Would you stop calling me that?"

"Nope. You threatened to call me 'surly wench' at work. If that's the case, I have every right to call you 'asshole.'"

"Are you sure you're okay to go home with him?" Andrew asked her.

I straightened, my lip curling up into a snarl. "What the hell is that supposed to mean?"

"I just thought you'd want to stick around and pick up someone for dessert," Andrew answered with a smile on his face.

Apparently my reputation preceded me.

My snarl turned to a sneer. "No, thanks. I'm full."

"And on that note," Caroline said in an attempt to deflate the subject.

"On that note, I'm calling it a night and taking 'drunkie' here with me." I stood and stepped back so Lila could get out.

"Well, it's been fun, all!" Lila said with a smile, then looked down to Andrew. "Drew…good to see you."

Before I could drag her away, the fucker climbed out of the booth and wrapped his arms around her. She floundered for a moment before hugging him back.

"You call me if you need anything, okay? I'll always be here for you. You know that, right?"

"I know, Drew," she said, then kissed his cheek. "See you."

One last wave and I grabbed her wrist. I'd barely had anything to drink, but was completely pumped up. A violent energy hummed through me, and I desperately needed some sort of outlet.

Jerome was still manning the door as we exited, Lila's unsteady steps making her weave and bump into people.

Jerome grabbed my arm, but I kept my eyes on Lila. "Yo, Nate, that chick has some serious issues. She's the clingy type, I can tell. Best leave her."

I smirked at him. "That shit runs both ways."

His jaw dropped, and he nodded slowly as he looked at Lila again. "All right, I see."

I said goodnight, then made up the distance to Lila, directing her to my car. It was nearly a block's walk to my car, and once we got there I held the door open. She reached out to steady herself, her hand on my waist, lips parted.

I reached down, under her skirt, and cupped her pussy, pressing my fingers against her clit. She drew in a breath, her eyes darkening.

The beast growled, ready to punish her.

"Sit, or I swear to God I will take everything out on you right here."

With a swipe of her hand across my cock, she slid down

into the seat. The car was nothing but a hotbox of swirling, dangerous energy. A heady combination of my jealousy, lust, and need. An explosive combination that would set fire to the air, and I was ready to feel the burn.

ESPITE HER GRUMBLING, I HAD LILA UP, OUT OF THE CAR, and over my shoulder. After the protests began, I ignored her. Though they seemed to stop when she noticed my ass.

A growl rumbled through my chest in warning. The drive did not cool me down. In fact, I was unhinged, volatile. I felt a vibration down to my core.

Off the elevator, into my condo, and pinned to the fucking wall as my lips crashed to hers.

Fuck her.

For making me feel things I shouldn't.

For the emotions that heaved inside of me.

For the possession my body demanded.

"Who is he, this *Andrew*?" I asked, panting as I dug my fingers into her hips.

"Andrew is my ex-boyfriend."

From my calves to my neck, every muscle tensed.

The fucker hadn't just longed for her, he'd had her. She'd been his. It'd been his cock inside her before me. She looked at him with those lust-filled eyes, begged him for more, gave him everything.

Fuck that.

I barely heard her call my name in the background before I kissed her again. The agitation swirled, morphing into a tornado that demanded destruction before it would release. Letting her go, I turned and drove my fist straight into the wall.

"Nathan!" Lila wrapped her hands around my wrist and pulled my hand out. Her gasp let me know she saw the other holes I'd created. "Why?"

"You. You do this to me. Every time… You make me so angry," I admitted, and reached out to caress her cheek. "I slept with my dress shirt on the other night because it smelled like you, and that pisses me off! I'm mad at myself and pissed at you for wrapping me around your little fucking finger."

"But I didn't…"

"I know!" I yelled, unable to hold back. "And that ticks me off more. I hate that you turn me on. I hate the way I need you all the fucking time. I don't want that. I *can't* want that. I *can't* want you…but I do. So fucking much I do."

"I want you, too."

No, don't say that.

"I hated every male that even looked at you tonight and wanted to hurt the one that dared touch you. I wanted to scream out *'mine'* to keep them all at bay. But I can't. I can't claim you like that. I *will* consume you."

"Why me?" she asked as she sunk down to the floor.

I stared at her, trying to understand where the hell the bottom of her self-hate was. Me asking the question was one thing, but it was the same one I'd been asking from the moment I first saw her. An answer that never came.

"What did you say?"

"I'm nothing. Drew leaving me proved *them* right. I'm nothing special. Plain, boring, pitiful, ugly Lila. Worthless."

"You shut that shit up right now!" I seethed as I squatted down in front of her. I'd hoped punching the wall would do more to calm me, but seeing how badly she looked at herself infuriated me. "*You* are beautiful, intelligent, witty, sarcastic, fun as hell to tease, and so fucking sexy I have trouble keeping my hands off you. You make it so hard to stay away… I want you so much. I've tried so hard, but you keep fucking drawing me in."

She blinked up at me. "Then why? Why can't we…"

I shook my head. "Because I can't. I can't love you. I can't allow myself to pursue you, Lila. A beautiful woman like you shouldn't waste your time on me."

"But, you said I wasn't 'that pretty.'"

I jumped back up and wished I had something to throw. "Shit. I was being a sarcastic asshole and was going to tell you I was joking, but you fucking threw me with your response. I'm used to women arguing against me, but you agreed. That shit is fucked up." I began to pace, jaw ticking as I tugged at my hair.

I was telling her things I never wanted her to know, but I couldn't stand seeing her so beaten down. She was everything I said and more, but we could never be more.

"Do you want to know what I think?" she asked as she braced herself against the wall to stand up.

"No. It doesn't matter."

"It doesn't matter that I want you?"

I squeezed my eyes tight. "Please don't."

I resorted to begging her to stop, because the beast prowled in his cage, desperate to get out, to take her, claim her and bind her to me.

Lila was still drunk, and I was thankful for her pause, but I knew she wasn't done. She was going to decimate me, destroy my resistance.

"We can't…be?"

"*Be?* Be, how?"

"Like we have been?"

I pushed the heel of my palm against my eyes. "You don't really want that with me."

It was a bad idea to give her an opening, to not shut her down once and for all.

"What if I do?"

"Drop it, Lila." I couldn't fucking talk about it anymore. We'd gone far past anything I could handle and entered into territory I couldn't allow, and somehow she'd almost convinced me that it was possible. That there could be more between us.

"Well, goodnight, then," she said as she turned toward the door.

I stared at her for a second before spinning her around. "Where the fuck do you think you're going?"

"Home."

"Oh, no. I'm not letting you out of my sight, drunkie."

It was to make sure she was okay. That was the lie I told myself to assuage the irresponsible motive of keeping her beside me. Slipping my hand in hers, I led her through my condo and into the master bedroom. With my hands on her hips, I directed her to sit on the edge of the bed. I began unzipping her boots, trying to get them off when I felt the warm, tingling sensation of her fingers sweep through my hair.

"So silky," she murmured.

My eyes closed, and I leaned into her touch, but then pulled away. She was doing it, drawing me in. I couldn't fall, couldn't get involved with her any more than I already was. Her small petting only reminded me of how starved I was for affection, how much I wanted it.

Once her boots were off, I lifted her to standing, then worked at getting her skirt off.

"You do know I'm not so drunk that I can't walk or undress myself, right?" she said with a small giggle.

"Shut up and get in the bed, Delilah," I commanded. Once she was settled, snuggled into the blanket, I pulled my shirt off and slid under the covers and against her back.

It'd been years since I last slept with someone, but there was no way I was going to let her out of my sight. The warmth of her skin soaked into mine and relaxed me.

How had I forgotten the simple bliss of human contact?

Halfway through the night I awoke, hard, my hips grinding against Lila's soft ass. It was softer, intimate, but still laced with the intensity that drove our attraction.

When I woke a few hours after that, it was to the sound of crying. I glanced around, trying to find the source as the bed was empty, and found Lila on the floor ten feet away, her arms wrapped around her.

"Lila?" I asked as I jumped out of bed. I looked around, trying to find a reason when a sob broke from her, tearing at me. "*Lila?*"

I dropped down in front of her, and she flung her arms around my neck. I wrapped my arms around her and pulling her close, my head in the crook of her neck.

"What happened? What happened to you?" she asked.

It clicked, the reason for her outburst. She saw what I kept hidden from everyone—my scars. The evidence that I was a dead man walking, that my heart shouldn't have been beating.

I tensed, the action pulled her closer, almost using her as an anchor to keep me from crumbling.

"Please, don't ask me that. Please… I can't…"

I can't tell you about what I lost, about why I am the way I am, about why you need to stay away.

The beast growled, but in pain instead of anger, crying out.

I kept her securely wrapped in my arms, keeping her from looking at them again, until her tears subsided. It was a reaction I wasn't used to from women. Most who caught a glimpse were a mixture of curious, disgusted, and full of a pity I couldn't stand.

Lila continued to confuse and surprise me. More so when she studied them further, her fingers reaching out to trace the large raised scar that wound around my hip.

I stared at her, completely confounded by her reaction. Leaning down, I caught her bottom lip between my teeth, drawing her attention away from my monstrous appearance.

Her eyes were a strange, beautiful gray and green mixture, and even in the darkness, gave so much away. There was more there, emotions I couldn't handle, ones that had the power to burn us alive.

"Push me away. You have to."

"No."

"*Push me away!*"

"*I can't!*"

Her tears returned, and I rested my forehead against hers. "Why? Tell me why…say it."

Torture me more.

"Because I want you! I want you so much it hurts! I need all of you, and I can't deny it anymore."

Part of me reveled in her confession, but part of me feared it, knowing full well the consequences.

I brushed a strand of hair behind her ear and cupped her face. "I can't give you what you want, beautiful. I'll only hurt you."

She shook her head, her fingers flexing against my skin. "It's okay. If it's you, I don't mind."

Fuck!

"Stop," I begged as I held my hands up. "Let's just go back to bed."

She paused, then nodded. "Okay…okay."

I helped her stand, and we climbed back into bed.

A woman was in my arms. A woman who had feelings for me. It wasn't a good situation, but I didn't know how much longer I could resist her.

THE PUSH AND PULL WAS MADDENING. NOT JUST WITH LILA, BUT within myself. I wanted more of her. I wanted more with her, but that was an impossibility. Logically, we could never be anything more than coworkers. The problem was that logic and the will of my cock were two entirely different forces.

Opposite ends playing tug of war while Lila sat next to me, completely oblivious of the battle she created in me. The blame for my mania rested solely on her.

Jesus. Every fucking day was a struggle beyond any struggle I'd ever experienced. Instead of day by day getting better, I fell deeper and deeper into a storm, churning and violent, and I didn't know how much longer I could hold on.

Lila wasn't a victim of the storm—she *was* the storm.

And I hated her for it. I hated the emotions, the way my dick got so fucking hard that I couldn't keep control over my actions.

She would be my demise.

Guilt crushed me. Every day with Lila was a deeper hole into a dark area that was full of the danger I'd avoided.

It took every ounce of energy to stay away.

We'd crossed the line of just sex. She wanted to be, to continue on with the warped relationship we had evolved into, but I couldn't.

Still, my dick was constantly hard, the memory of being inside her a driving force of multiple-times-a-day masturbation.

I managed to keep my distance throughout the week, but come the weekend, I failed.

Multiple nights in a row I tried to stay away but ended up at her door. The resulting anger in my failure only served to up the intensity. Everything was harder, needier, and borderline abusive, and it wasn't all coming from me. She inflamed my sexual deviancy, accelerating an already high sex drive.

Another night of resisting, of sitting alone in my condo willing myself not to go to her. I was going to do it, resist her call.

I sat on the couch, my dick hard, begging to fail again. The urge was great, so I slid my hand into my pants and pulled it out. The head was red, angry, beads of precome leaking out. All I did was think about her, remember her mouth, her pussy wrapped around me, and I was aching for release.

The sound of my doorbell shook me from my thoughts and sent an ice-cold shock through me. It was enough to cool my dick down.

Looking through the peephole I saw her, and a groan rolled through me. It seemed, though I had managed to stay away, she couldn't.

Fuck.

Why? Why couldn't I stop this? Why was it so hard to stay away from each other?

"Go away, Delilah," I said through the door.

She shook her head. Her unmasked eyes were almost lifeless but held an edge of desperation.

"No."

She needs us.

She shouldn't.

With a sigh, I twisted the two locks and swung the door open.

"I can't save you," I said, holding my hands up.

She shook her head. "I'm not looking for a savior."

"I can't love you." Definitely not. "So what is it you want?"

Her head tilted slightly to the side, fingers twisting in front of her as her brow scrunched while she contemplated.

Most women would have lashed out at me, but she kept coming back. No matter how many times I tried to push her away, she stared up at me with those beautiful, empty eyes and called to the beast.

"I want you to not stop," she said.

I blinked at her, stunned. Stopping was necessary for her survival. "I have to."

She shook her head. "No, you don't."

I needed to stop my internal comparisons of her to average women. Lila wasn't and would never be average. I didn't know what happened to her, but I did know it created the tortured, empty soul in front of me.

And the darkness from that was a beautiful pit that my own darkness wanted to crawl into.

"I know you want me as much as I want you," she said.

Even though her words were said with clarity, they lacked the strength. She wasn't sure, which was odd to me as I'd pretty much attacked her with how much I wanted her on more than one occasion.

"Want is a passing fling, and it will pass."

"I don't want it to."

She stepped forward, a determined look on her face. I blinked down at her, once again surprised by her tenacity. Normally she was so submissive to everyone, wanting approval, clawing at favorable emotions. She placed her palms against my chest, fisting the loose fabric of my T-shirt.

"What are you doing, Lila?" I asked as my heart kicked into high gear, hammering inside my chest.

She pulled on my shirt, yanking me down to her level. Her lips ghosted mine, fucking obliterating my resistance down to a small thread keeping the beast at bay.

"I need you, Nathan."

A groan left me as I shuddered. Fuck. A few more words and there would be no way to stop myself from taking her to my bed and fucking her until we both passed out.

"I need your body over mine, your cock inside me. I need you to touch me. Bite me. Mark me."

My cock thumped hard in my pants, barely restrained by my boxer briefs, while my breath picked up.

Fuck, I wanted her, needed her just as badly as she did me.

I reached up and cradled her head in my hands, my fingers fisted in her hair. The last fraying edges that held me back began to snap.

What was it about her? Why couldn't I stay away?

She was wrecking me, and I reacted like any other animal fighting against their end.

"You're killing me."

My lips were on hers, drinking her in like she was an oasis in the desert.

My dreams were often filled with nightmares. Some I remembered, but more often forgotten. Glimpses of memories mixed with horror. It was my wife. Always my wife.

But something shifted one night.

"You're not helping me, Nate. You're not helping me. Why aren't you helping me?" Grace screamed, her body melting, morphing.

I shook, watching as my wife's blue eyes faded, the hue changing to a familiar gray-green.

Lila.

She looked down, her hands rising. They were covered in red, her face pale. "So much blood," she said, then collapsed to the ground.

I sat straight up in bed, gasping for breath. Sweat covered my face. A scream filled my ears, and as the room came into focus, I realized it was me. My whole body shook, a wave of nausea rolling through me.

I swung my legs over the edge of the bed and fumbled for the switch on the bedside lamp. It was blinding, but necessary as I pulled open the drawer and dug through the bottles. As the names passed by, I became more and more frustrated. I was tempted to take them all when finally I found the name I was looking for—Xanax.

The pills inside were small, and I emptied a few onto my palm before tossing them in my mouth. I'd perfected taking pills without a drink, and the smaller ones were easy to do.

My nightmares had shifted, and it was no longer the woman I was missing, but the woman that I had.

The bed bounced a little and I quickly shut the drawer.

She sat beside me as I tried to calm down. The problem was, I couldn't. It was overpowering.

Why was it Lila?

I jumped at the feel of her hand cupping my face. Her eyes were filled with worry, and I leaned into her touch. I needed the soothing, but more importantly, the reminder that she was fine. That she was alive.

"Ssshhh," she soothed as she brushed strands of hair that were stuck to my sweat-covered forehead. "It's all right, baby. Everything's all right."

I pressed my lips to hers, needing the connection, to feel her. We lay back down, and I wrapped my arms around her, ducking my head into the crook of her neck. I needed to keep her safe. Protected.

She ran her fingers through my hair, and it didn't take long for her to lull me back to sleep.

KEEPING MY DICK OUT OF LILA WAS QUICKLY BECOMING A complete joke. Between the teasing, I took any excuse and opportunity to get inside her. After shoving my cock down her throat at the office, I was hating us both for my lack of control.

I kept a cool disregard toward Lila as we entered our building. It was necessary after what I'd done. Sure, it was after hours, but I'd still lost control at the office again.

Though there was no way I regretted having my cock down her throat or the way I came with her nose pressed against my abs. She deserved it for teasing me.

As we entered the elevator, I made sure to punch the button for my floor along with Lila's. When the doors closed, I was left with no moving air and her so close. I could almost feel her looking at me, and when I glanced at her, that wide-eyed, blank expression stared back, only this time with a bit of expectation.

I needed to tell her it wasn't going to happen, that we needed to stop, that I wasn't going to break and she shouldn't either. All of that was decimated by my fucking stomach. How a stomach could make a high-pitched sound and turn into a gurgling rumble, I'd never know. The wonders of the human body. It was especially loud echoing off the metal walls of the elevator.

Lila giggled. "Hungry, are we?"

The tension fell from me, and my lips twitched up. "Maybe just a little."

The elevator slowed and pinged, then the doors slid open. She stepped off and turned, her hand extended.

"Come."

Come where? On her? With her? "Lila, I…"

"Have dinner with me. Come."

I shook my head. "You don't have to cook for me."

"Well, I have to do it for me, and it's usually enough to feed four. So, come."

I stared at her hand as I contemplated her offer. If I went with her, I knew there was no stopping me from fucking her. Acceptance equaled sex, pure and simple. It may have been an offer of food, but it was also an invitation for so much more. What lay in the more was what worried me. Sex wasn't all Lila wanted from me.

The doors started to close, and I made the decision that could be the beginning of my destruction, all because I couldn't stay away from her.

I followed her down the hall, and resisted the urge to touch her while she unlocked her door. Thankfully, with seconds before I just grabbed her and pinned her against the door, she got it open and stepped inside, ushering me to follow.

"So, how long have you lived in Indianapolis?" she asked as she disappeared into the master bedroom.

I wasn't sure getting to know the details of each other's

lives was a good thing, but what could a few generic answers hurt?

"My whole life, with the exception of college. What about you?" I asked as I pulled my jacket off, followed by my tie.

"Indiana native, born and bred," she admitted. "I moved to Indy just before college and stayed. No reason to return anyway. Not much demand for lawyers in the middle of nowhere."

Her entire life in a few miles' circle? With what little I knew about her I began to wonder if she'd ever left the state.

"You didn't go out of state for law school?"

We moved into the kitchen, and I watched her chest expand before a sigh escaped. "No. Too much to pay out of state tuition. I'll be paying off my school debts for another few years as it is. Even with my grants."

"Yeah, I don't have those. My parents paid for my undergrad and Harvard Law."

"Wow. How was Harvard?"

"Hard," I chuckled. "And the east coast... That is an experience. Very different from here."

"You know, that mask of yours is slipping a lot lately."

I stared at her before shrugging my shoulders, my smile fading. "There's no point in the pretense around you."

Not with all we'd been through the prior weeks.

"But I still don't know your secrets," she said as she rifled through the fridge.

"No, but you know there *are* secrets. That's much more than anyone else. It's nice not to have to always pretend everything's perfect."

Less fucking exhausting, even with as dangerous as it was to get close enough to someone for them to see.

"So, why pretend, then?"

"It makes things easier." I reached up and rubbed at my neck. Her questions were getting a little too in depth, too close to me. "It didn't take long to learn that after… People don't really want to know that your knee and wrist ache every day, your body hurts in ways you can't describe, that you're plagued by migraines and nightmares, or your depression and anxiety continue years later."

Fuck.

It just spilled from me, part in agitation and part because I had a feeling out of everyone I knew, she might be the only one to understand. Nobody understood, but from what I'd learned about Lila, I knew there was so much she kept hidden. Whether for emotional stability and protection or just trying to fit in, Lila's charade was just as orchestrated as my own.

"What about you?"

Her spine straightened almost imperceptibly. "What *about* me?"

There was no way I was going to let her play that fucking game after what I just told her. "You really want to play that game? Do you want me to say it?"

"No," she whispered.

"Why, then?"

She let out a huff, her face scrunched as she set a can of pasta sauce down a little hard on the counter. "The same. It's easier to say I'm fine then go into detail about how I put out a confident front, but inside I'm holding the darkness at bay and one word can send it crashing down."

One word?

Those two little words confirmed some of my suspicions. Verbal abuse was rampant in her life at one time, probably her childhood.

I tilted my head to the side as I looked at her. "You confound me."

She stared back, her brow still scrunched.

"You have such a poor view of yourself." It was a constant with her that I didn't understand, and wasn't sure I wanted to. There was a strong sense that I would be very violent against another human if I knew the details. "How did you get this way?"

She kept her eyes away from me. "Doesn't matter. Damage done, and I'm working to get past it."

Bullshit answer for the win.

We were a fucking pair.

I leaned against the counter and watched her move. It was fluid, smooth, but there were nuances in her posture. The way her head was always bowed down, elbows kept close to her ribs. Even her footsteps were small and light to avoid making any sound. She may have been out of it, but she was far from over it.

"Hiding it doesn't help you get past it."

She set a pot in the sink and turned on the faucet, filling it with water. Her avoidance tactics were well honed, but not with someone like me.

"No, it doesn't. You know that all too well. The thing is, I've at least gotten a little better over the years. Have you?" she asked as she set the filled pot on the stove.

"Your eyes say differently," I said as I ignored her question.

"I said I've gotten better, not that I was healed. Downers don't help. That's why I don't go out drinking with people… you've seen what happens."

I had. Years of repression, of sadness and despair, came pouring out of her. Darkness that she drowned in. She risked the memories for a few hours of shutting it all down.

"Yes, but that also shows you aren't better."

"You make me better," she whispered.

I froze.

No. No, no, no.

Those words were the exact reason I didn't want to get so involved with her. Not that I didn't want her to get better, but her saying that it was me and the way she said it—they were tells that she had feelings for me. Feelings that could get her killed.

"You make me feel like I'm all of the things they said I wasn't. Beautiful, smart, sexy...worth something."

"Who are 'they'?" I asked after a moment of silence as I tried to ignore what she was saying. "What did 'they' do to you?"

She slammed the box of pasta down on the counter. "You want to know? You're certain you want me to tell you how every day I was told how insignificant I was?"

The way her voice shuddered cut at me.

"You're not forthcoming with information, and I get that, I do. I hope one day you'll be able to tell me. As for me... Well, when you're young, and the people in your life tell you these things *every day*, you begin to believe them. They become ingrained into who you are, and I've worked damn hard to push them away. Years of therapy. I've seen a psychiatrist from the time I was seventeen. Twelve years later, I have more confidence, but everything still haunts me."

Her hands shook as she stared down at the counter. Broken and beaten down. What happened to me was instantaneous, but Lila was stripped away little by little until she was barely human by the time they were done with her.

"I've done that to you, haven't I? I've said something to trigger you?"

When I first met her, I was certain I said something. She turned to me and shrugged before returning her attention to the counter.

"You didn't know. Alcohol is a double-edged sword for me. It helps me sleep, but my depression spikes."

"Yet you drink every Friday, letting everything come back." I'd seen it, the transformation in her. I didn't know anything about her insomnia, because I seemed to fuck her to sleep.

"Stalking me now?" she said with a teasing tone in an obvious attempt to change the heavy mood that surrounded us.

"No, just observant."

"Well, Mr. Observant, can you hand me the bread sitting next to you?"

Diversion was obviously one of her coping mechanisms. I'd seen it before, but with just the two of us in the most honest conversation we'd ever had, I was a bit surprised.

I handed her the uncut loaf, then moved my hand to caress her cheek. She was so beautifully broken, and I wondered how different she would be if she'd grown up in a loving home.

"You are so much more than pretty. That was what I wanted to say to you that night. Instead, I was inadvertently mean to push you away." I pushed her back with my body until she was settled against the counter, my forehead against hers. Those intriguing eyes of hers stared at me. "How do you do this to me?"

She tilted her head in a tentative move, and I waited, unmoving, as she moved to press her lips to mine. It was a rarity for her to make the first move, but when she did, it just made me want her more.

I didn't move at first, didn't breathe, just to test myself, but there was no resisting her. I'd long given up on that. She parted her lips, and I slipped my tongue in, then bit down on her lower lip. It was so much softer and intimate and had my cock hardening as lust took over.

"Fuck, you taste so good. Could fucking eat *you* for dinner," I said as I rocked my hips, making sure she felt what she did to me.

"Please."

A shudder rolled through me at the simple word. I fucking loved it when she said it, when she begged for me.

"Please what?" I grabbed her ass and pulled her closer.

Her hands fisted in the fabric of my shirt. "Please, Nathan, I need you to fuck me. I need you inside me. I've waited all day."

It took me only seconds to pick her up and put her on the counter, my dick pressing against her hot core.

"You like that? Little wanton slut begging for my cock. Is that what you want? Me to shove my cock in you? Make you scream?"

"Yes, fuck yes!"

She pulled my lips down to hers. The touch, the taste, of her fueled the need to get inside her. Lila managed to get my cock free, her small hands stroking me.

"Fuck." I groaned. "God, you are so fucking insatiable."

That was part of the problem. Her need for a connection skyrocketed her sex drive to a level that matched my own.

"Good thing you can keep up," she said as I pressed forward.

A gasp left her as inch by inch disappeared inside her.

"So wet for me," I groaned as I pulled out, exposing the

glistening sheen on my cock. I slid back in and held it there while I took her nipple between my teeth.

She bucked against me, trying to get me to move, but I wasn't having it. I fisted her hair and pulled her head back, forcing her body to arch, her neck exposed.

There was excitement in her eyes, and I glared at her.

"I'll fuck you when I'm good and ready. Until then you will sit there with my cock shoved up your cunt and be happy it's there."

She let out a moan, which became hitches in her breath when I slipped my hand between us and found her clit. I teased it and her nipple, but before long, the desire for friction won over and my hips began to move in short strokes.

I kept teasing her and pulled on one of her nipples with my teeth. She was tight around me, but I didn't realize how close she was until her body tensed, then released, a small, high-pitched whine leaving her as she shook.

"That's it, baby, come all over my cock."

The feel of her squeezing me only heightened my need to come. I let go of her hair and moved to grip her hips, giving me the leverage I needed to pound into her.

Lila was still sensitive, her cries and screams fucking music when each thrust bottomed out. She was left as nothing more than a vessel to receive the pleasure I gave her.

"Fuck!" I hissed as I slammed into her. "God fucking damn tight pussy."

Each thrust in drove me close as she squeezed me harder, building up to another milking orgasm. She shattered, falling apart around me for a second time, and I lost it.

"Shit, shit, shit!" I cursed as I slammed my hips all the way against her, my cock firing off in the mind-wiping pleasure I craved.

The tension fell away, our harsh breaths in time as we slowly came down from the ultimate high. "Lila…fuck, Lila."

She shook her head against mine. "No. No fuck Lila. Lila done for tonight. Try back in the morning,"

I chuckled against her neck and kissed the skin there.

"I suppose I could wait a few more hours, maybe fuck you while you're asleep in the middle of the night. Wouldn't that be a nice way to wake up? My cock buried inside of you?"

A moan slipped through her lips. "Oh God!"

"I'll take that as a hell yes, Miss Palmer."

"I am all for wake up calls like that, Mr. Thorne."

I let my imagination begin to drift, when reality interjected. The pot we had on the stove was emitting a steam cloud. Stepping back, leaving her warmth, was always hard.

Though not as difficult as I watched my come drip from her pussy onto the floor.

I helped her down before stepping to the sink for a towel. It was a good thing I had only gone a few feet because Lila's legs gave out, and she stumbled.

My new mission was to make certain she had difficulty walking every time. I chuckled and placed a kiss on her neck.

"Hmm, maybe we should have something delivered instead of putting you near a pot of boiling water right now."

"You may be on to something," she agreed as her legs gave out and we sank to the ground, laughing.

After she had some time to recover, I ran up to my place and grabbed my stockpile of delivery menus. An hour later, we were stuffed with fried rice and cashew chicken.

We watched some television, then moved to her bed. I had her in my arms, her head on my chest as I began drifting off to sleep.

"Hey, Nathan?"

"Hmm?" I was almost asleep, no strength to actually form words.

"I'm yours, just so you know," she mumbled.

My eyes shot open, and I looked down at her. Her eyes were closed, her soft breath against my chest.

The beast purred at what she said, but it was panic that overtook me. I had let her get too deep.

Lila's words didn't sit well. She had developed feelings for me that seemed to grow deeper every day. I didn't want to think about it, and I wished she'd never said anything.

It left me agitated, the anxiety piling upon me a little more every day.

Her words spurred on the nightmares that terrorized me. They'd morphed. No longer just of my wife, but many starring her.

I didn't want to put her into harm's way. That was the whole reason I tried to keep my distance. The problem was that she was just another drug to me, and like all the others, I'd become dependent on her without even knowing it.

I was burning through some of my medication faster than normal just to keep my heart from beating out of my fucking chest. The stress, the weight of her declaration, was too much for me to handle. I'd been running and avoiding for years, and suddenly there was a declaration hanging in front of me that could make everything come crumbling down.

I tried to keep things lighter, our usual banter and sex, even though my dreams were turbulent.

A week later when she handed me the key to her condo, I froze. A key meant a lot. A key implied a relationship of sorts. And a key also was almost too much for me to handle.

Still, I took it, and gave her one to my place.

Turned out having her key came in handy for more than just going over for a fuck. It also made me feel better knowing her door wasn't unlocked.

I was used to seeing Lila in mainly two forms of clothing—work attire and loungewear—so when she stepped out onto my balcony in a knee-length dress with a sweater looking every bit innocent and corruptible, it was hard to keep on schedule.

Come here, little girl, and sit on my lap, the beast purred.

She stepped closer, almost close enough to reach out and run my hand around her exposed thigh.

"I didn't know you smoked."

"Sometimes," I said as I blew out.

She stared at me with those eyes, digging into me. Lila was smart, observant, much more so than she let on.

"It bothers you that much…my feelings?"

Did it? The easy answer was yes, but it amazed me that she'd picked up on it just by seeing me with a cigarette. Smoking was a habit I'd almost given up until she opened up to me.

"Yes. I don't want you to feel that way."

She took a deep breath and moved to sit next to me. Her fingers landing on the scar on the inside of my forearm, a few soft caresses on the white lines before she pulled my arm to her for a drag. It was a move I wasn't prepared for. She always seemed so innocent, but when she expertly took a drag, I remembered there was a lot I didn't know and didn't want to know about her.

Like ex-boyfriends that suddenly show up.

The anger that lit in my veins…two of the holes in my entryway were because of that fucker. Andrew was too familiar with her, too casual, too intent.

Andrew wanted her.

"What?" she asked, making me wonder what kind of look I was sporting.

"I don't like the way he looks at you."

"And?"

I scrunched my face, hating the emotions, the admissions. But a grin spread as I realized how I could get my point across. I reached over and slipped my hand between her thighs and cupped her pussy.

"For me only."

She stared at me before shaking her head. "You are such a fucking contradiction."

"What?" Maybe she had caught on to just how screwed up she made me.

"I wish I knew what was going on in that head of yours sometimes."

I leaned over and snuffed the cigarette out on the ground. "No, you don't." I tapped my skull. "It's dark in here."

And dangerous. And so fucked up I didn't think she'd be able to handle the load.

Just knowing about the beast would send her running.

I stood and held my hand out to help her up. "Ready?"

She nodded and slipped her hand in mine. I wanted to keep it there, but once she was upright, I let go and we headed out.

"Are we starting with shots?" I asked as we walked to the bar. Nipps had become a regular part of my weekly routine.

"Sounds perfect."

Two hours and two shots later, I was working on my

second beer and munching on chips from the nacho plate we'd ordered.

I pulled out another cigarette, amazed how fast I fell back into them, though I hadn't fully stopped. They were just a crutch, something that gave me a feeling other than pain.

"So with all the sleeping you're doing lately, why still drink?" I asked.

It shouldn't have amazed me that my dick had the power to cure insomnia. I'd just never tested it out before.

She reached for my hand and took a drag from my newly lit cigarette. I watched intently as her lips wrapped around the end, her cheeks hollowing out as she drew in, and my dick stirred. It'd been half hard from the moment I saw her in her dress, and the ideas of what I could do with her began to form.

"I need to unwind after dealing with you and your fanclub all week."

I chuckled. "They are fucking something. I just don't understand how they think that's attractive. I mean, yeah, breasts are great, love them, but showing me your rack isn't going to get you a ride on my dick."

We both laughed, but were soon interrupted.

"Delilah Anne Palmer!"

We turned, and a growl left me as the image of her fucking Mr. Perfect ex-boyfriend appeared.

"Smoking? You worked so hard to quit, and now you're at it again?"

Scratch that, Mr. Fucking Perfect Boy Scout.

She let out a sigh. "It was just a drag, Andrew."

"A gateway drag."

Is this douche serious? I almost laughed.

The sound of his voice irked me, but not as much as his

goody-goody disapproval. She was a fucking adult and could do whatever the fuck she wanted. And I was right that she had smoked in her life.

She didn't seem to like his chastising either. "What are you doing here?"

He pulled the bar stool out from beside her and sat down like he was invited to our fucking party before signaling to John.

"Well, I was thinking we could have a celebratory drink."

Three days prior, Jack had announced a new employee, and it infuriated me when Andrew walked through the door. He hadn't been around the office much in his first few days, but his appearance at the bar, knowing full well she'd be there, was a taste of things to come.

"Whatever."

What a fucking joke.

That was the moment the fucker noticed me. He had been so fixated on her, he was oblivious to everything else.

His expression soured, and I resisted flipping him off.

I was here first, asshole.

"What are you doing here?" he asked.

The guy was just asking for a fucking beat down. I didn't like him to begin with. His whole savior complex made me want to puke. Add in that he stuck his dick in Lila at one point, and I was ready to shove my fist in his face to get him the fuck away from us.

"It's Friday night, this is the closest bar to my house, and I needed a drink." Not that I owed him any fucking explanation.

"Cool. Just stay away from Lila."

The beast growled while I practiced my counting-to-ten skills. The last thing I needed was to call my parents to bail me out of jail.

"Andrew!" Lila admonished him.

Every muscle tensed, and I shifted to stand. I couldn't fucking stand the guy, and I was more than ready to lay him out. "What did you say?"

Andrew's body shifted as well, both of us ready to beat the shit out of one another. "You heard me. You're bad news, I can tell."

Bad news?

My lip curled up. "What the hell do you know about me? Nothing. So shut the fuck up."

Andrew stood. "I've seen the way you look at her. Stay the fuck away."

"What way do I 'look' at her?" I asked as I stood.

"Like she's another notch to add to your bedpost."

I stepped forward, but was stopped. Lila's hand pressed against my chest, a burning point that seared me. Her small frame was no match for the two of us, and I hated that she tried.

"All right, boys, back up."

Andrew backed off like a good little puppy, but I refused to let it go. I wasn't going to be blasted by a shit like him.

"I have to go to the bathroom. Do you think you two can be civilized?"

No.

"Don't worry," I said as I downed the rest of my beer. "I'm on my way out."

I had to get out before I hurt my hand on his face.

I pulled out my wallet and threw forty bucks onto the counter, then walked away. The noise and the crowd had picked up, and I looked back to find their attention solely on each other with Lila clearly not happy. Dangerous ideas formed, and instead of leaving, I changed course from the front door to the side and the hall the led to the restrooms.

I was going to prove to him that he wasn't wanted or needed. And I was going to punish her for ever having him inside her. I didn't fucking care that it had been years. I didn't like it.

There was an alcove for the fire door, and I hid there until she approached the door and I grabbed her wrist and pulled her in. She was lost in a haze of confusion of the situation, but by her submission, she knew my touch.

I had her lips against mine and climbing onto the sink in seconds, legs wrapped around my waist, hands gripped to my shoulders, and her fucking hot pussy against my dick. I sunk my teeth into her shoulder for mark number one.

"But you left," she said between pants.

I released her skin and licked it lightly to soothe the reddening mark. "I couldn't exactly follow you into the bathroom to fuck your brains out with your knight in shining armor watching, now could I?"

By the time I was done with her, he would fucking know she was taken.

Cover her with my come and mark her as mine.

18

MY ANGER GREW WITH EACH STEP BACK TO MY CONDO. IT should have been gone. I fucked Lila in the bathroom, gave her a new pet name of Honeybear, and came all over her face and chest. She was covered in come and I made sure to smear it all over her skin to dry. The smell of come wasn't strong, but it was distinct.

It was the thought of her being there with him and not me. Talking with her, laughing with her. And I knew he was eye fucking her.

Would he try to make a move? Try to kiss her? Lila was pretty submissive—would she submit to his advances?

Fuck.

I almost turned around, returned to the bar so I could drag her out and the fuck away from him. Their familiarity, their history, drove me insane. There was an ease in their relationship that we neither had nor could have.

I hated him. Loathed him for returning to her life.

Three steps in the door, and my fist was in the drywall when it should have been against skin.

I hated him. Hated the fact that I hated some inconsequential guy all because he knew the woman I was fucking in more intimate ways than I ever could.

My knuckles throbbed, and I pulled my hand out. There was no broken skin, but one knuckle did appear to be swelling.

Great.

I froze at the sound of the doorbell. My parents were in Chicago for the weekend and Lila had a key. No one else knew where I lived.

One glance through the peephole, and I pulled open the door to a normally timid Lila who was lit up. Her eyes were wide, jaw set as she launched at me, pushing me back into the wall.

"You, sir, are a fucking bastard."

She was angry, livid, and it was a fucking turn-on. The beast was ready to turn her around, press her against the wall, a fuck her.

"What the fuck was that all about?"

I smirked at her. The only reason she was back mere minutes after me was because…

"He noticed." I leaned down and whispered in her ear as I pulled her closer. "Good."

Her hands smacked against my chest. There was really no physical strength to her, and her anger amused me.

"I can't fucking believe you."

"You're the one who said you were mine," I said, throwing her own words back. "I was just making it known."

She struggled and pushed away.

Well, fuck that.

I crossed my arms over my chest.

"You're always trying to push me away, but I want you to

think about it. I mean really think about me no longer being around...or better yet, me with another man, screaming out *his* name as *his* cock is buried in me. Tell me, what do you *think* now?"

Another man's arms around her? His cock buried in her warm pussy, come dribbling out.

Hell fucking no! Mine! She's fucking MINE!

I grabbed her wrist without even thinking. Impulse was my truth. The truth I didn't want to face or admit.

My breath picked up as I looked down, a shake beginning deep in my core. I let go, but she grabbed my hand.

"Shh," she soothed as she caressed my fingers with her thumb.

I drew in a stuttered breath. It was all too intense on an emotional level, too intimate. I didn't want the feeling that clawed in my chest, didn't want to want her so fucking much the idea of her being with someone else made me see red.

Her gaze flickered behind me. "Did you punch another hole in the wall?" she asked. "Were you angry that you let yourself go again and showed me the real you?"

I froze. Where the fuck was she going?

"Did you do that because you were pissed at taking me in a public restroom, or because you claimed me as yours?"

All of the energy drained from me.

"What does it matter?" I asked with a sigh.

"What does it *matter*?" she mimicked. "We've been going with the flow, and then all of a sudden... I don't get you."

"You're the one who wants to 'be.' I told you it was a bad idea," I spat as I picked up the glass of bourbon I'd forgotten about when we left. It burned on the way down, but I needed it for the conversation she started.

"Yes, but your actions back at the bar? Laying claim to me caveman-style? Being possessive and jealous?"

Fuck. She was right. My need to one-up Andrew, to get him to back the fuck up, let the beast divulge the greedy and selfish desires I kept from even myself.

"You changed things."

Changed?

No!

Memories of all the photos of death and destruction the Marconi dealt over the years flew through my mind. If things continued, I would condemn her to be another photo in a file with his name on it.

I turned and grabbed hold of the glass, then swung my arm out with all the frustration in me, sending it shattering against the wall.

"Fuck!" I tugged at my hair. "Why was he there?"

"*Who?* Andrew?"

"Who the fuck else?" I asked, not caring if I sounded like a condescending ass. "He doesn't know shit about me!"

"Well, he seems to think he knows *something*," Lila said.

I began pacing, my gaze anywhere but her. The way Andrew talked about me, the venom he spewed meant he'd talked to people about me.

"With all the rumors, he probably believed them. He seems the type."

Lila held up her hand. "Before I touch that last part…what rumors?"

I stopped and stared at her. Since the beginning, I told Jack that I needed anonymity, a clean slate. The problem was not everyone could keep their damn mouths shut. There was a posture to gossipers. The stare and whisper, looking around. They didn't see me at first, but their demeanor would always change when they noticed me.

While I knew that most of the office didn't know anything about me, some remembered my name from stories in the news. They recognized me.

"Lila, you're intelligent, so I know you've figured out transactional law and contracts are not my area, but I can do it."

She nodded. "You don't have the personality, and no one graduates with honors from Harvard Law to work contracts at a law firm in Indianapolis, albeit a large one."

"Exactly."

I froze as realization dawned on me. We'd reached a point, a crossing. The next words would change things.

We already changed things.

As much as I hated to admit it, they had. I pulled at my hair in agitation, my jaw locked down. Andrew knew rumors, but I didn't want Lila to know rumors.

"The last few years...hell, they've been hell..." I trailed off. How much could I tell her? My hand clenched my chest, and I fisted the fabric there. "I can't go through that pain again. If I love you, then that's something they can take away from me. Take revenge on me by hurting you. I can't deal with that." The strength left my voice, the next words barely a whisper. "Not again."

The whispered thought of her being gone tore at me, and I closed the distance between us. My lips on hers, tongues tasting each other as I pulled her so close there was no space left between us.

Before things got us sidetracked, mainly my ever-growing constant need to be inside her, I slowed our kisses.

I reached up and caressed her cheek with the backs of my fingers.

"I'm not worried about you being hurt by me, Lila. I'm worried about you being hurt *because* of me."

There. An admission I hoped would appease her, because the energy flowing through me was going to explode soon, a fight in which I would drag out her darkness. Something to appease my own, appease the beast screaming inside me.

I returned to pacing, the agitation crawling up my throat, constricting me. She was a nervous mess, but I was a motherfucking hurricane.

A shudder rolled through me as I tried to reign in the emotions that were trying to explode. There was so much. So much I did wrong.

I was stuck, alive, standing in front of a woman who made me feel something, and I fucking hated it. I'd paid for my sins and I refused to pay again, but for some fucking reason, it felt like nothing had changed since the morning I woke up.

Nothing except the fragile woman in front of me that infuriated me. It was her fault I was voicing my pain. Because I met her and her irresistible call.

She fucking caused the flare in my chest, the anxiety that beat like a war drum in my veins.

My entire body was tense with anger and frustration, and I saw just how much so when Lila's body leaned away from me.

"You think being a federal prosecutor is great. You work hard to put heinous criminals away, hopefully for good. You don't think about the repercussions. About how the ones you're prosecuting or their families may be angry with you and want revenge for you trying to uphold the law and make people safe. You don't think about how someone will try to take your life because they blame you for ruining their life or their loved ones. They don't care who else gets hurt in their quest to get to you. Sometimes they even threaten them to scare you."

I moved to the couch and sat, my eyes fixed on the fireplace, agitation leaking from me in the form of my right leg bouncing at a frantic pace. The energy couldn't be expelled fast enough and I picked up the only thing left on my side table, which was a sandstone coaster, and twirled it in my hand.

In my periphery, Lila moved closer but remained silent. She was so close to me, too close. They would come, and I would lose her.

A snarl ripped through me, and I pulled my arm back and threw the coaster against the fireplace where it shattered before falling to the floor and joining the pieces of glass.

"I was cocky. I thought nothing and no one could touch me. I was very wrong."

So very fucking wrong, and I paid the ultimate price. My life was penance for that attitude.

Lila dropped to her knees in front of me.

Each word was fucking torture.

"I couldn't do it anymore. I couldn't handle it, not after… I tried, I did. I failed miserably when not even a month back in, I exploded in the courtroom."

"But you're not a prosecutor anymore," she said.

If only it were that simple. Vendettas rarely are, especially not with the head of a large criminal organization very pissed that you put his daughter in jail.

"Do you think that matters, Lila?" I asked. "This condo? It isn't even under my name. Because I'm still alive."

I couldn't take it anymore, couldn't stand another word about the past, about the shit I brought down on myself.

It was her fucking turn.

Her gray-green eyes stared at me with pain, but they were also devoid of so much.

"Why are *you* so empty?" I asked, turning the tides. If I was opening up, she sure as fuck was going to let some out as well.

She stared at me. I could see in her eyes the way she tried to find words to answer, and I had a feeling she was going to try and brush it off like she'd done so many times before.

"I can see it as clear as day. It's one of the many things that drew me to you. You're empty. You wear a mask to hide it, to make yourself seem somewhat normal, but your face… Do you know how expressionless it is when you think no one is looking? I provoke you to get some kind of reaction like you provoke me to feel. Have you ever been happy?"

She continued to stare at me, unable or willing to answer, but I saw the shake begin in her hand.

"Is that why you chose law? Contracts in general, because it's cold with precise guidelines? The people at the office don't see it. They think you're frigid, but I know you have a loving soul. The problem is you were never shown love, right? That's very cruel, to grow up without love."

For too long I'd gone with a hatred built up in me with no outlet. From the very second I first saw her, I knew there was something broken about her. Even since then I'd seen snippets of whatever horror laid in her past, but nowhere to direct the anger that had formed. No person to hate, to hunt down.

"Shut up!" She jumped to her feet, fists clenched at her side as she shot me daggers with her eyes.

Even though she pushed me, she resisted when it was turned on her. I moved to stand in front of her, to leave her no space to run until she let it out.

"Why? Because you don't want someone to point out what you're lacking?" I hit with low blows, words to incite her. "That's why things failed with you and Andrew, isn't it? He couldn't take your darkness, couldn't fill your void. He seems like the type to want to fix something that's broken."

"Shut up, shut up, shut up!" she screamed as she beat her fists against my chest. "Please, it hurts!"

The tormented look on her face was heartbreaking, but she needed the evisceration of her pain.

"Why?" I pressed.

Her face scrunched up as the pain overtook her. "Because I was never wanted, I was never good enough, never smart enough, never loved! He *hated* me. I was in the way of his happiness, shackled to him."

He?

"He hated that my mother died and forced me upon him. A child he never wanted from a woman he knew for a day. The things he said, the things he did, the looks he gave…so many times, he wouldn't even give me that. It hurt more than when he smacked me or grabbed me and yelled. Those were the only times he ever touched me. He was my father. He was supposed to love me. *Protect* me!"

The blood in my veins turned to ice. Fuck.

It was one thing to speculate, but another to have it confirmed.

"My stepmother, she ignored me. Oh, God…the nasty things she would say to bring me down. She knew he wouldn't stop her. He encouraged her. Then there was Adam…"

Fuck fuck fuck! A grown fucking man wouldn't stop a woman from abusing his child? What the fuck kind of bastard was he?

What worried me the most was the lost look in her eyes and the way she trailed off. Her arms crossed her chest as her entire body shook.

"He took high advantage of being able to say and *do* whatever he wanted."

Do?

Do?

What the *fuck* did he *do* to her?

"He hated it when I moved in, hated his beloved stepfather bringing him a sister, and made it his personal mission to make me the most alienated and bullied kid in school. I kept my head down, my mouth shut, and prayed for someone to see me. For someone to love me… I still don't know why I never killed myself. I thought about it, a lot."

Her voice cracked at the end.

I stood there staring at her, completely numb, watching as she crumbled before me. Sobs tore from her, each one a searing pain to my chest. I pulled her to me, holding her up as she fell apart.

I stroked her hair in an attempt to calm her.

"You're dead inside, just like me."

"That's not true," she said with a shake of her head. "You have very strong emotions, violent almost."

I let out a maniacal laugh full of bitterness and regret "You don't get it." I pulled back to look at her. "I wish I was dead," I said, letting out my darkest secret. "I wish the paramedics had taken five more minutes to get there."

I heard the smack before I felt it. My vision blurred as my head jolted to the side. My gaze snapped back to her, stunned as to what happened. Her hand was up, and tears slid down her cheek.

"Please, don't leave me," she whispered through broken gasps.

"I wish the battery on the defibrillator had been out," I pressed on. "That way they wouldn't have been able to restart my heart. Because then I wouldn't feel dead inside, in pain daily. Because I wouldn't be here, hurting you."

How much more of this can we take before we break?

I didn't have an answer, but I continued on, telling her my story without telling her everything. Morbid details of the condition I was left in.

"I'm angry because I'm alive. My heart, my soul…they're gone, dead, but my body remains. This is my purgatory."

"No, no, no, no! Please, please, Nathan… I can't fathom… I *need* you. You make… I'm falling… Please, please, please." The words bounced out between gasping breaths.

Lila broke, shattering in my arms. Tears streamed down her cheeks as she yelled, begged, pleaded with me to not leave her as her fists beat on my chest.

Not leave her?

She leaned into me, her body somehow revolting. I wrapped my arms tighter around her, but she pulled back, her hands smacking my chest.

"No!" she screamed as she attempted to push me away.

"Lila," I said her name in an attempt to get her attention. She was borderline hysterical, and I was afraid she was going to start hyperventilating. I grabbed her arms and tried to get her to see me, hear me, anything. "Baby, stop!"

"No!"

With every smack, I tried to restrain her arms, but she managed to pull away. It was pissing me off. The moment I had a hold of her, I walked her back into the wall and pinned her there.

"Calm down," I growled.

"Say it!" she cried out.

I closed my eyes and let out a shuddered breath as I fisted her hair.

"I want you," I said before crashing my lips to hers.

I told her. Not everything, but more than she could even fathom. What I used to do, what followed me, and the empty life I led.

Anger fueled revelations, spewing emotion based words at each other. Snippets of her damaged past, of those who harmed her, but it was only the surface. The scars they laid were so much deeper than she let on.

I knew, because we were a matched set of empty landscape. Neither living nor dead.

The darkness grew, overpowering, taking us both over as our pasts exploded out in a cathartic release.

What followed was an emotional power play with our bodies, and for the first time, Lila took control.

She forced me to feel, to confront and accept, to understand that even if I only mattered to one person, my life had meaning.

In return, I made her feel how good my cock could feel in her ass.

WHEN LILA SLEPT WITH ME, SHE WAS OUT. A COMPLETE and deep sleep that lasted through the night. After our confessions and admissions, things changed.

Her sleep wasn't as smooth. I would wake to her normally still body jerking. Deep dreams that led to restless nights. She never woke, but as I stared down at her, there was no way I could let her continue to sleep.

Tears streamed down her cheeks, her arms covering her face against an invisible attacker.

"Lila," I whispered as I shook her. No response. I tried again, the volume of my voice increasing with each attempt.

Worry overtook me, my shaking increasing.

She shot up, gasping, her eyes unfocused.

I'd never seen her like that. The sheer terror, being held captive in a dream I couldn't wake her from.

She ran, stumbling her way to the bathroom, the sound of her heaving echoing around the tile walls.

I knew my own reaction to night terrors, and I watched from the doorway. Her small frame shook, trembling so hard it was visible from the hairs on her head down to her toes.

I was very familiar with the bodily effects of nightmares, at least the panicked throwing up. The other side was the mentality she was left with once her heart stopped trying to beat out of her chest.

It took a few minutes for her to calm down enough to stand, and it was hard to keep myself from rushing forward to help her. She wobbled over to the sink and began brushing her teeth. I followed slowly, making sure there were no sudden movements.

She hadn't looked at me yet. The closer I got, the tighter her muscles became. I watched her closely as her breath sped up, her movements faster as the shaking increased.

"Lila?"

There was no response, no inkling of recognition that she heard me.

"Lila."

With her head still down she turned and tried to maneuver around me. I threw my arm out in front of her. I had to pull her out.

"Lila!" I yelled out.

She flinched, her eyes glued to the ground, refusing to look at me as she stepped back. Small steps until her back hit the wall.

It was the conditioning her family put her through. She was trapped in memories, locked in a state of fear.

"Lila?" I lowered my voice, aiming for as gentle and soothing as I could. There was a pause, then I took a step toward her.

Her harsh breaths stopped, her body frozen on the spot.

What the fuck did they do to her?

If she was that afraid, her childhood was much worse than she'd ever let on. I wondered if she even had the ability to talk about it. Her body may not have been riddled with scars like mine, but it was obvious to me she suffered much physical abuse over a long period of time.

"Lila?" I coaxed again.

I reached out, and the anger of what they'd done to her spiked as she tensed. She was bracing for the pain. I hooked my fingers under her chin to raise it so I could look at her, but she pushed back, refusing.

A growl left my chest, anger filling me. If I ever met who hurt her, there would be hell to pay. I trailed my hand down her jaw and around to the base of her neck before fisting her hair and tugging.

Finally, our eyes met, and an ache seeped into my chest. The absolute fear that looked back at me was devastating. I waited for her to see me, waited for her eyes to clear, for any flicker of recognition. To bring her back to the present and pull her from the ghosts that clawed at her.

Long, hard beats of my heart I used to count, waiting as the number increased, and still she was gone. It was more than two minutes before the fog began to lift. Her body was the first to remember as her chest rose, bowing into me.

It was my cue, and I pulled her to me, her whole body relaxing into mine.

My touch brought her back. My body against hers.

The beast purred.

I pressed my lips to her, my tongue prying her mouth open. When the last resistance left her, so did my own. I pushed her against the wall, my hands gripped her body, my fingers dug in as I claimed her mouth.

When I pulled back for breath, our eyes locked. I released her hair and brushed the loose strands from her face.

"Tell me."

Her eyes slipped back into the fear-filled frenzy, looking anywhere but me, looking for a way out. I gripped her jaw and brought her attention back to me.

"It's just you and me. Now, tell me."

"A dream," she whispered. "It was just a nightmare, that's all."

I let out a sigh, making the decision that going back to bed wasn't going to work. She remained all over the place, and until I got her to fully let go, the night wasn't going to get any better.

I stepped away and she gasped, her hands reaching for me.

It stabbed at me. I knew she was broken, but the depth was deeper than I imagined.

"Come on."

She was wound so tightly, and I knew one way to relax her. I reached in to turn on the shower, my hand waving under it, waiting for the warmth to make its way through the pipes.

I jumped at her hands on my skin, on my scars. I couldn't remember the last time someone touched them, and the caress of her fingers was feather light.

I let her continue, but it was difficult knowing her attention was solely focused on my battered skin. When the water turned warm, I grabbed her hand and moved her in front of me.

Tears slid down her cheeks. Tears for me.

I walked her back into the shower, watched her eyes widen when the water hit her cooled skin. We showered in silence, letting the water wash over us.

I flinched again at the touch of my scars, my chest clenching. Her fingers followed the line down my ribs. It wasn't the first time, but the shock of being touched was still an adjustment.

When the water was warm enough, I pulled her in front of me. Tears slid down her cheeks, leaving me amazed how she could be upset over what happened to me after what just happened to her.

I walked her back, a gasp as the water hit her skin. She began to relax, but as she washed her body, I noticed she was focused on me. After rinsing off, she reached out to my scar.

After what happened to her, she seemed transfixed on my skin, something she'd seen and touched many times before. She was soft and gentle and felt pain on my behalf without knowing what happened.

How the fuck could anyone hurt such an innocent soul?

The intimate touch as she moved around became more than I could handle. It was silent as we explored each other, my hand shaking as I caressed her still tense body. She was still stuck in her mind, so with each pass I reminded her where she was and who she was with.

There was nothing to fear with me. I pulled her hand up to my lips and kissed each knuckle. The gesture was too much for her, a hiccup leaving her.

I more than anyone knew the power of ghosts. Memories so real that you lose a sense of reality and time.

There was no space between us. Skin on skin as I kissed every part of her I could reach. With each kiss, her body relaxed, and I morphed from reverent to possessive.

"Relax, baby," I whispered as I turned her in my arms. "Do I have your attention now? I need you here with me."

She nodded and let out a sigh, some of the tension leaving her. It wasn't enough.

I ran my hand down her side, caressed over the curve of her hip before slipping between her legs. She was wet not only on the outside, but the inside as well. Slowly, I slid two fingers inside while my other hand teased her nipples.

"Come back to me, baby. Don't let them take you from me."

The more I worked her over, the more she shook. I ground the heel of my hand against her clit, eliciting a long, drawn-out moan as her hands reached back to fist my hair.

"You are *my* cock slut, *my* sex goddess, and *my* beautiful girl. That's all you need to know."

She rocked in my arms, her breaths coming out in pants. With every thrust of my fingers I pulled her back until she froze. I worked my fingers faster, my teeth on her shoulder, and she let go.

Every muscle tightened, then released, her pussy pulsing around my fingers as she lost all strength. Her whole body was limp against me.

I held her tight to me, placing light kisses on her shoulder as I ran soothing circles across her skin.

"Feel better?" I asked with a kiss to her temple. "Are you okay now?"

She managed to nod, and I continued holding her.

It was frightening seeing it on the outside in comparison to my own experiences. One I didn't wish on anyone.

HATED ANDREW.

The next morning he was outside our building, waiting for Lila to come down. I really couldn't stand him or the way he drooled over what was mine. What was the worst was the fact that they were touching.

Andrew's presence was grating. I couldn't stand having him so close, trying to angle into what was mine. He drove my possessiveness to a new level, one I'd never experienced before.

An hour later, when we arrived at the office, I fucked her in the elevator for it, destroyed her panties, and took the scarf that hid my marks. All out of anger, out of spite. There was no way he wouldn't see and understand, truly, that she wasn't fucking available.

I had her fucking panties in my pocket if he wanted fucking proof of ownership.

Still, later that morning, he was fucking leaning against Lila's desk, forcing me to listen to his inane chatter. The blood pumped violently through my veins as I imagined the brutality I would deliver to his boy-scout face.

"Lila, it looks like you've got some dirt on your neck," Andrew said.

The words drew my attention, and I turned just in time to see him reach out and try to brush it away. Lila sat there, rigid, waiting for him to realize and probably wondering what to say in response.

Andrew bent down, his eyes narrowing before he stopped and pulled back. "Oh, I see," he said.

Yeah, take that, fucker.

There was a definite awkward tension between them, and I wanted to laugh.

"So, I was thinking that little gyro place for lunch down the street. Sound good?" he asked her.

Fucker didn't know when to quit. Even if it was just as friends, even if he understood she wasn't available, he was still trying to fucking get in.

"Yeah, um, they have really good chicken there," Lila replied.

I stared at Andrew, the image of my fist hitting that pretty-boy face. He really needed to fucking leave.

Andrew's eyes met mine, and he startled before glaring back. "What?"

I mashed my teeth together in an attempt to stay calm. "Nothing. Just trying to get some work done in here. Your persistent talking is distracting. Go bother someone else."

The fucker actually tried to bait me, which only excited the beast. His posture told me he was ready, but just when I was about to stand and show him just what he was dealing with, Lila let out a loud sigh.

He looked down to her and relaxed a bit. "I'll see you at lunch," he said to Lila before finally getting the fuck out of our office. I suddenly had an inkling of understanding of Lila's frustrations at Jennifer and the slut parade.

As soon as he was gone, Lila turned to me. I glared at her before mouthing, "Mine," and returning back to my work.

She was having dinner with the fucker. For the first time in weeks, I was alone for dinner. I tried to work it off in the gym, running at near full speed until I couldn't breathe.

Over the past few weeks, I'd lost some muscle mass, and it was noticeable. Not so much in the mirror as in my level of pain. Before returning to work, I ran almost every day and weight trained three to four days a week.

It paid off by reducing my pain and increasing my flexibility, but not enough that I could go without pain meds. Since I met Lila I let a lot of things slip, but mostly because my workout was in a very different form.

For almost two hours I pushed myself. Repetition after repetition of weights until failure. None of it helped the violent energy that surged through me.

By the time I was done in the gym, one of our building's few amenities, it was seven. I stopped by the guard desk to say hello on my way to the elevators. It was really just an excuse to check the cameras to see if her parking spot was still empty instead of going out to the lot.

I went upstairs and took a shower. Busted a nut in there, and still, my veins thrummed.

She was with him, the man who wanted what was mine. Once she'd been his, but that obviously didn't work out, so his forced injection into her life drove me insane. Even more so when Lila divulged she had barely spoken with him in the six months prior to him joining Holloway and Holloway.

Ever since that night at the club, he seemed to pop up everywhere.

There was no waiting for her at my place.

It was almost nine when I used my key to open her door and still, she wasn't home. I mashed my teeth together, my fists clenching and unclenching.

Only minutes had passed when I heard movement on the other side of the door. I moved to stand in front of the door, not giving a fuck if Andrew was with her. If he was, fuck it. He was going to get quite the show of my cock in her cunt.

The door slowly opened, and Lila's eyes widened at the sight of me. She was alone.

"Nathan! You scared me."

No response, no words. The moment she was through the door, I shoved it shut and spun her around into the wall. I pressed against her, pushing her chest into the drywall.

"He's getting on my last fucking nerve," I spat in her ear as I tugged at her jeans while rocking into her ass, pushing them over her hips.

"It was just dinner," she said, her hands splayed on the wall, purse still hanging from her arm.

"That's not what he thinks. He's trying to get back inside you, but that's reserved for me alone."

Mine! Fucking mine!

"Yes."

With a hard tug, I got her panties down her hips enough to expose her. It was all I needed, just enough room.

My dick pressed against her, lined up, and then I thrust forward, pushing as much in as I could. She was tight and hot, and it only took a few bruising slams of my hips to add wet.

With one arm I pushed her into the wall, and with the other, I pushed her hips down as I drilled into her. There was nothing but the pleasure of her warmth coaxing my come.

"You're a fucking cock tease, Lila, but you're *my* fucking cock slut."

"Yes," she whimpered.

My thrusts were hard, brutal almost. All of my anger and frustrations I funneled into Lila in the way I pinned her to the wall with my cock. It was her punishment, the pleasure all for me. She was wet, moaning, but it was my show, and I was so worked up.

"Take my fucking cock, whore. Fucking cream on it."

My balls were tight, and there was no drawing it out any further. I didn't want to.

My fingers dug into her hips as I shoved into her, my cock firing off in a powerful explosion. With each stream I expelled my irritation, all of the high-strung, powerful emotions dissipating.

As my muscles relaxed and I came down from my ultimate high, I felt my knees start to buckle. My legs gave out, a combination of my workout and the fuck I gave her, and I fell to the floor, landing on my back.

"Nate!" Lila cried out, rushing over to me. "Are you okay?"

My heart slammed in my chest, my lungs burning as I tried to get a full breath.

"Don't ever fucking go to dinner with him alone again."

She sat down next to me. "Is that an order?"

"No, it's a request. I can't fucking take it."

Her lips formed a thin line. "That's a big request. We were talking about seeing a movie this weekend."

A growl rumbled through my chest as I glared at her.

She took her bottom lip between her teeth, but I saw a pull on one corner.

I narrowed my eyes at her. "Miss Palmer, are you baiting me?"

She reached out and trailed a finger down my chest, then down the length of my spent cock.

"Maybe."

"Are you sure that's wise?"

"Well, you were the only one who just got off…"

There was a playful glint in her eyes. It never seemed to matter how far I went, how off-the-handle wild I went with lust and anger, she always wanted more.

FOR FUCK'S SAKE, THIS GIRL IS AN IDIOT.

Jennifer sat on my desk, fucking sat on it, to try and entice me. Acting like a moron wasn't going to make her more attractive, it actually made her much less so and made me question the quality of her work.

During her inane yammering, my phone buzzed in my pocket. The first thing I noticed was the low battery notification from failing to plug it in overnight. The second was a text from Lila.

Change of plans. Caroline is coming over. I can't hide you from her any longer. I trust her. I'll come over—

The phone flashed the low battery warning at me and dimmed before I could finish reading.

Can't hide me…

I knew Caroline was her best friend, and that Caroline was fiercely protective of Lila. It worried me that someone would know, because the more people knew, the more chance the Marconi could find out.

At the same time, I felt that Caroline knowing was a very

good idea. That way, if anything happened to us, she would know who was to blame.

Nothing will happen to Lila.

You don't know that.

We won't let it.

I wanted to believe that, but I had a past that proved I wasn't invincible and that those I loved paid the price.

While I hadn't had much interaction with Lila and Caroline together, I knew Lila, and I was well aware of the reputation Caroline knew from my time at the club. Talking wasn't going to do it. If we wanted Caroline on our side, I had to be there to show her.

"So what do you think?" Jennifer asked.

I hadn't processed a word of what she said.

"I'm sorry, I missed the last part."

She pointed to a line in the contract in my hand. "Does that word sound right?"

I glanced down, then looked to her. "It's good."

"Really?"

I nodded and shoved the paper back at her. "All good."

Jennifer got the hint and headed out, leaving me with my plotting.

I knew Lila would talk me out of it, so I left before her, making her think I was headed home. Instead, I headed to the grocery to pick up something for dinner and a bottle of wine.

Lila's car was in the parking lot when I arrived, so I headed straight to her condo. Upon entering, I didn't hear anyone, but as I set the bags down in the kitchen, Lila came around the corner.

She was out of her suit and in some sleep shorts and a T-shirt.

"Hey. I picked us up some food to make dinner with. I was thinking that chicken bake you made a couple of weeks ago. God, that was good."

Her eyes were wide, and she glanced down the hall, then back to me.

"What are you doing here?" she asked in a hushed whisper as she stepped up to me.

Nervous energy rolled off her, her gaze continually flickering back down the hall. I pulled her to me and groaned at the faded patches of skin on her neck.

Mark her again.

I didn't need the beast to tell me that. I was already leaning down, lips and tongue teasing her, both in a mental and physical way. Perhaps it was more torture than teasing, due to the circumstances.

"Mmm, well a song on the radio said something about disrobing, then probing. I was thinking we could do a lot of that tonight."

I slid my hand under the hem of her shirt and moved up to her squeeze her breast before tweaking her nipple between my fingers.

"Fuck," she moaned.

Once I had her focused on me, I picked her up and put her on the counter, trapping her as I pushed my hips between her thighs. The little shorts she had on gave me easy access to her pussy, and I slipped my fingers across her slit, making sure her clit got lots of attention. She bucked against me as her eyes darkened.

"You like that, don't you, my little whore?" I hadn't meant to go quite so far, but as always, she turned me on too much to stop.

Her eyes fluttered. "I love your fucking dirty mouth."

I slipped my fingers inside her, making her gasp.

"Mmm, I love it when you say 'fucking.' I like being in control, fucking you how I want. You're so willing to please me, and I love watching you come." I accentuated the last words with hard thrusts into her. "No one is as beautiful and sexy as you when you're coming undone around me."

She tried to hold back, to stay quiet, but I didn't want quiet. I wanted Caroline to hear her.

"Nathan, didn't you get my text?" she asked, pushing past my distraction.

"You sent me a text? My phone died after lunch." I saw her text about Caroline, but she could've sent another after my phone died.

She froze for a second, her hands moving to my chest. "Crap!"

There was no pushing of me away. I had her trapped in pleasure. Slow, deep strokes as I moaned against her skin.

"You taste so fucking good."

"Nathan, please…wait." Her hands fisted into my shirt and there was a vain, weak attempt to push against me.

"You've made me wait all day; I'm not waiting any longer. Wearing that skirt to torture me…you little cock tease." I slid my free hand up her shirt, her skin hot against my own.

"You don't… *ah!*" she cried out as I pinched her nipple. "Hold on! W-what skirt?"

What skirt?

The skirt.

"The skirt you were wearing the first time I fucked you in our office."

My dick twitched, ready to recreate coming inside her.

"Nathan, don't be mad."

The sound of a door closing hit my ears, and I froze, waiting.

"Lila, is there someone here?" I asked, knowing full well by her panic that Caroline was already somewhere in her home.

"I tried to tell you…the text I sent."

"Shit," I growled. The excitement that we were about to be caught was too much. Fantasies of being caught while inside her were rampant.

"Oh. My. God!" Caroline's voice rang from the hallway.

"Fuck," I whispered with a sigh. I'd have to try my fantasy out another time.

I turned to Caroline, my hand still between Lila's thighs, fingers soaked. I removed them and lifted them to my mouth, sucking up her juices before looking back to Caroline, who stood there with her mouth wide open.

"Hi, Caroline. Dinner?" I asked as I stepped away from a flushed and thoroughly turned-on Lila, who was suddenly panicking.

There was silence as I washed my hands. Caroline seeming to be at a complete lack for words. I went about the task of putting groceries away as well as starting to prep for dinner.

Minutes passed before Caroline finally spoke. "Nathan?" It was on the shrill side, indicating she had no clue who Lila was really with.

Out of the corner of my eye, I saw Lila standing close, their voices low, but I could still make out the words of surprise before Caroline dragged her away.

A few minutes passed, and suddenly Caroline was inches in front of me.

"*You.*" She stuck her finger in my face. "Hurt her, and I'll fuck you up. Understood?"

My eyes popped open in surprise. Half in fear of the small, brown-eyed woman staring me down, and half in shock of how fast she accepted me in Lila's life. In the background, Lila let out a little giggle.

"Understood," I said with a sharp nod.

Her gaze narrowed on me. "Are you being safe with my girl? I've seen you with some floozies."

Yes, she had, which was one reason I was surprised by her acceptance.

"I'm clean. Promise."

"Better fucking be, bucko."

She smiled and relaxed, stepping back to lean against the counter. "So, you two…" She waved between us. "When did all of this start up? Did it happen one day here, or was it an office tryst, one-night type of thing?"

I froze mid slice, remembering how I'd lost all control. Gauging by Lila's silence, she was thinking the same.

"Seriously? In the office? In *your* office?" she asked, our reaction giving it away. "Wow, you're my kinky idol now, Lila."

"What? I…he…" Lila stammered.

"I bet it was hot."

"Of course it was hot," I said as I looked to Caroline, then gestured to Lila. "Look at her. She is fucking gorgeous and sexy as hell. Sin should be her middle name."

A grin spread on Caroline's face. "So, have words of love been shared?"

I froze as a sick feeling rolled through me. The blood fell from my face as memories flashed in my mind of the last woman I loved.

No, I couldn't love Lila. I wouldn't allow myself to.

"What did I say?" Caroline asked.

I turned toward Lila, and our eyes locked. By the worry on her face, she knew Caroline had gone too far. I set down the knife and moved to wash my hands.

"I think it's about time you took over. I'm going to go change."

"All right. Thank you," Lila said.

On my way out, I saw the sadness in her eyes and stopped to place a kiss on the top of her head. It was hard not to slam the door behind me. Not that I was angry at Caroline. Under normal circumstances, in a normal relationship, it would be fine.

Neither Lila or I was normal. Caroline's question simply highlighted it and served as a reminder of the love I'd lost, a reminder of why I could never love Lila.

As I changed my clothes, I tried to remind myself why I decided to interrupt their night. It was for Lila's sake, to make it easier for her to tell Caroline, to make sure Caroline knew and understood. That way, if anything happened, she would know it was my fault.

No! We will protect her.

I can't protect myself.

That was why even what I was doing was bad. If they saw, if they knew…

With a sigh, I tried to shake off the remnants. After changing into jeans and a T-shirt, I headed back down.

"How's dinner coming?" I asked as I entered.

Lila looked nervous, while Caroline looked about to cry.

What the fuck?

Caroline walked to me, her phone clutched in her hands. There were tears in her eyes that looked at me with pity.

"I'm sorry. I Googled you. Don't worry. I won't say anything to anyone, even Lila. She wants to hear it from you when you're ready," Caroline blurted out.

I froze and stared at her.

Shit. I was not expecting her to do that in the few minutes I was gone. I swallowed hard and kept our eyes locked.

"I need to request that you please make sure you do. Only a few trusted people in the office know. I stress this because what you learned isn't the whole story, nor wholly true, and I don't want rumors spreading."

"I promise. I won't say a word. It's not my place anyway," she assured me.

"Thank you, Caroline."

During dinner, Caroline thankfully steered the conversation clear of anything about my past, but she did have a nasty habit of bringing up Andrew's name. By the third time, I caught on, her sly smile giving her away. Lila must have told her about our mutual hatred of each other.

"Wait, you call Jennifer and all the others what?" I asked.

"The Boob Squad," Caroline said. "I've watched them adjust their clothes and fluff their boobs up to make them pop out before they go into your office. It's hysterical to watch. Dress code all day. Need to see Nathan? Boobs out!"

Well, that explained something.

"They will forever be the B.S. from now on. And don't worry, I don't buy any of the B.S.'s BS," I said with a chuckle.

After a few hours, Caroline headed home and we went about cleaning up dinner.

"Did your phone really die?" Lila asked as she handed me some of the dishes.

I smirked at her as I ran them under the water to rinse

them off. "Yes, it died after lunch."

"How long after lunch?" Her eyes narrowed at me.

My smile broadened. "Sometime around when you got coffee. I was surprised to find she followed you home. I thought she would come over later."

"Oh, God, you did read it and came over anyway?" she asked.

"Technically, I read half of it…then my phone died."

"Unbelievable!"

"I thought it was a good idea. One of your friends should know, in case…" I trailed off.

Thankfully Lila didn't pry.

"You couldn't have given me a heads up? I was freaking out!"

Her reaction was priceless and worth it.

I leaned down and kissed her neck. "I'll make it up to you."

"How?"

I gave her a waggle of my eyebrows. "Oh, I think I have a few tricks up my sleeves…and down my pants."

She shook her head and rolled her eyes. "Do you, now? I'm not sure I'm convinced of your professed prowess."

My mouth popped open. "Are you challenging my ability to make you come, and come often?"

I loved the smile that spread and the way she bit her lower lip. It was the lightest I'd ever seen her. She seemed relaxed and, though still unsure, a little more comfortable in her own skin.

Once the dishes were done, I had her over my shoulder and headed to the bedroom

"Nathan!" she cried out.

"Time for bed, number one."

"Number one?" she asked.

"Yes, you're number one in the Boob Squad."

"Says who and why?"

A jolt went through me as she grabbed my ass, and I smacked her ass in return.

"Because you show me a hell of a lot more of your tits than they do. Way more of them, and way more often."

I threw her down on the bed and climbed to hover over her, my knees pushed hers out, allowing me to settle between them. Her hips tilted as I pinned her arms above her head.

She was still smiling at me, and I couldn't stop from doing the same. There was something lighter about us, even if it was just for the moment. However, as she continued to rock against my cock, the mood shifted.

"Something you want, baby?" I asked. Her response was only to lift her hips and look at me with those fucking erotic eyes of hers. "Words, Delilah. Tell me in words what you want."

"Kiss me," she said.

"Where?" I rocked into her, groaning as her breath picked up.

"Everywhere," she whispered.

I crashed my lips to hers and immediately found her tongue. As sweet as ever, and even more so after dessert. After a minute I released her lips.

She was so free at that moment, so beautiful and happy. Not only that, in her, I felt a sort of peace that was infectious.

"I meant it, you know," I said as I caressed her cheek.

Her eyes fluttered as she looked at me, her brow scrunched. "Meant what?"

"When I told Caroline how beautiful and sexy you are." It fucking pissed me off that she'd been treated so badly. I still didn't know the extent, but it was obvious it'd been bad. An ache settled into my chest just thinking about what she had possibly gone through. "I don't know how anyone could ever tell you different, but they were wrong. Believe me, baby, they were so wrong about it all. It kills me and pisses me off to no end to know that there are more of their lies rattling around inside that head of yours."

Her eyes began to water, and she turned away from me. "You can't know they were all lies," she said in a small voice.

I cupped her cheek in my hand and brought her eyes back to mine. "Yes, I can. I may be fucked up beyond repair, but I can still see the truth. You deserve so much…you deserve a loving heart and a caring hand, understanding and kind words to erase the false ones."

There was nothing I wouldn't give to be the one, but there was no way. One day, we would end. One day, the beautiful woman beneath me would meet someone who could do more for her than I was capable of.

Her arms wrapped around me, and she buried her head into my neck as a sob broke loose. She shook against me as I held her tight, petting her hair.

"It's okay, Honeybear, I've got you."

For now, I've got you.

Forever.

I wished I could agree with the beast, but I knew our reality.

HATED ALARM CLOCKS. I ESPECIALLY HATED THEM WHEN THEY were early in the morning and took Lila from my arms.

Every morning I awoke with her in my arms was torture when she left them. I watched her slide off the side of the bed, her hair a knotted mess thanks to my hands. Inches of beautiful pale skin speckled with my marks slipped away from my body and into my view.

Naked, beautiful flesh for me to drink in. I watched her arms rise above her head, stretching her sinful body. She glanced back to check if I was awake, and our eyes met.

No "Good morning" or anything. That wasn't our style.

It was in the way her lips parted. Sometimes she would bite her lower lip, other times her tongue would peek out and wet her lips.

I continued to watch as she walked into the bathroom and listened in as she started the shower. My getting up took longer. While she showered, I stretched. It was something I fought against, but it turned out to be the best thing for me to make it through the day. It helped reduce my daily dependence on pain pills, which always left my mind in a fog.

Over the span of a few months, I'd fucked Lila everywhere. In the elevator, in the office, the parking lot, almost every inch of her condo, and a lot of my own—I couldn't get enough of her. The need to be inside her was a sickness, a madness that consumed me.

We fell into a routine of sorts over the following month, an unrehearsed dance where we both understood the moves, sliding through each day seamlessly together.

Every night with her in my arms is a perfection I never thought I would experience again. Even if was just in her room, we were something more than I ever expected.

As I stood, my hard cock bounced against my abdomen before sticking straight out. The question I asked as I stretched out my quads on my left leg was how I was going to handle my morning wood.

The shower turned off, and I heard the glass door open. It was short, which meant it wasn't a hair washing day as those always took her longer.

There was a repetitive snap and pop as I pushed my shoulders back, my spine and ribs releasing muscular tension around them. Lila stepped out of the bathroom, her hair tossed up into a clip, a towel around her. She cocked an eyebrow at me as she moved to her dresser and pulled out some undergarments. The corner of her mouth pulled up as her gaze lingered on my naked body and morning erection. Our eyes locked for a split second before she disappeared back into the bathroom.

I glanced over at her bedside clock, then down to my cock. There was time.

My dick bounced with each step I made toward the

bathroom, toward the sweet smell of her soap and the delicious scent of her skin. It made my dick harder, and the site of her profile made it even worse.

She was naked with the exception of a tiny little thong, her skin still pink from the warmth of her shower. Her arm moved at a fast pace as she brushed her teeth. I was hypnotized, watching the rhythmic bounce as her tits jiggled. Soft, supple flesh I wanted to bite into. Her nipples were hard, probably from the cool air. I wanted them between my teeth, pulling, the combination of pain and pleasure making her walls lock down on my cock.

The lines of her body as she bent over to rinse out her mouth, the way her ass stuck out, made me twitch. I stepped through the door onto the cool tile floor. As she stood up, I was behind her and I pulled at her hips, forcing her back, bending my knees so that my dick rested between her perfect ass cheeks.

Our eyes met in the mirror, and she slowly returned to standing. My fingers flexed on her skin, a groan coming from deep in my chest. Her lips parted, eyes clouding.

I tugged at the thin fabric of her thong, pushing it to the side as I flattened my hand on her back, coaxing her to bend over. A small bend of my knees and the head of my dick found its home. She wasn't wet yet, but she would be soon.

I pushed forward, the dryness taking a few thrusts before I was all the way inside. Her silence broke into the erotic song that only got me harder, cries of pleasure as I worked my way in and out, her juices soon coating my shaft.

"Fuck, baby," I groaned, my eyes glued to our connection, watching my cock stretch her open with each thrust. "Such a good little slut taking my cock whenever I want."

Every time I bottomed out inside her, she let out a mewling

cry. One that drove me faster, made my cock harder. Each provocative sound was so erotic my balls drew up, making me come that much faster.

A few hard, fast strokes, and I slammed into her, my cock jerking with each pulsing stream of come.

She gave me the greatest high. Being inside her, all around her, consuming her. I needed her daily. She was the only reason I moved through any type of life.

The problem was the volatile situation my addiction put us both in. No matter how much I wanted her, how much I *needed* her to make it through the day, I knew the outcome. I knew the pain I was going to cause her, cause us both, but I couldn't stop. Every time I tried, the inevitable outcome was a massive breakdown of will.

I hated her. Hated the way she made me feel. Hated the absolute dependent need I had for her. Hated the way she made me break.

It was her fault my cock couldn't get enough. Her fault I couldn't stop. If she'd just pushed me away like I asked, she'd be safe.

Instead, I was hooked. Unable to let go.

Each day that passed brought us closer to June, closer to the anniversary of the accident, I grew more afraid. Nothing but pain was headed our way, and I was powerless to stop it.

I took a quick shower, and when I stepped out, Lila had her makeup on and was slipping on a skirt. Almost every day she wore a skirt, and somehow I had yet to bend her over her desk and shove it up her hips.

"Anything sound good for dinner?" Lila asked as she slipped her blouse over her head.

"If we had time, I'd say pot roast." The temperature fell for the week, and a hearty bowl of warm comfort food sounded good.

"We can do that this weekend."

I nodded in agreement. "What about a chicken dish? Maybe some pasta on the side?"

"I'll look for some recipes today and go to the grocery after work. We've overdone my pasta bake."

I chuckled. It was my fault, really.

"At my place tonight," I said.

Her lips pulled up into a slight smile, her head bowed in a bashful way. "Okay."

After all the time we'd spent together, all the nights she'd slept in my bed, and the idea of dinner at my place made her oddly shy.

At the end of the day instead of following each other home, Lila headed for the grocery. Part of me hated that I couldn't go with her, but it wasn't worth the risk.

My jacket gone, followed by my tie, and I was about to lose my shirt when the doorbell rang. Figuring it was Lila with her hands full, I ran to the door and swung it open.

It wasn't a petite blonde with bags stuffed in her arms.

"Dad," I said in shock at the man in the hall.

"Did I catch you at a bad time?" he asked.

I ushered him in and tried to find the best way to answer that. "I just got home from work."

"How is that going for you? We haven't talked in a while."

We hadn't talked in over a month.

"Good. A bit boring at times, but it keeps me busy."

I directed him to take a seat, but I couldn't join him. Nervous energy was eating me up as Lila was due any minute. How was I going to explain her to him?

"We need to talk, son," he said, his tone serious.

I nodded, my jaw clenching. How was it those words could still inflict fear in me as an adult? The way he used his Dad-voice made me feel like I was a kid in trouble again. It was a tone I was very familiar with. I was a model student, but I got into my fair share of trouble, too.

And I was, once again, in trouble, even if he didn't know the extent.

"First, though, how are you feeling?"

I shrugged. "Fine. How are you? How's Mom?"

"We'd be better if we saw you more often."

Knife to the heart. My father was never one to pull punches, but he somehow always managed to be caring and diplomatic.

"I know. I'm sorry. First it was the adjustment, then the long hours."

He nodded in understanding, but before he could respond, we both froze at the sound at the door.

Fuck.

I heard the lock and the door as it opened. Lila had arrived, and I was fucked.

"Nathan?"

I froze, my eyes locked on my father's.

"Who is that?" he asked.

"That's…it's complicated." I begged him with my eyes to not ask any questions yet as I called out. "In the living room."

I clenched my jaw in time with the clicks of her heels on the hardwood, my gaze locked on my father. I watched as he stared at the hall, the way his eyes widened when she came into view.

The clicks stopped, and Lila's unsteady words filled my ears. "Oh, I'm sorry."

She stared at my father for a moment before looking to me, and I beckoned her to my side. It was a necessary move to calm us both down, because I could almost feel the anxiety flowing from her.

I wrapped my arm around her waist, her beautiful eyes filled with a cross between curiosity and concern.

"Lila, I'd like to introduce you to my father, George Thorne." I moved my gaze from her to my father. "Dad, this is Lila, my…my Lila." Every muscle tightened, and I pulled her closer as I awaited his reaction.

A gasp left him as he stared at her with emotions that tore at me. Emotions of surprise and joy, which were the reason I never wanted them to meet. Because as much as I wanted her, as much as I needed her with every breath, we were doomed.

Like Romeo and his Juliet, we were a tragedy. A semi headed straight for a collision with a slab of concrete.

There was only decimation in our future.

He held out his hand. "Lila, it's a true pleasure to meet you."

My fingers dug at her clothing as she left my side and stepped forward to slip her hand in his. "You as well, Mr. Thorne."

Dad smiled at her. "George, please."

When his features morphed from a cautious happiness to slacken, I glanced down to follow where he was looking. I tilted my head back and cursed.

Fuck.

Her arms were bare, exposing the bruises that she gained daily when we fucked. Lila noticed as well and pulled her arm free.

"Are you staying for dinner, George? I'm making chicken marsala."

He forced a smile, but his jaw was noticeably tight. "No, no thank you, my dear. I would love to, but Mrs. Thorne is expecting me home soon."

I didn't want to have the coming conversation with my father, and I didn't want him to tell my mom. Add that in with the bruises, and the air was thick with an uneasy tension as Dad looked between us.

"Well…I'll just let you return to your conversation, and I'll go work on dinner," Lila said as she stepped away from me again, severing herself as a shield for the coming conversation. "It was very nice meeting you, George."

He gave her a nod, but she'd barely left the room before he let loose. "Nathan, are you…hurting her?"

I blinked at him and almost stuttered. "What?" Hurt her? Hurt my Lila? Was he insane?

"Son, she has bruises on her biceps and wrists. Are you abusing that girl?"

I shook my head and held my hands up. "No. Never. Jesus, Dad."

"He is not hurting me," Lila practically yelled as she stormed back in, her hands resting at the hem of her shirt.

Beneath the fabric were worse bruises, bite marks, the evidence of my depravity for her. A sight I wouldn't allow him to witness.

"Lila, no." A sliver of her milky white skin peeked out from between her skirt and shirt, but I managed to stop her before things got worse.

"No. He has to see." She continued to pull at the hem while I pushed them back down. "I will *not* allow your father to think you are abusing me! That you are *hurting* me!"

I pushed at her hands again, forcing them down. "I said no, baby. Only I get to see you without your clothes, even if my father is a doctor."

The little vixen wasn't backing down, and the beast purred while my dick twitched, excited for the explosive fuck that was to come.

A crackle filled the air as we faced off. I waited for her to back off. There was a strength in her, a determination that fueled her in a way I'd only seen a few times before. She was submissive to a point, awkward to the outside world, but beneath the scars, I had a feeling my girl had the strength of a goddess.

"Fine," she said, the fight leaving her.

I would win anyway.

She moved her hands up to her hair and pulled it away.

Yeeessssss. Ours!

Mine.

Fuck I loved to see the marks I'd left on her skin. The proof that she was mine. I'd marked her in every way I could. There were still more ways, but I couldn't risk any more than I already had.

Even my father's gasp couldn't tamp down the pride I had for them.

"I'm an easy bruiser, Mr. Thorne. Malice and hate does not mark me. Nathan's passion and need do. I know the sting of an angry hand, and *that* is something Nathan does not have with me."

The beast whimpered, and I reached up to caress the marks. Her skin beneath my fingers was electric, filled with the heat I so desperately needed.

I leaned forward and pressed my lips against her skin, soothing the bite mark I'd left the night before. So engrossed was I with my lips on her that I didn't even notice her reach up and pull my collar back to reveal her own marks on me.

"See? He's not doing anything to me that I don't want him to. We just get a little…carried away, is all."

Dad cleared his throat, and I realized I was getting a little sidetracked. One last kiss to her skin, and I backed off, slipping my hand in hers.

"I'm sorry, Lila, Nathan. I was just concerned." He let out a hard breath before steadying his gaze on me. "It's apparent your anger is getting out of control. I mean, look at what you've done to the entryway in the past few months." He motioned to the chunks of missing drywall. "I was just worried that you… Darren told me you haven't been by in months. He wanted me to let you know he won't refill your prescriptions anymore unless you get back in to see him."

Fuck.

Fucking fuck fucker fucking making me…

I released her hand and rubbed my face, mashing the heels into my eyes. "I know, I know."

I'd been putting it off, mostly because I knew I'd be too tempted to ask about Lila. Darren was her doctor as well, but I hadn't told her yet.

"This is serious, son. I want you to get better. I want to see you smiling again. I want to see you happy." I didn't miss his eyes glance over to Lila. "But you'll never be any of those if you don't get help."

I couldn't stop the snort that came out as I rolled my eyes. "Yeah, because the last three and a half fucking years of therapy have done wonders."

"It only works if you actually want help and work at getting better. Not going in months, not talking to him about your new relationship… Things are changing for you, and you need some support to help you get through this, work through this. To move on, so you aren't weighed down any longer. You deserve it, as does Lila." I saw the concern etched into his features. Everything he said was true, but I couldn't risk it. "You're going through your meds at a much faster rate than usual. David also told me you missed your last appointment."

"I had to reschedule it, that's all," I snapped. I had a long list of doctors, but only two that I saw regularly—one for the head and one for the body. "And I'll call and get in with Darren this week."

"Because you're out of meds?" he asked, though it was more of a statement.

I nodded.

"Well, I should be headed out now before your mother begins to worry." He stood and walked over to me, his arms wrapping around me for a hug. "I love you, Nathan."

I pulled him tight and nodded. "I love you too, Dad."

He then turned to Lila and pulled her into a hug. "Thank you, Lila. Please take good care of him."

Lila froze, my father exposing one of her social flaws. The awkwardness in her, the inability to understand social cues, was astounding. I had a little insight into her past, much more than she did to mine, but I knew whatever happened to her stunted her in so many ways that she had no knowledge on how to handle some situations.

"Have a good night. I hope to see you at dinner sometime soon. Your mother misses you," he said, shoving the knife further into my heart. "Oh, and don't forget to bring this lovely young lady with you. Your mother would love to meet her. It was such a pleasure meeting you, Lila."

"You too," she said as he stepped through the door.

I stared after him, my gaze moving to Lila every once in a while. No words came to me in reaction to what had happened, and she offered nothing.

"Dinner?" she asked.

My stomach rumbled, deciding to answer for me. We both let out a laugh, which broke the tension.

Once fed, a different kind of hunger took hold. I tried to fend it off with cleaning up the cooking mess we made, but having Lila right beside me and remembering what she'd done, I was worked up.

There was a swimming rule of waiting thirty minutes after eating, and I wondered if that applied to sex as well. I decided it didn't matter.

I pulled her into my arms and gave her a light, teasing kiss. Lila refused to be teased again and wrapped her arms around my neck, holding me in place as she stretched up.

Deeper, harder until I was pushing her up against the counter.

"Come on, Honeybear, let's move to the couch. I need a new batch of bruises on my body so I can scare the neighbors..."

She rolled her eyes at me, at the pet name I'd given her, but she didn't complain. I had a feeling she liked it, even with its ridiculousness.

I sat down on the couch and found the remote.

"Why is it that you don't want me to see Andrew, but your fan club can hang all over you?" she asked as she stood in front of me, her legs straddling mine. "That sounds like a double standard to me, Mr. Thorne."

I reached up and grabbed her waist, my thumbs caressing her skin.

"It's simple. I have no interest in any of them, and I have never touched, nor will I ever touch, any of them. Andrew, on the other hand, has shared a bed with you, been in a relationship with you, had his cock inside you." A growl rumbled through my chest, my fingers flexing on her hips. "I know he wants you, and you have every opportunity to go back to him. He wants to take what's mine."

"They want what's mine," she said. "And how do you know Andrew wants me?"

I sighed and quirked my brow at her. "Delilah, I know you're naïve in some regards, but trust me, he wants you back. I've seen the way he looks at you. And, yes, the girls may want what's yours, but have I ever touched them? Have I ever given any indication I wanted to pursue any of them? I don't want to pursue anyone."

"You pursue me," she said.

I froze as her words sliced through me. It was true, I had pursued her.

"Yes. Against my better judgment."

"What does your judgment tell you to do?" she asked.

"It says that it's better for you if we weren't together, but that line of thinking makes me want to go mad, and I find it even harder to let go of you."

"So…you're saying…that your heart pursues me?"

Is that what I'm saying?

Yes.

"Your head rejects me, but your heart wants me?"

For months I'd tried to work Lila out. Early on, I got a generalized overview of her. She was dead on, the same words having gone through my mind before.

I tightened my grip and pulled her close, down to my lap, and leaned my forehead to hers.

"I'm sorry..." she trailed off, her hands smoothing across my back and shoulders.

I pulled her flush and grazed my lips down her neck and across her shoulder. With my teeth, I moved the thin strap of her tank top to the side, letting it drop around the curve of her shoulder.

Time to show her how much my body wanted her.

"OH, MY GOD. COULD YOU QUIT FLAUNTING YOUR TITS around? I'm getting so sick of looking at yours, I can hardly stand to look at my own. And, by the way, if he hasn't taken the bait yet, he isn't going to."

I was officially a fan of Caroline. She was a badass, take-no-prisoners, can't-keep-her-opinion-to-herself kind of woman, and the exact opposite of Lila. That made her the perfect best friend.

It was hard to keep a straight face as she chided them. The encounter wouldn't have happened so epically before she found out about Lila and me. She still would have given it to them in some way.

"Whatever, Caroline," Kelly sneered as she grabbed Tiffany's arm and stormed out.

Once they were gone, I let it out in shoulder-shaking laughter. The moment was cut short as Andrew stepped in seconds later, stifling my good mood.

"Morning!" he said with a huge smile.

Fucking boy scout.

I glared at him and was met with a glare of his own before he looked back to Lila and Caroline.

"Did I miss something?" he asked.

"Just Caroline showing the Boob Squad why she rocks," Lila answered.

"Awesome!" He reached out to Caroline for a high five. "Oh! Hey, Lila, guess who I ran into last night?" he asked, plopping down on the chair in the corner of our office.

"Who?" she asked.

"Teresa," he said.

I'd never heard the name, so I returned to work, listening on the side.

Lila let out a small gasp, quickly earning my attention back. "I thought she and Armando were still in Europe."

"Yeah, apparently Joan found another kid that needed a home and, well, you know Teresa."

"Yeah. She never passed up the opportunity to help any child," Lila said.

The words caught me and I glanced over, shocked to see a soft smile on Lila's face.

"What are you two talking about?" I asked.

The three of them looked at each other like they were trying to decide if they should let me into their special club. It seemed that decision rested on Lila.

"Well, umm, Teresa was my foster mom for a little while."

Foster mom?

In all our talks, in all the times we pulled information from each other kicking and fucking screaming, being a foster was a subject that was never mentioned. My stare must have been powerful, because Lila looked away, which Caroline took as a cue.

"Come on, Andrew," Caroline said as she slid from Lila's desk and took hold of Andrew's arm. "Let's go get some coffee."

"Umm, okay," he mumbled, oblivious as to what was going on.

"What?" I asked once the door clicked closed.

She had her lip between her teeth, a nervous habit, as she seemed to gather herself. A long sigh left her before she began.

"A few months after my sixteenth birthday, I contacted a children's law center to be emancipated from my family."

I stared at her in shock. "Jesus fucking Christ."

I knew she hadn't told me everything.

"Joan, she was my lawyer… In fact, she was the one who got me interested in law. Anyway, we never made it to court," she said with a steadying breath. "Child services stepped in. Joan knew of a couple who liked to help out teens in situations such as mine, and so I moved to Indianapolis between my junior and senior year and finished out high school here."

The abuse she suffered was far reaching both in time and effect. It still wasn't enough to silence her strength, her will to get away.

She seemed reluctant to tell me more, because the subject was difficult to talk about, but she pressed on. "Teresa is a sweet, loving woman who was very patient with me. She was my first hug."

"Your first *hug*?" I was going to be sick. Sixteen when she had her first, most basic sign of affection. No fucking wonder she was a mess.

"My first real hug since I went to live with my father," she said in clarification. "Armando worked with me, showing me that what my father and stepbrother did was not how most men behaved. It took me a long time to trust him. I waited for the insults to slip from his lips, but only words of encouragement and caring ever came from him." Tears filled her eyes, and a small smile formed on her lips. "Armando was a bit awkward, but that made him more endearing. Noah was also there, and he helped as well."

"Who's Noah?" I asked. It was the first I'd heard any inkling of a family outside of her abuse. If they were people she loved, why didn't she talk about them?

"Noah lived with Teresa and Armando when I moved in. He's a year older than me. He came from a more abusive home than I did. He was headed to college that fall, something he never thought he would do. He showed me what a brother was supposed to be like. He was better adjusted than I was to people."

She had to be taught how men really were. How badly had I fucked with her in the beginning? All that hatred and blaming her and taking my frustrations out on her. Was I any better?

"Do you want to know what my favorite Disney movie was?" she asked, drawing my attention.

I forced myself to relax as I looked at her. "I want to know anything you want to tell me."

"Cinderella. I used to pretend I was her and a prince would come and take me away," she said as a sad smile tugged at her lips. "It was when I was fourteen and Adam kicked me so hard he broke two ribs that my dream came crumbling down."

A wave of nausea rolled over me.

"The hospital, of course, believed the story my father told about what happened."

Her lips pursed together, and I wondered if anyone ever believed her. Surely someone had to be suspicious.

"He told them we were roughhousing when the truth was

Adam was pissed off, and I was an available punching bag. It was then I realized that if I wanted out, I had to do it myself. No one was going to come rescue me. There was no prince on a white horse."

Every muscle in my body was taut, and the need to destroy rippled through me. "Did he do that to you often?"

She shrugged her shoulders. "It was mostly verbal. Yeah, he'd push me into walls every day, but a few times a year he would go off, and I'd be in the hospital again. I was 'clumsy,' you see. Clumsy Lila hurt herself again. Tripped and fell down the stairs. Can't walk across a flat surface without falling. Clumsy, clumsy Lila."

She was holding back from me. The reactions I'd witnessed, her night terrors. No, those weren't the result of what she'd just described, but a situation much worse. She was skimming the surface for my benefit and possibly her own.

"Did your father hit you?" My teeth were clenched tight, anger consuming me. She twitched at my question, an involuntary response. "Fuck."

"He would slap me, but he never punched. He couldn't stand to look at me, and if his eyes met mine, he would snap."

He never punched her, but her stepbrother...

My hands were fisted in my lap, violent energy coursing through me at the speed and energy of a freight train.

"Why, then?" What about her eyes set him off?

"Because he was staring at his eyes on the face of a woman he slept with once, years before, and he hated her for ruining his life. He hated me."

My brow scrunched. "Your mother?"

"She died in a car accident when I was five. Steve, my father, knew about me, but didn't want anything to do with me.

When she died, he was listed as my guardian. I don't think she ever meant for me to go with him, but her own parents were dead, and she had no other family. I'd never met him before that day."

Torn from her mother in a cruel twist of fate and dropped into hell. I couldn't stop images of a smaller, thinner, frightened Lila from filling my mind. Skittish in her movements, reluctant in others, as she adjusted to life without fear.

The sadness morphed into anger. Her father, her flesh and blood, hurt her over and over. He *encouraged* his stepson to abuse her and, God forbid, use her.

The horrors she endured made my blood boil and pump furiously through my veins. My hands shook, teeth mashing together. I wanted to find them and bash their fucking skulls in.

Lila was innocent and so fucking pure in the world, and they corrupted it, twisted it, for fun.

I wondered if my parents still had my bat from when I played baseball in high school.

"He was married by then, and his wife had a son of her own. They all hated me for disrupting their family. It was the talk of the town because he was prominent in the community, so he couldn't ditch me once word got out. I wish he had, but they had to think he was the kind of man that did the right thing. So, he took me home and ignored me. He refused to soothe me when I was upset, and he would yell and scream instead. He put on his proud father face when out, but when at home, I was left to fend for myself. Child protective services would be all over his ass these days."

"How did you survive?"

She scoffed, a reaction that surprised me. "He taught me independence through neglect. That was probably his downfall."

The overpowering need to touch her, to soothe her, took over, but we were at the office, so I was limited to reaching across the desk to take hold of her hand.

"You did nothing to deserve it. You know that, right?" I asked, needing to know she understood she did nothing wrong, that she was innocent.

She nodded in agreement, but I wasn't sure she meant it.

As we returned to work, I continued to look over at her from time to time, concerned how she was handling the ghosts. There was nothing I could do at the office, but once we were home, I would show her.

She was stuck in the void of her own memories, the emotions that drowned her as a child. I knew Lila was stronger than she believed. The fact that she got out of that situation by herself told me that. She didn't let them break her completely.

That evening, I tried to show her affection.

When she came around my cock, I felt a shift.

I'd been breached.

FUCKING HATED THE PAIN. MOST DAYS IT WAS MANAGEABLE, BUT with the spring weather, pills were sometimes my only solace.

I'd spent months pretty much blessedly free from migraines, but they seemed to be back with a vengeance. Between the stiffness and pain, I could find no comfort or reprieve.

Scar tissue tugged, exacerbating my symptoms. It felt like the black hole I'd lived in for years was swallowing me up again.

Lila's touch seemed the only thing able to soothe me.

"This hurts you a lot, doesn't it?" she asked as she trailed her fingers down my scar.

"Yes. There were broken bones, sliced muscle, and chewed-up organs. Lots of damage that left lots of problems."

She felt around at my ribs, digging in a little until she found what she was looking for. Following a line, she counted when she found the remodeling on each rib.

"Five?"

I nodded. She took hold of my hand and placed it against her ribs on the left side in almost the same spot. The same remodeling bumps, only smaller.

"Your stepbrother?"

She nodded.

"Do you have a plate here?" she asked, her fingers deftly dancing across my wrist.

"Yes."

"And your knee?"

We both glanced down at the second largest scar on my body.

"Completely decimated. The femur shattered at the knee. There's so much metal under that scar."

Her brow knitted, and she snuggled into my arms. "I wish I could take it all away."

I wish I could take it all away from you, too.

The next day things got worse, and I was numb to the world. After work we stripped and I pulled Lila into bed. She lulled me to sleep by running her fingers through my hair.

I considered myself to be the type of person who could get along with just about anyone. It seemed the accident may have busted that up as well, because after more than a month, I still couldn't stand Andrew.

Ever since he popped back into Lila's life, I hated him. The way he looked at her gave him away. Work luncheons didn't happen often, and they were usually with large clients of the firm. Four attorneys—Andrew, Benjamin, Lila, and myself—sat around a table with the CEO of a regional chain of grocery stores to talk about the takeover of a city-wide local chain.

It was past the lunch hour, the restaurant mostly empty as the hostess guided us back to a small private room. The moment I saw the large, round table, I adjusted my position from Andrew, making sure Lila was not next to him.

Instead of Andrew on her other side, it was Benjamin who was seated there. I'd seen him around Lila before and it was obvious all his attention belonged to his wife.

As the talks began, I placed my hand on Lila's thigh. That was the start, the catalyst. I teased her mercilessly until she had to get away.

To avoid suspicion, I waited a few minutes before excusing myself and following her. I snuck in the ladies' restroom and slipped inside her.

Quick, dirty, and exactly what I fucking needed to calm the jealousy that raged inside me.

"We need to get back out there," Lila said as I regained my breath. I had her bent over, using a wall support as I fucked her.

My cock was spent, the agitation of Andrew's presence lessened. Another minute, and I stood and pulled out. Some come dribbled down to the floor.

"Come on, Honeybear, we better get cleaned up real quick and get back out there before they send out a search party," I said as I stuffed my dick back in my slacks.

She was smiling as she straightened back out. It took a few minutes, but once everything was back in place, we headed back to the private room.

"There she is," Benjamin said with a smile. "And she found Nathan."

We sat down, and I noticed Andrew was avoiding looking at Lila, which was odd.

"We sent Andrew out to find you two, but he came back empty-handed," Benjamin said.

My jaw twitched as I glanced at Andrew. Fuck. That was the change in his demeanor. He heard.

"I caught her coming out of the ladies' room and dragged her outside with me for a minute," I said, coming up with the most plausible lie I could, but the cloud around Andrew didn't change. "We had something we needed to discuss."

As lunch wore on, my suspicion that Andrew overheard us became more concrete.

"You were a very bad boy today, Mr. Thorne. I don't know if I should let you in tonight," Lila teased that night when we were in the elevator of our building on the way home.

The corner of my lip pulled up. "Oh, really? And how are you going to manage that when I have a key?"

"Hmm, good point." She tilted her head and tapped a finger against her lips. "I could deny you access."

"Could you?" I asked in challenge. I knew for a fact she couldn't, but I really wanted to see her try.

"I think I could," she said, standing straighter.

Challenge accepted.

I leaned into her and pressed her into the elevator wall, one hand on her hip, the other cupping her face as I leaned in to whisper against her ear. "Could you?"

I ghosted my lips across her cheek before pressing them to hers. She relented and wrapped her arms around me, pulling me in as close as possible. Her hands fisted my hair, pulling me back to look in her eyes.

"Could *you?*"

"Never," I admitted. "I could never deny you."

That was my issue from the beginning. From the moment I met her, I was fucked. It took little effort on her part.

Our want became a raging need, and by the time the elevator pinged for her floor, our clothes were a mess. We stumbled out into the hall, bumping into walls as hands grabbed.

I let out a groan as her tongue ran along my exposed collarbone, while I worked to pull her skirt up. We were frantic, unbalanced as I pulled her leg up to my hip, causing us to fall against the opposite wall.

It was exactly the leverage I needed. I got her other leg up, and she locked them around my waist, pulling my hips in, letting my cock press into her heat.

I rocked into her as I nipped along her jaw, completely overcome by the drive to be inside her.

"You aren't going to walk straight when I'm done with you tonight."

A moan slipped from her lips while I continued to trail my teeth down her neck. I was ready to fucking pin her to the wall with my cock when we were interrupted.

"What the fucking shit is going on?"

We stopped from shock and turned to find Andrew a few feet from her door.

I groaned and turned my head back into her neck.

"Fuck. Fuck, fuck, fuck, fuck," I hissed against her skin.

I straightened and stretched my neck, the beast waking in excitement.

"I told you to fucking stay away from her!" Andrew yelled, his face red, body tense. He was itching to punch me, but wouldn't do anything while I was so close to Lila. "And I told you to stay away from him!"

What the fuck right did he have to tell her that? She wasn't his.

I let go of her legs and let out a hard breath before starting down the hall. Everything was tense, readying for a fight. It was long past time we had it out.

"What fucking right do you have to fucking say that to either of us?"

His lip curled up, and he stepped forward and attempted to lean over me, but there was only an inch between us and he wasn't intimidating.

"I can't fucking stand you," he seethed. "Now, get the fuck away from her."

"Make me," I said in challenge, our faces inches apart. "If she wants me to get away from her, *she* needs to tell me, not some overgrown, jealous Neanderthal."

Lila's small hand pressed against me, the heat from her touch calming me enough to listen to her.

"Boys, we need to get inside before my neighbor comes out, and you both know how she is."

Lila turned to the door and fumbled with her purse in search of her keys. It was taking too long, so I pulled mine from my pocket and handed them to her.

"Here."

The fucker gasped in shock.

Yeah, you don't have a key, do you, asshole?

She ushered us in, handing me my keys.

"Are you kidding me? He has a fucking key? To your condo? Hell *no*," Andrew growled.

Lila threw her bags down and slammed the door shut before turning on him. "Andrew! You don't know anything about what is going on, so shut up."

"He's fucking playing with you, Lila. Open your eyes. He sticks his fucking dick in anything that has a pussy!"

I closed the distance between us and got right up in his fucking face, ready to deck him. He had made me blood-thirsty from the moment I first met him.

"You don't know anything."

"How long have you been stringing her along? Making her think she's different from the other girls?"

"As I said, you don't know *anything*. Because if you did, you would know the only woman I've been with for almost four months is Lila."

The expression fell from his face, and he looked toward Lila. She wasn't impressed by any of our posturing. There was a satisfaction that sunk in as his eyes grew wide. Fucking finally he knew—he understood.

She didn't want him. He finally knew all the marks left on her were from me.

Lila was mine.

"No. Him?" He pointed toward me. "It was him at the bar? It's him who marks you? *Him* who understands you?"

Lila simply nodded, refusing to elaborate. Which was good, because he had no right to our relationship.

I stepped up, getting his attention. "Yes. Me. I see her. I'm the one who sleeps with her every night. It's my cock shoved in that fucking tight pussy of hers," I growled. My arm shot out, and I pointed to the door. "So, get the fuck out of here so I can pin her against the wall and make her forget that anyone other than me has ever been inside her."

He needed to fucking go. He didn't belong.

Suddenly, his hands were fisted in my jacket as he pulled me so we were face to face.

"You don't deserve to be in the same fucking room as her."

I pushed him off with so much force, he stumbled back.

"What the fuck is your problem? You just can't let her go, can you? Wasn't it you who left her?"

What the fuck kind of claim did he think he had on his ex-girlfriend?

"And what do you know about me, Andrew? That I fucked around with women over the last two years? Yes, that's true. I needed an outlet for my anger, frustration, and sexual needs. Who the fuck cares? She doesn't." I gestured to Lila.

"If that's all you know and that's all you care to know, then leave," she said.

Andrew stared at her, and I could see the hurt, but I really didn't care.

"This is a breach of both of your employment contracts. You know that, right?" he asked.

"Of course we know," Lila said. "Are you planning on saying something so we'll both get fired? Is your prejudice of Nathan that great? So great you would endanger my job as well? And my happiness?"

"I… Lila…" He let out a sigh as he begged her with his eyes. "I don't want to see you get hurt, and I think he could damage you."

"Nathan has no devious plan, no ulterior motives. He's a good man, and you need to open your eyes and see. Because all you're looking at is the act, what he shows you, not the real man."

Fuck, I wanted to kiss her.

"Now get the hell out of my home, and don't fucking come back until you're ready to know him—ready to know us. I'm an adult and can make my own goddamn decisions. I choose who I want to be with. And it's him. He's the one I want."

Fuck, yes, we are, the beast growled from his cage.

His body slouched in defeat. "Good girl."

Good girl? Was she a fucking dog, or was he really that clueless as to how strong she could be?

She smiled back, and he turned to leave.

His love for her in whatever capacity could render him an ally, as much as I hated to admit it. Much like Caroline, he did have her best interest at heart, and I had to commend him on that.

"If you want to find out some truth—as true as the news will give you, anyway—then do what Caroline did and Google my name," I said. His eyes met mine, the animosity gone. "And once you've done that and found some truth, then you can come and try to tell us what kind of person I am, but not before. Because I guarantee your opinions will change."

He nodded and headed to the door.

Seconds after the door clicked closed, I had Lila pinned against the wall as I devoured her mouth. It was what I needed to calm down and I slowed, nuzzling her.

"Mine," I said.

Her fingers caressed my cheek as she smiled up at me. "Always."

WASN'T SURPRISED THE NEXT MORNING WHEN ANDREW CAME UP and wrapped his arms around me in a firm hug.

"I'm sorry," he whispered too low for Lila to hear.

It wasn't an, "I'm sorry I was such a douche," but an, "I'm sorry for what you went through."

We pulled back, and I stared him in the eye and nodded. Andrew gave me a sad smile, then glanced to Lila.

"I won't say anything."

Lila didn't understand, and her curiosity was getting the better of her. She knew more truth about what happened to me physically, but unlike Caroline and Drew, she didn't know what I'd lost.

There was no longer animosity between us, which confused Lila to no end. The fire had died, and he accepted that Lila was mine. A friendship formed, and it was the first one I'd had in years. I'd forgotten what it was like to talk to someone who didn't walk on eggshells around me.

I begged Lila to give me time, but I wasn't sure there would ever be enough time to prepare me for that conversation.

Scandal hit the office a week later, and suddenly Lila and I were on edge again. The rumored relationship between two Holloway employees turned out to be true. The non-fraternization was so strict it even covered those working in two different departments that didn't interact. For all anyone knew, they could have met at a bar and found out later they had the same employer.

It wasn't the same for us. Our small office only seemed to shrink while the tension soared.

"Your birthday is coming up in a few weeks, right?" Lila asked one afternoon as I flipped through a file.

Every muscle froze as a barrage of images flew across my vision and a sudden flare of pain erupted in my chest.

"I don't celebrate my birthday."

I didn't have to look at Lila or say another word. She didn't ask any questions or even speak. Most people would verbalize their internal questions, but she silenced hers.

In fact, Lila barely asked questions about me, and only delved into my past when something brought it up. Like my Harvard T-shirt. We both knew all she had to do was Google my name and any questions she had would be answered, but she never did.

Which only made our situation volatile. She was waiting on me to open up, but it would never happen. I cared for her, but I didn't think I could and would ever tell her. It was too deep, a hole I didn't want to go near. Why would I jump into that kind of emptiness and drag her in with me?

Just the thought of my birthday sent the darkness crawling in like a fog.

The fog grew with each day, wrapped around me with each passing hour. Every day, it got thicker and darker. Lila had me so distracted that the date crept up on me, but the second she reminded me, albeit unintentionally, everything turned.

The anniversary was a blanket of oppression stifling each breath. With each day, the darkness closed in. My hands shook, anxiety buzzing through my veins.

It all leaked into my time with Lila. The only way to release the pressure and the pain was hard, rough fucking.

"Nate, you shouldn't be doing that," Grace said.

I quirked a brow at her and looked down at the game of chess before me.

"Why not?" I asked.

There was something eerie about all of it, but I couldn't put my finger on it.

"It's dangerous."

I rolled my eyes. "It's just a game, Grace."

"No. It's not. You're blind," she said.

"I don't understand."

"Look, Nate."

I stared down at the pieces on the board. Instead of the normal pieces, there were people. On the opposite side of the board were men dressed in dark suits. The king was familiar. A frightening familiarity. The queen beside him was a woman I knew well.

"Grace?" I picked up the piece and, sure enough, it was my wife.

The eyes popped open, and she looked surprised before she began screaming, but no sound came out. I set the piece back down, the dark eyes of Vincent Marconi looking back before lifting his arm, gun in hand, toward the other side of the board.

I was the king, and beside me was a broken and frail looking queen that was an unmistakable tiny version of Lila.

"What is going on?" I asked.

"It's a choice."

I scrunched my brow. "A choice? I thought it was a game."

"Choices are moves in games. You chose to go left instead of right."

The queen moved left, putting her in the intercepting path of Vincent's gun.

"Each choice is an action and as such, has a reaction. We're all pieces on a game board, but look at your side. There are no pawns left to protect you or your queen. One lonely rook, one beaten knight, are all you have left."

"He destroyed it all," I whispered.

"No, he didn't. You did. And you will destroy her."

"No." I shook my head. "Never."

"What about me, Nate? We were forever, and now we're never. The only similarity is ever. Life isn't guaranteed, but ever is always there. Ever is the catalyst for life and death. At any time, in any way."

"I won't. Lila will be fine."

"Lila will be dead."

"Don't say that!" I screamed and grabbed her by the arms. "Don't you ever fucking say that again. She will live, even if I have to die."

She began to glow, morphing. Blue eyes turned a clear gray-green. I wanted to smile, kiss her, but red droplets began to cover her, and her eyes stared at me in a hauntingly familiar empty look.

"I'm already dead."

Shaking woke me, and my eyes snapped open. I was out of the bed in seconds, my leg stiff from sleep causing me to stumble as I made my way to the bathroom. I leaned over the sink and turned on the cold water, splashing it on my face.

A dream. A fucking terror.

I felt Lila behind me, staring, but I couldn't look at her. The image was too fresh, her body mangled and bloody, and I was to blame.

I heard her call, saw her reach out of the corner of my eye, but I couldn't respond. I shied away from her, from her out-stretched hand, and crawled back into bed.

The dream only called out my harsh reality and what being with me ultimately meant for her. It was something I ignored because for the first time in years, I felt some measure of happiness.

But my happiness was not worth her life.

I would keep her alive even if it killed me in every way possible.

My mood, my situation, did not improve. My heart beat a furious pace at almost all times, my anxiety at epic levels.

"Do you want to do anything special for your birthday?" Lila asked one afternoon.

My birthday?

The shock alone sent a spear of pain through me. How did she know?

It was an innocent question, but to me, it was a dagger shoved into my chest. "Please don't say that again, and don't tell anyone. I don't celebrate my birthday…not anymore."

Lila didn't say anything or ask any questions.

When the actual date rolled around, I retreated into myself, something Lila took notice of. I was hard with her, the devastating energy driving me. I needed the mind-wiping come, needed it to drag me under and make me forget. Shine light on me, guide me in the emptiness.

What was worse was two days later. Halfway through the day, I left without a word. Jack would understand, and there'd be no trouble, but I couldn't even tell Lila. I had to get out of there, had to drown myself just to get past the day, past the hour. The countdown to 9:16 pm.

I shouldn't have even stepped inside the office. There was no way I'd be able to handle it.

The moment I was home, I pulled the vodka from the fridge and took a long, hard pull straight from the bottle. It was only a third full and wouldn't last long.

Deep inside I shook, from my core expanding outward. I wasn't good to be around, nothing but a destructive force.

The draw to see her moved me to the closet and the box that lay hidden. I hadn't even acknowledged its existence since that day months before when it tried to pull me under. But I needed it, more than anything. I needed to see her, to see them, to completely submerge myself in the pain.

I threw the blankets and sheets off, uncovering the box and pulling it into the middle of the closet. My hands shook as I flipped the lid, the beast howling inside my mind, but I was driven by the need to see, to rip open the scars of my heart.

A vice wrapped around my chest as I lifted the lid, getting a glimpse of my wife for the first time in over a year. Tears filled my eyes as I looked over the top photo, the one I used to have sitting on my desk. Jack stood between us beaming with pride, my wife's eyes sparkling.

Life was so easy, simple then. At least that was how it seemed looking back. Photos of us in college, my Harvard graduation were in there. Then came our wedding photos. We were so young and naïve, ready to tackle the world.

I took another large gulp of vodka as the tears slowly trailed down my cheeks.

I pulled a small jewelry box out and opened it up. Inside sat the only remnant of that wedding—my wedding ring. The small ring of gold was the only thing to survive the crash intact, not even a small divot in the smooth surface. They managed to get it off before it had to be cut off due to the swelling from my broken arm.

I finished off the bottle, my mind a complete wasteland. I needed more, so I picked myself up from the disaster zone I'd created, slipped the ring into my pocket, and headed to the kitchen.

Once there, I stared into the fridge and the six pack of beer that sat on the shelf, one of the bottles missing. I'd been drinking the same brand for over a decade. My wife had brought it home one day in a mixed package of different beers.

My chest expanded, and I let out a howl, all of my energy concentrated as I tried to force my pain out. Loud and wounded, but it wasn't enough to expel the churning despair inside me.

Nothing in me was salvageable. I shouldn't have taken the job, but it was just another piece in a long line of my failures.

I grab hold of anything in the kitchen not tied down and threw it, dinging walls and sending shards of debris everywhere, screaming as I let it all wash over me and take over.

My breath was hard, the kitchen a mess of broken glass and ceramic. I opened the fridge again and pulled out the package of beer. In less than a minute I had the top popped and the first bottle drained.

Two more in hand, I grabbed my cigarettes and headed out to the porch. It was warm, the day too nice outside for the destruction inside me. I was a bomb, explosive and destructive.

Numbness moved through me as I finished one beer and opened another.

I lost my entire life—my home, my job, my family, my health. Everything that I was, gone in an instant.

The ring in my hand was a reminder of how fucked up I'd become. I stared at it, remembering the moment she slipped it on my finger.

It was a symbol of love, and now it was a symbol of loss.

"Nathan?"

Lila's voice penetrated through the emptiness, and a searing pain cut through me as I continued to twirl the ring in my fingers. I wasn't going to let her end up like my wife. Loving me was a death sentence.

I had to let her go.

"You shouldn't have come today, Lila," I said, my voice hollow even to my own ears. I reached down and picked the bottle up and took a swig. "I can't control what I may do. I'll hurt you. I don't want to hurt you."

Run. Run while you can. Don't let me destroy you.

"I'm not going anywhere. Tell me what's wrong." Determination laced her voice.

There was no holding it back from her. She'd seen the ring. "Four years ago today, everything fell to ruin. Leave, Lila."

The pain whirled inside me, growing and heaving.

"I'm not leaving, not when you're finally talking." She stepped closer.

I needed her to understand, to get away from me, to save herself before it was too late. "I don't just mean today. Leave me. What we have is fucked up."

Save yourself.

"It may be fucked up, but it's helping us both. We need each other."

"I'm not good to be around."

"You are. You *are* good to be around," she said, her voice breaking.

No!

The violent energy surged, and I stood and flung the bottle against the wall. Liquid and shards of glass sprayed everywhere. In my periphery, she jumped, perhaps frightened of me for the first time.

I wanted to break something, mangle, hurt myself on the outside until the pain went away on the inside.

"You don't fucking get it! I lost *everything* that mattered most. My family. The family they stole from me, and the one I pushed away for their own safety."

I stepped forward and slammed my lips to hers, my hands fisting in her hair. The anger and pain was too much to handle. The first bomb exploded.

"Leave me," I begged. "I can't lose you the same way I lost her."

It would kill me.

Her hands ran up and down my back. It was supposed to be soothing, but instead stroked the destructive fire in me.

"I'm here, take solace in me. I need you."

Take *solace?* There was no comfort for me, no peace, not for me.

A growl ripped through me, and I walked her backward and into the brick wall. "I can't fucking *do* this to you. I won't." I refused to drag her down with me, to let my nightmares become reality, to let the past repeat itself.

I pinned her arms to the wall, the pull to her as strong as the push away.

"It's okay," she soothed. "I want you to do it, let me take your pain."

"Push me away and leave. Please, Lila!" The desire tore through me and combined with everything else for a perfect storm as I ripped her shirt off. "I don't want to break you."

The resistance, the last wall, crumbled and everything flooded in.

I drowned in the pain, drowned in her.

Hands clawing at her skin, begging for some sort of release from it all. I picked her up and walked her inside, pausing to tug my own shirt off. We made it to the bed and I had her beneath me.

I couldn't touch her enough, taste her enough.

Nothing was enough for what was the last time.

Inside her was pure pleasure, but it couldn't combat my mental state, couldn't push through the noise, through the pain.

Lost in the fog of my own mind, I thrust forward. I couldn't see anything, hear anything, barely feel anything. Rougher, harder, deeper to find her, but it was like I was fucking the wisps of fog in the nothingness.

I couldn't find my way, couldn't stop. With each thrust, I fractured more as I searched out the thing that connected us, but I couldn't find it.

I pushed harder, faster, running from it all. Each slam was like a hammer strike, cracking and shattering everything around me, but I still couldn't break through.

My whole body was tense, breath caught in my throat as I exploded, my dick twitching with each pump of come. I let everything out in her, poured it all in stream after stream.

The air was gone, muscles tight as I gasped. The energy

dropped, dissipating the cloud that blinded me.

I stared down at her, at my Lila, as my mind came into focus. I was inside her still, which meant I'd been fucking her, but somehow it didn't feel real. Her eyes met mine for a brief moment before rolling back.

Ice shot through my veins as I looked down at her, felt the burn of scratches on my skin.

What did I do? What the fuck did I do?

The beast whimpered as I unclenched my hands. My nails, which were short, popped out of her skin leaving crescent shaped marks. Some were so deep that I'd cut the skin, leaving little trails of blood with the red tinge of her skin.

Guilt flooded me as nausea rolled through me. It was my fault. I lost all control.

No more. I refused. I wouldn't play the game anymore. I wouldn't hurt her.

I physically *hurt* her, and it made me sick.

Seeing her like that, damaged, because I physically did it to her, cleared my mind. The pain was new, fresh. It hadn't had years to build up, but only moments of remorse.

My Lila.

My Lila that I was destroying.

I pulled out, shuddered at the feeling, watching as some of my come spilled out. The sight before me left me reeling. Tears still slid down her cheeks, her skin covered in pink and red. It was not her normal look of well fucked.

She looked beaten, abused, and it made my stomach turn, the sick feeling increasing. I did that to her. I hurt her. It wasn't someone from her past, but me, someone she trusted.

There was more pain circulating through me than any one person should handle, and I just made it worse.

I threw on some clothes before wrapping her up in a blanket. She couldn't stay. I had to make it a clean break. Firm. It was the only way I could handle it and stick to it.

The most difficult thing I'd done in years was take her to her room and leave her. The most painful thing was saying… Goodbye.

Lila,

I can't do this any longer. I refuse to hurt you again. Please keep your distance, and I promise I won't come to you anymore. We'll act like we never happened.

Nathan

M Y CHEST CLENCHED, AND I RUBBED THE SPOT WITH FIRM pressure. A familiar pain was flooding in, and once again it was all my fault.

The doors to the elevator closed in front of me, the number twelve disappearing before my eyes, leaving me to stare at my own lifeless reflection. The weight of my decision hovered above me, poised for the right moment to crash down.

I saw her long before I ever met her; Lila, my cohort in crime at work and at home. Across a sea of asphalt and cars was where I caught my first glimpse of the woman who would do the impossible and awaken a long dead part of me.

She was unassuming, skittish even, captivating me with the way she walked. There was nothing particularly special about it; maybe it was just the way the light reflected in her natural blonde hair. Whatever it was, my eyes were glued to her. She became more intriguing when her demeanor changed as two men approached: her body rigid, pace slowed, and eyes down. It was subtle. Not many would notice, but I did.

The caged beast inside me also noticed and pulled at his chains, growling. He didn't like that they made her feel that way. I was about to go to her, launch myself at her, the beast wanting the strange siren, when a hand clamped down on my shoulder and pulled me back to reality.

I shouldn't have taken the job when Jack offered it to me. In fact, the only reason I did was to have something to keep me busy, keep my mind off everything. To keep the days passing as I waited to die.

Every day was the same; a spiral down to hell. I knew my family was waiting for the call that I'd offed myself. I'd been tempted, hundreds of times, but I never went through with it.

I wished I had. Better to destroy myself and not take her with me.

The throbbing behind my ribs was damn near crippling and made my legs shaky as I tried to brace myself in the elevator while it moved. No one would ever find out the level of asshole I'd achieved.

I'd done it. Done what I thought I couldn't.

I left her...the one good thing I had in my purgatory.

So, why did it hurt so bad that my eyes stung? I could barely breathe or think. Shouldn't I have been proud I finally found the inner strength to do what was best for her?

I blinked and swallowed, but the lump of shame in my throat wouldn't budge.

It was a necessary separation. I couldn't keep hurting her, and that night I *physically* hurt her.

She deserved more, so much more than me: an angry, depressed, broken man. I couldn't give her what she needed—love. So, I did what I had asked her to do.

I left.

Once more my eyes stung like a son of a bitch, but there was no room for tears. I didn't deserve them.

Visions of her collapsed and passed out after I lost control and took her assaulted me. It'd been too much, too rough. I begged her to leave, told her I couldn't control it. Not today.

Today was the day it all resurfaced. The pain, the agony… *my wife.*

The life, the love, and the family that was taken from me.

The last time I saw her surfaced, her eyes open…staring, blank, void, empty…dead.

The medically induced coma they placed me in kept me from even saying goodbye. I was unable to attend her funeral.

The elevator signaled that I reached my floor, and I was left with heavy steps as I walked out and down the hall. I entered my condo after having deposited Lila back into hers, leaving her.

I shut the door behind me, leaning on it as it clicked closed. All of my belongings I'd retrieved from her place dropped to the ground, landing on the tile floor below.

My hands moved to my hair, tugging and pulling on it as the air around me became suffocating. I felt something digging into my palm and released my grip to find out what it was.

I opened my hand, and in it rested a jagged piece of metal.

Her key…the key to my place. I took it from her key ring and returned the one she'd given me.

The weight was becoming too much, almost crippling. The animal inside me was stirring, the part of me that wanted her more than I wanted to admit.

Gone. She was gone. I left.

Mine! the beast howled. ***She. Is. Mine!***

No. She deserves to be happy and loved. I can't give her that.

I leaned my forehead on the door, pounding my fist on it—hoping the door would give way and I'd have an excuse to run back to her. Any excuse to end the agony in which I was beginning to drown.

"Stay here! You have to."

Arguing with myself probably couldn't be seen as sane, but my head and heart were warring. My feelings for her had become so strong.

Mine! he roared.

"Lila…"

Mine!

"Oh, God, what have I done?" I doubled over, the crushing weight of my actions coming down on me. "I need you. I need you so much."

Get. Her. Back!

"I can't. No. I won't…I won't hold her down, hold her back. Someone will worship the ground she walks on, love her."

We can do that. No one will ever understand her like we do.

"Someone will try. Someone will want and love her."

Someone like Andrew?

My voice broke down to a whisper. "Yes, someone like Andrew."

No! Mine. Not Andrew's. Mine. I need her!

A crunching sound that had become all too familiar in recent months filled my ears. I looked down to find my hand embedded in the drywall.

My knuckles began to sting as I stared at my arm still lodged in the new hole. I pulled my hand out and surveyed the damage. I spun around, looking at all of the holes that the entry walls contained. All were created because of her. Because

I wanted her and tried to deny it. Because I wouldn't face the truth about what was going on between us. Because I was angry at her for making me feel for her.

That was the moment I came crumbling apart at the seams.

I grabbed at the edge of the drywall and pulled, tearing a chunk from the wall.

It wasn't enough. At a frantic pace, I began pulling, large pieces coming off in my hands. The dust filled the air, clouding it, just like my mind and my heart. I needed the reminder of her gone.

I'd gotten one section down before it let loose; the pain, the loss, the anger. Nothing was safe from my path of destruction.

I pulled half a sheet down in one tug, tossed it to the side and manically finished the demolition of the remaining, offending plasterboard.

Every tug, every pull, I tried to push her memory away. The feel of her skin, her body beneath mine, her smile, her laughter, her mind, her taste, her need.

She needed me. I knew that. I needed her; something I was just beginning to understand.

I left. Separating us.

I screamed out, cursing myself, my life, and cursing her, though innocent, for entering my solitary existence and turning my purgatory upside down.

My hands snapped the wallboard off the nails that were holding it onto their wooden supports. In my fury I tore, pulled, and yanked the walls down until there was nothing left.

No holes. No walls. No reminder.

Nothing.

I stood, breathing hard, in the middle of the entryway. Sweat poured down my face, plaster dust clung to my wet skin and clothing. The air was thick with a white haze, the drywall bits covered the floor, beaten.

And still I could feel her presence.

I fell to my knees, the dust floating back into the air.

My arms itched from the powder coating my skin, and I coughed, gagging on the chalky substance hovering in the air. Didn't matter. I deserved to suffer.

My body began shaking as I sat there in defeat. In the future, I would mourn two losses of my love on that date: my wife and my Lila.

I wouldn't let what happened to her happen to Lila. I couldn't. Lila would live. Lila would meet someone worthy and start a family. Lila would be happy.

But not with me.

A sob erupted from my chest, startling me. The sting of tears in my eyes was disconcerting as my loss crushed me. I mourned them; one taken from me, and the other I threw away.

Tears spilled down my cheeks, my body finally having had enough; enough fighting, enough feeling.

Enough.

THE NEXT MORNING MY ALARM WENT OFF, BUT I WAS ALREADY awake. My eyes were glued to the ceiling, staring blankly at the white expanse. In the time I was staring, I noticed the nail pops, small cracks in the plasterboard, and the all-consuming ache in my chest.

I slept terribly; tossing and turning, fighting nightmares and periods of insomnia.

As I lay there, I realized it was the first night in months that Lila wasn't next to me in the bed. Her delectable cherry blossom scent and warmth filling the room. It'd been months since I'd awoken without her soft body curled into mine, our limbs entangled.

Instead the bed was cold.

No good morning kisses.

No morning sex with my goddess.

No sweet smiles from my Honeybear.

No Lila.

My Lila.

An hour later, on autopilot, I was dressed and walking to

my car. I noted hers was still in her parking spot a few down from mine. In the rearview mirror the dark circles around my bloodshot eyes made them stand out; evidence of my sleepless night.

I arrived at our office and breathed in her sweet scent that still lingered there. Sitting at my desk, I went straight to work and braced myself for her entrance. It was almost seven thirty; she would be there any moment.

Halfway through the Anderson contract, and still no Lila. Odd, as it was a few minutes past eight. Then again, after what I'd done, I didn't expect her to come in early.

At eight forty-five, she still wasn't there.

I checked my phone every few minutes to make sure I hadn't missed her call. My leg started bouncing in agitation. In my head, I began to spin different scenarios of why she was late, some of them causing me to worry about what might have happened to her.

The Boob Squad left me alone, obviously noting my mood. Thank God, because there was no way I could deal with them that day.

By nine fifteen I was pulling at my hair when Caroline stuck her head in to say good morning and stopped as she noticed the empty desk.

"Where's Lila?" she asked.

I kept my focus on my work, refusing to meet her eyes. "I don't know."

She closed the door behind her, and her tone, when she spoke, contained enough force to draw my attention. "What do you mean you don't know?"

I shook my head, my brain trying to find the words so she could understand. "I couldn't keep hurting her, Caroline."

There was a knock on the door before Andrew entered. I watched his bright smile fade when he noticed the scene in front of him. "What did you do?"

I leaned forward, my elbows resting on the desk, my hands pulling at my neck. "I ended it. I hurt her, and then I ended it."

"You fucking moron!" Caroline screamed at me.

At the same time, Andrew yelled, "I can't believe I fucking trusted her with you!"

Caroline's hand collided with my right cheek, and I welcomed the physical pain. "You...She's in love with you!" My head swung back to meet her fierce gaze, my eyes wide in disbelief. "Do you have any fucking clue what you've done?"

It felt like the floor was falling out from beneath my feet.

No, oh please, no. Don't love me. Please don't let it be true. They'll kill you. They'll kill you like they did her.

"Give me your key, and I swear to God, if she...if she isn't all right, I will kill you!"

I stared up at Caroline, believing her threat. "I don't have her key. I gave it back."

"And how did she take all of this?"

"I don't know. She passed out. I...I took her and placed her in her bed. I told her in a letter, though I'm sure she understood with my actions, and I switched out our keys before I left."

"You fucking coward!" Andrew said; every muscle was tense, and I wondered when he was going to hit me. I deserved it.

I flinched at his words but agreed with him.

"We need to check on her, and we need to do it *now*," Caroline said, pacing in front of me. "I'll call her cell, if she doesn't answer, we are going over there and *you* will get us in."

I nodded in agreement, my chest tightening.

She was all right. She had to be. She was just upset. She would be fine.

I tried to convince myself over and over. It wasn't enough. Opening up my desk drawer, I pulled out my anti-anxiety pills and took one, then stuffed the bottle into my pocket.

Caroline wasn't able to get ahold of Lila, so we headed out, leaving word with Jack's assistant about the situation, but leaving out the part about my relationship. The assistant hadn't heard from her either and confirmed she would alert Jack of the situation and our absence.

I let out a sigh of relief that Jack wasn't available. I wasn't sure I could face him right then, or lie to him, anyway. He knew me too well and could call my bullshit. One look and he would know. He would know that we were something more.

We all piled into my car, and ten minutes later we were in the parking lot of our building. Her car was where I had last seen it, cool and unused, in her parking spot.

"Mike!" I called out as we rushed in and up to the desk. "Have you seen Lila Palmer today?"

"Lila? No, she hasn't come down yet," he replied, a bit bewildered by our entrance.

I began to shake, Andrew had begun pacing, and Caroline was biting her fingernails. None of those were good signs.

"Can you ring up and see if she answers?"

"Sure thing, Mr. Thorne."

He let it ring nine times before hanging up and shaking his head.

"We need your help. Lila didn't show up to work, and her car is still here. We're unable to reach her by phone, and we're worried there's something very wrong. We need to get into her apartment and make sure she's okay; can you help us with that?"

"Well, we do have keys for emergencies," he said, his voice shaking and his jaw tense, making it obvious he was now infected with the same worry that plagued us.

"This is definitely an emergency." My voice cracked with the force of my emotions.

Something was wrong. I could feel it in my bones. My inner beast that had been silent, brooding, was whimpering and pacing.

Please, please, be all right.

Mike unlocked a hidden safe behind the desk and pulled out a bundle of brass keys. Andrew wouldn't stop pushing the elevator button, all in hopes it would get there sooner, and when it finally did, we all rushed in.

The soft elevator music could not dissolve the building tension as we climbed up to the twelfth floor. Mike was out first, and we followed behind to Lila's door, anxiously awaiting him to unlock it.

I was trembling, my stomach knotted. I felt like I was on edge and afraid of what we would find on the other side.

The door swung open, and we burst through, all of us calling out for her.

"Lila!" I rushed toward the family room. In my periphery, I watched Andrew head right toward the kitchen, and Caroline make straight for Lila's bedroom.

I stared after Caroline, and a few seconds later, her voice broke the fear. "In here!"

I stood frozen, afraid of what I was about to see. It shattered when I watched Andrew run out of the kitchen.

I rushed after him, my eyes frantic in their search for her as I entered the threshold.

The sight before me caused my knees to go weak, my legs

threatening to give out, and my balance shifted my weight backward into the door frame, my hands grasping it for support to keep me from falling.

No. No, no, no, no, no, no! No!

Please! Please, Lila, please!

No, no! Please be okay, please be okay!

My mind was frantic, begging for hope.

Lying on the floor near the foot of the bed was Lila; her hips were twisted, shoulders against the floor, arms splayed, head tilted to the side. She was naked, just as I had left her the night before.

Her pale skin showed the deep bruises of my body's assault on hers. I had been too hard, too rough, too much. I was out of control, and I knew it.

The world stopped—everything stopped—when I reached her eyes. Her beautiful gray-green eyes were open, the lids unable to close. They were glazed over, empty, flat, void.

Images of a night years before, another set of eyes, flooded my mind.

Empty.

Void.

Dead.

My stomach turned, and I propelled my body to the adjoining bathroom to heave into the toilet. I hadn't eaten, so only bile and acid were expelled; my stomach retched to purge my mind.

My ears were ringing, and I couldn't hear anything that Caroline and Andrew had said from the moment I saw her lying on the ground.

Caroline's voice erupted, breaking through. "Mike, call 911! Oh, Lila!"

"Is she breathing? Please say she's breathing!" Andrew begged.

"She is! Lila? Can you hear me? Lila?"

I wiped my mouth and walked back into the bedroom where my Lila lay, alive but unresponsive.

"Goddamn son of a bitch!" Andrew roared before his fist collided with my jaw.

I stumbled back against the wall. His hand grabbed at my suit and brought me back up to face him.

"This is what you fucking said to her?" He held up the letter I'd left her. "I thought you understood her. I thought you cared for her. You fucking destroyed her!" He looked at me with absolute contempt, and his tone was murderous. "You fucking stay away from her. You don't talk to her, you don't fucking look at her." For a moment, I got a reprieve from his animosity as he turned to look at Lila's lifeless form. "Do you have any idea what you've done?"

"It's better this way," I whispered as Caroline covered her body.

"Like fucking hell it is! She was getting better, we could all see it. That was your doing. You were healing her. Now…she's barely functioning."

My stomach clenched again, my breath catching. "I warned her from the beginning. I begged her to go. I hurt her, Andrew."

"*You* did this to her. She trusted you. You know what happened to her and you just confirmed everything they ever told her. You knew how broken she was, and you went and fucking crushed her. You were healing her, and now? She may not recover from this." He was seething, glaring down at me, his nostrils flared.

The room remained quiet after Andrew stopped yelling at

me. We waited on pins and needles for the paramedics to come and take her away. I couldn't drive, and Andrew wanted nothing to do with me so he grabbed Lila's keys and took her car, while Caroline shoved me into my car and drove us. We arrived at the hospital not long after the ambulance.

Since I wasn't family, they wouldn't tell me a thing no matter how many people I cursed, yelled, and spat at. It was a nightmare, one from which I was afraid I might never wake up.

Sometimes it was good when members of your family worked at a hospital, but sometimes it wasn't. The times when you screwed up and destroyed a beautiful woman? There they were without invitation.

My mother looked at me with such pity, while my father looked disappointed.

We'd been there about an hour when a familiar form walked down the hall toward us.

"Darren?"

"Nathan?" Darren Morgenson, my therapist and friend, wrapped his arms around me in a hug. "What are you doing here?"

"I fucked up." The words slipped out, because that was all that was going through my head.

He pulled back and studied my face. "What are you talking about?"

"What are you doing here?" I asked, diverting talk away from me. I didn't think I had it in me to tell him I'd destroyed my own heart and an innocent one in the process.

"I got a call, one of my patients. Poor girl's had a

breakdown, it seems." He shook his head. "I haven't seen her in months, and now this. She's so fragile; I always wondered when she'd break."

My eyes widened, and my stomach dropped. "Lila Palmer?"

I begged to all the Gods that I wasn't right, but I already knew I was. Darren was her therapist as well. I'd seen his name plastered all over her medications.

He blinked at me. "Yes. How did you know?"

"He's the fucker who broke her," Andrew said from behind me, sticking his hand out for Darren.

"Hey, Andrew, how are you doing?" Darren asked, trying to hide the momentary look of frustration toward me regarding my actions that caused all of the fuckery that was going on. His eyes shifted to Andrew.

I exhaled, and my shoulders rounded forward, crumpling in on myself. Every moment away from Lila made my bones ache and my muscles tense up. Yet, there I stood—rooted in place, helpless to do anything to change any of it.

Andrew's lips were set in a thin line. "I'd be doing a lot better if Lila was at the office."

Darren nodded in understanding. "I take it you know what happened."

Andrew jerked his head in my direction. "Like I said, *he's* responsible. You'll need to ask him."

I tried to meet Darren's gaze, but I couldn't. I was drowning in my shame.

"What is he talking about?" Darren turned to me. "Look at me, Nate. What the fuck is he saying?"

"I had to." I managed to choke out the words.

"He left her this." Andrew handed Darren the note, and I cringed.

Darren gasped as he read it. My eyes flickered over to him, and I could tell he was furious.

He looked back at me, anger and pain in his expression. "You just undid six years of therapy in four sentences. Four fucking sentences!"

He stormed off down the hall to her room, leaving me to drown in my growing self-hatred.

It was not what I wanted.

We stayed for a few hours, but Lila never woke up.

Darren and her other doctors came out, looking for her family. None of us were, but Caroline lied and said she was her sister. Darren knew better, but he didn't correct her. They were sisters in spirit.

Self-induced psychological coma, they told Caroline. Lila had retreated into her own mind, unable to take the pain and harsh new reality I'd created.

D AYS PASSED, AND LILA WAS STILL UNRESPONSIVE, TRAPPED IN the recesses of her mind. For the second day in a row, I found myself leaving the office at five and rushing over to the hospital.

Work was utter hell. I hated being away from her.

Nothing changed in the ten hours since I'd last been there. I walked into the room with quiet steps up to the bed. She looked so peaceful, like an angel. The constant beeping of the machines, along with the low rise and fall of her chest, put to rest the creeping fear that she was gone. I clung to each breath and beat.

She was still there, alive, and she would return.

I hoped.

My hand reached out to move a stray strand of hair from her face, but I stopped myself. It was one thing to see her, to smell her, and to feel her presence. It was another thing entirely to touch her.

This is for the best, I reminded myself.

I turned and walked back out to the hall. Once there, I leaned on the wall and stared at the room across the hall. A shiver ran down my spine, and my body shuddered as memories flooded back to my mind.

I pushed them away and slid down the wall to sit on the floor. My mind turned over to the beeping of the machines that let me know my Lila was still with me. After a few minutes, my heart began to beat in time with hers.

I sat there listening, thinking, feeling, until after midnight when a nurse came by and told me I couldn't stay any longer.

When I returned the next night, her door was closed, and through the small glass window I could see Darren and a few other doctors looking at the monitors and talking.

Taking my position again, I slid down the wall, coming to rest on the cold, hard floor. I closed my eyes, my head tilted back, and I listened to the steady beep of the machines.

I heard the door to her room swish open then click closed. I didn't know if he saw me or not, but he knew I was there.

He sighed. "Why are you sitting out here? If you came this far, why don't you go in and see her? She knows you're here, after all."

My head snapped up. "She's awake?"

I watched Darren turn to look at me, a sad smile on his lips. "No, not yet."

"Then how do you know she knows?"

"Her heart rate's been steady all day. It picked up about fifteen minutes ago," he said, then quirked his brow. "How long have you been sitting out here?"

I stared up at him in wide-eyed shock. "About fifteen minutes."

"That's what I thought." Darren slid down to sit next to me. "What are you doing?"

"What do you mean?"

"Here. Why are you here? You broke her, yet you come by every day and sit outside her room."

I sighed. "I don't know. I just... I feel such a pull to be near her. I hate that I did this to her...but it's better this way."

"Better than what? You may be saving her from the possibility of being harmed by Marconi, but what do you call that in *there*? Three fucking days she's been unresponsive." He hitched his thumb toward her room. "In that room, they're talking about moving her to a facility I don't want her to go to. She has no next of kin... Well, none that would come. She just has you and a small handful of friends. Friends who have lives. What do you have, Nathan?"

I sat there, staring at the room on the other side of the hallway.

He answered for me. "Nothing. You have nothing. You had her. A beautiful, broken woman who would have done anything for you. A woman who loves you, and you were selfish."

"*Selfish?*" My voice rose in indignation, my head snapping to look at him.

"Selfish. You did this for your protection more than hers. The thought of losing her the same way you lost your wife crushes you, doesn't it?"

"I... How do you know she loves me?"

"Way to deflect there, Nathan. Don't worry, I won't forget. And I know, because if she didn't love you, she wouldn't be in her current state. And if you didn't love her, you wouldn't be sitting out here in your expensive suit, on the floor, outside her door in a *hospital*."

I cringed at the word, just as he probably knew I would.

After spending months in a hospital after the accident, I hated them. The smell alone made me sick. Especially there, in that wing, sitting across the hall from the room that had once been my home.

There was a sudden shrieking plea that rang out from her room. Lila was screaming, begging. Darren jumped to his feet and threw the door open, rushing into the room.

I turned, my fists slamming on the wall while her screams echoed around the hall. My eyes were screwed tight, but the tears leaked through as I listened to my Lila cry out.

Her screams and pleas cut through me, tearing me. I wanted to run in and take her in my arms and never let her go. I wanted to chase away her fears and self-doubts. Declare my undying love, want, need, and support.

"No one wants me!" she wailed.

My heart splintered. "*I* want you," I whispered into the wall. I held my body tight and tense to keep me from running to her, to keep my heart from ruling.

I felt a warm hand on my fist, and I looked up through bleary, tear-filled-eyes to find my mother staring down at me with a sad expression on her face.

"It doesn't have to be this way, Nathan."

"Yes, it does. She's safe this way…without me in her life."

I continued to listen to her pleas and sobs as Darren worked on calming her. It was my punishment. I had done that to her. I needed to hear it. Every cry and sob I created. I broke her.

My chest tightened, constricting my breathing.

It's better this way.

She's better off without me.

I repeated those words over and over in my head, trying to convince myself that I had done what was best for her in the long run. A mantra, as I remained in the hall, listening to everything that poured out of her. My heart broke more the longer

I listened, but it was my punishment. I had to hear her pain, because she was what mattered most.

But if I walked through that door and saw her, I might shatter. I'd much rather sit outside, listening to her scream, and let her be comforted by Darren. He knew what to do. He always did. I couldn't offer her any solace; I didn't have it in me anymore.

All my fucking fault. All of it.

They released Lila the next day, and I was left without any outlet to her. At least in the hospital I could be near her, but it was much better that she wasn't there any longer. However, I was not better.

The beast within me paced, and I grew restless. Sleep evaded me, and I was lucky to be getting three or four hours a night. It was never in one shot either; forty-five minutes here, thirty there.

When Monday rolled around, I was anxious yet elated. I would see her again, and maybe that would soothe me some. I was happy she was returning to work because that meant she was awake. Over the previous few days, I found out just how much I'd grown used to always being around her, how much I was addicted to her.

I arrived at the office early, as insomnia had me up before five, and anxiously awaited her arrival. I was a nervous wreck and had no clue what to do or how to act. I just knew I was miserable, and I guessed that she was worse.

Worse was an understatement when she arrived a little while later. What walked through the door and into our office was not the Lila I knew. My heart ripped again. She looked… different. Almost as if she'd reverted back to that time in the parking lot. Her eyes were directed to the floor, hair down. She didn't look my way. She didn't acknowledge my presence.

It was difficult to look at her, knowing I'd done that to my Lila, but it had to be that way. Didn't it?

I could smell her, and a calm spread through my every nerve. She was there. She was alive. That was what mattered.

Alive.

She continued to avoid looking at me while booting up her computer and sorting through the piles on her desk. Still no acknowledgement.

"Good morning, Lila," I said. I was going to say more, but refrained when she cringed. My chest burned, the knife twisting deeper.

It was better that way.

The days passed just the same, silence prevailing between us. I hated it. Every moment was torture, and not just on me. Lila wasn't even trying to hide the pain, her façade blown away. Stuffing herself into work to avoid thinking, perhaps?

I knew that was what I was doing. Distracting myself with contract after contract.

On her fourth day back, it was so busy I didn't even take a lunch break. I ran to the lobby, picked up a quick deli sandwich from one of the vendors that occupied the first floor, and ate at my desk. I almost picked up Lila's favorite, but I had a suspicion it was a bad idea.

She never left her desk, other than to get more coffee or

some water. She drank her coffee black, so I knew she wasn't getting any calories there, and I hadn't seen her eat anything.

I glanced over at her and cringed. She'd lost weight over the last week. Not a lot, but noticeable. I knew I was to blame.

She's in love with you!

Caroline's words rang through, interrupting my thoughts.

There were only two hours left before she was to leave, Jack making sure she didn't overdo it, and I had a feeling she wasn't eating at home.

I knew I wasn't.

"Lila, go eat something," I said, my eyes never leaving the screen. I needed to stay detached to keep myself restrained. That was why I hadn't engaged in conversation with her since her return.

"No." Her fingers didn't even skip a beat on her typing.

My jaw twitched. "Go."

"I'm not hungry." Her voice was detached, but held the beginnings of annoyance.

I slammed my hands down on my desk.

Dammit!

In my periphery she jumped, but kept her head down. I startled her. She did look my way as I stalked out and down to the break room. I surveyed the contents of the vending machine and found there wasn't much of anything healthy, but at that point, she just needed something in her system.

Her favorite granola bar was there, so I entered my money into the slot. After retrieving it from the machine, I returned to the confines of our office. I threw the bar onto her desk, and it landed right in front of her.

"Eat it," I demanded.

"No."

"Eat the fucking granola bar before I shove it down your throat." It was taking all my control to keep from yelling at her; I was so angry that she wouldn't just take it.

Her hand wrapped around the package, and I smiled on the inside. My body sighed in relief that she was doing as I asked, but was quickly proven wrong when she threw it against the wall. It shattered inside the wrapper with a crack before falling to the floor.

"Oh, I've heard that threat before," she spat up at me. Anger was boiling in her eyes, venom lacing her tone.

My eyes grew wide as I remembered the last time I'd given her a similar threat. My chest ached, longing for the time when things were different between us. Times where my possessiveness was allowed to get the better of me, and my cock ruled.

Her anger was new, confusing, and I didn't know what to do. Something that scared me, but made me proud at the same time. I hated that she was going against me, but at the same time happy she was fighting back.

'D TAKEN TO DRINKING AT NIGHT, WHICH WAS NOT GOOD FOR anything that got in my path. The alcohol reduced my inhibitions, and the beast was let out. All my anger and pain was unleashed upon my surroundings.

I wondered if I was like a drug addict going through withdrawal. I had all the symptoms, my physical dependence on Lila showing its ugly self.

My depression and anxiety spiked, and I craved her more than I ever had before. I *needed* her.

My condo was a mess: the drywall still laid on the floor in the entryway, various pieces of furniture were knocked over, and the closet in the master bedroom was ransacked. Clothes, shoes, belts were strewn all over the floor. Casualties of my search for something, anything, that was hers.

I emptied the hamper and found a shirt of mine she had thrown on one night and found it still smelled of her. I sighed, having enough of a fix to calm me somewhat.

I was a mess, and it was my own fault. We could have been together. There were ways.

But there was no thinking on that day, only pain. It was for the best…for her.

We can give her what is best, what she deserves. We used to be that man. We can be him again.

Seeing her in the hospital, unresponsive, had been unbearable, but she was awake and she would get over me and move on. Get married and have a family.

Our *family*. *We could have been a family; we could have made a family with her.*

I shuddered at the thought, my eyes turning toward the small wooden chest lying exposed in the closet after my search. My mind moved back to another "made" family. My hand caressing the bump that lay between her hips, the ultrasound showing the life we had created.

Gone. All gone.

My wife.

My little boy.

"Happy birthday, Daddy!" she said with an excited smile while I opened the box she handed to me.

We were spending the weekend at her parents' place for a combination belated birthday-slash-Father's Day party.

Within the box laid a black picture frame. Behind the glass was an ultrasound picture with an arrow pointing between what appeared to be legs with the words "I'm a boy!" printed on it.

I smiled as I looked from my wife to the picture containing our child. Miscarriage after miscarriage, and finally we were going to have our family. I leaned forward and captured her lips, conveying my love for her and for our child.

"I wish I hadn't missed that appointment."

"It was the first one you haven't been able to make. I think that's pretty good, especially with your schedule," she said, her hands

running through my hair.

"But, I missed this." My fingers traced the form of our child.

"But what a great birthday-slash-Father's Day gift! Besides, you won't miss any more."

I was pulled back by the frightening reality her statement held.

No, I didn't miss any more because there were no more to miss. She didn't know—none of us did—that just a few short hours later I would lose them both.

They said he wouldn't have survived outside the womb, even if he'd survived the crash and they'd gotten to him in time.

I saw the evidence photos; he didn't survive the crash.

I pulled the shirt back up to my face and inhaled, breathing in Lila's lingering scent. It was amazing how even the tiny bit that remained could calm me. What was I going to do when there was no more scent?

Her soft, warm body haunted me. I wanted to feel her in my arms. Just…feel her. Lila, *my* Lila.

My hand unconsciously rubbed at my chest to try and soothe the ache that lay beneath.

You can still fix this. Get her back! the beast spoke. **Lay claim to her, make her ours! Marry her!**

No.

Why?

And give Vincent Marconi someone else he can take from me?

We can protect her!

I couldn't protect *them*; how was I supposed to protect Lila?

I looked up at the clock; fifteen minutes past eight. She was running late, past her normal seven-thirty. I tried to ignore the thought that sprung forth about the last time she was late, but it caught me nonetheless.

The phone on my desk rang and, in my daze, I answered it without looking at the caller ID.

"Nathan Thorne," I said in greeting. There was a whimpering on the line before Lila's voice broke through.

"N-Nathan, i-it's Lila."

There was something wrong, off in her voice, and I found myself on edge—my body leaned forward, bracing for the impact of her words.

"I-I'm n-not going to-to make it… Oh, God!" she cried out, and I heard the pain and fear. Mine was rising to meet hers. Her speech faltered, and I was unable to make out what she was saying. "Won't…be in…"

"Lila? Lila, are you okay?" My anxiety was skyrocketing faster than my heart rate. Her pain came out in whimpers and gasps. She was having a difficult time breathing.

"So…ung…so much b-blood," she whispered more to herself than to me. "I d-don't know where…w-where it's com-coming from."

Her voice grew in pitch near the end. My stomach dropped, and the blood fled from my face.

"Lila, what happened? Where are you?"

"C-crash. N-not far… St-t-star-b-bucks," she struggled to say.

I jumped up from my chair. Voices of the rescue crew were in the background, asking her questions, gaining vitals. What sounded like a chainsaw started, and I feared they had to cut her out of the wreckage.

Crumpled metal and mangled flesh flashed before my eyes, and a vise formed around my chest then began to tighten.

"Lila! I'll be right there. Do you hear me? Lila!"

There was no response before the line went dead. I slammed the phone down on the receiver and ran out of our office. I rushed to the elevator bay and pushed the down button at a frantic pace in a fruitless effort for it to arrive faster. The doors sprung open, and I barely registered anyone was coming out as I pushed through and entered into the cab.

"Nathan!" Jack's voice rang out, drawing my attention. "Nathan, what's wrong?"

My eyes met his, and I knew he could see the fear and desperation. "Accident. Lila's been in an accident."

His eyes widened, but he remained silent as the doors slid closed. I didn't know how much I had just given away, but at that moment I didn't care; nothing else mattered. I needed to get to Lila. She was all I cared about.

I paced as the elevator descended to the plaza level and dashed out as soon as my body could fit through the gap in the doors.

Panicked, I ran. She was about half a mile away, and I could get there faster on foot.

I had to get to her. I had to tell her. I couldn't lose her.

Please...don't go!

The rain had let up to a sprinkle, but it didn't matter if it was down-pouring; I was too focused on reaching her.

I turned the corner, and it all came into view. Gawkers stood around, blocking me. Police cruisers were everywhere, fire trucks and ambulances, but I couldn't see her car.

I ran up to the line next to a cruiser when it came into view. The sight almost brought me to my knees, and it would have if the need to see her and make sure she was all right hadn't been so great.

It had been a direct hit to the driver's side. It was a crumpled mass of metal that once resembled her sedan. The door had been ripped off, and I could see blood on the upholstery.

That night began to flash again, overlaying on the scene in front of me. Another car, another crumpled, bloody mess, with another woman I loved.

My heart rate increased and my chest tightened with each step forward, my body shaking.

"Hey, hey! You can't enter!" a cop called out to me, stepping in front of me.

"Please, I have to… Lila!" I yelled as I pushed past the officer. "Oh, God. Lila! Love, no! No!"

My vision started to darken, and my heart beat wildly in my ears. It was sprinting. I knew the officer was trying to stop me, but I pressed forward, searching for her. Another officer came up and they tried to restrain me.

"Get your fucking hands off me. That's my girlfriend! Lila!"

An ambulance gurney came into view, and on it laid a woman. Her left hand was lying over the side, limp, stained with red.

"No!" I screamed, my knees buckling. Another image filled my mind, almost an exact parallel from the photo of my wife's hand to Lila's.

The officer attempted to slow my descent to the ground. My heart was beating at a furious pace, my chest caving in to the point that I was grasping, clawing, at whatever was keeping me from breathing. My vision was blurred and getting darker with each beat until I could see no more.

I had a vague feeling of people surrounding me, talking to me, and then I heard a familiar voice, breaking through everything.

"Help him! He's having a panic attack!" Caroline cried out.

I didn't even get to breathe a full breath before I felt a prick in my arm and everything turned black.

IT WAS BRIGHT, SUNNY, AND I HAD TO SHADE MY EYES FROM THE LIGHT. Something stirred at my side, and I looked down to find my Lila snuggled in. Her head tilted up; her intriguing gray-green eyes met mine briefly before snuggling back into my chest. My arm was around her shoulder, and I leaned my head down to breathe her in, kissing the top of her head. I let out a sigh and pulled her closer, reveling in her warmth.

I looked around and found we were outside, lying in the middle of a park, people all around us. People all around, yet there we lay, re-laxed and content. I felt something move on my chest and looked down to find Lila's hand resting over my heart, a diamond glinting from her ring finger, a small band seated just beneath.

I couldn't pull her flush to me, so my gaze moved farther down and saw that her stomach was large and swollen. My hand reached out to rest on her belly. I felt a kick against my palm, and my heart swelled at the feeling of life beneath it. A life we had created.

She shifted and sat up. "Anna!" she called out. "Anna, come back away from the pond!"

I looked to where she called, and my breath caught in my chest.

A small girl, who couldn't be more than four, turned to look at us. Her light brown curls were bouncing as she ran toward us, hands waving in excitement. Her eyes lit up just before she threw her tiny body on top of me.

"Daddy! Daddy! There are fishies in the water!" The joy rolled off her tiny frame, her smile consuming her face.

Her unique gray-green eyes stared up at me, identical in color to Lila's, her hair the same shade of brown as mine. Other elements of Lila could be found in the shape of her lips and the angle of her little nose.

My hand reached out to touch her face, but instead of meeting flesh, my hand fell right through her as she dissipated between my fingers.

The sky turned gray, dark clouds tumbling into view. My gaze turned back to Lila. She was still curled into me, but her body was limp and skinny, no swell in her stomach. I looked to her hand. It was now bare of the rings that had been there, and blood covered her skin.

"Lila," I called to her, shaking her, but she didn't wake. "Lila!"

"Lila!" I cried out. My eyes snapped open, my breathing hard, as I looked at the ceiling. I could hear the beeping of various machines next to me.

I sat up and looked around, trying to orient myself, and recognized my family in the room. My mind fought back, trying to remember how I got there. Visions of Lila's crumpled car, her bloodied hand hanging from the stretcher, came back at once. I swallowed back the bile that rose in my throat as the panic set in again.

I had to find her. I needed to make sure she was all right, that she was…alive. She had to be alive.

Please, she has to be.

I pulled back the sheet and swung my legs over the edge.

There was a tug on my hand, and I ripped the heart monitor from my finger. The machines began beeping wildly, alarms going off.

"Nathan, honey, it's okay. She's alive," I heard my mother say. I could tell by her tone it was a plea in hopes I would calm down, but it didn't work.

I could vaguely hear and see my parents in the room along with Darren, Trent, and Erin. They were talking in whispers, but I couldn't concentrate on that. I had to find her.

Please be okay. Please be alive. Please don't leave me!

"Lila!" I cried out for her, my panic rising.

"She's all right, Nathan," Darren said to me as he stepped to the side of the bed. I didn't believe him, I couldn't. I had to see for myself. I swatted at him, pushing him aside.

My feet landed on the cold floor, and I took a few steps forward before a sharp pain pulled at my wrist. I looked to find an IV line attached in one hand.

"Lila!" I called out again.

"Mr. Thorne, please, lay back down!" a woman in green scrubs directed upon entering my room. I ignored her, pushing past her and out into the hall, the IV tube in my hand as I dragged the stand behind me.

Darren followed behind me, arguing with the nurse; him telling her to let me go, her telling him I was disturbing patients.

I didn't give a fuck if I disturbed patients; *I needed* to find my Lila.

"Lila!" I called again. My chest was throbbing with each step, tears stinging my eyes. She had to be here, somewhere, she just had to be.

"Mr. Thorne! You need to return to your room!" the nurse screeched at me.

"He has to do this, Mary. Just let him go," Darren said to the annoying nurse.

"Lila!"

The IV stand caught on something in the hall, and I pulled on the tube, dislodging it from the bag.

"Don't pull that out!" another nurse scolded as they all chased me down the hall.

"Lila!" I wailed. A sob was growing, about to release while tears began streaming down my face.

I looked into each room, one at a time, the irritating nurses following right behind, yelling at me, threatening me. Darren and my parents then started yelling at them.

"Lila!" I was begging for her to answer, but with each room I came to and didn't find her, my desperation grew.

My heart was hammering in my chest, the ache growing. My vision began to dim again, dread setting in.

I reached a room near the end of the hall and leaned on the frame, bracing myself while my limited vision wildly searched for her.

And then I saw her. She was bandaged and beaten to hell, but she stared back at me with wide-eyed recognition.

My vision returned, and my body relaxed while I took her in. Lila was alive. Thank God, she was alive.

Her eyes met mine, and relief flooded every part of me, tears stinging at my eyes. Joy that my nightmares hadn't come true.

I wasn't too late. I could fix this, fix *us*.

"Lila!"

I stumbled toward her and took her hands in mine as I leaned my forehead against hers. "Oh, thank God. Thank God, you're alive."

I couldn't stop the tears. She was alive, fucking alive.

Every emotion of happiness and relief swept through me. The thought of losing her broke everything open inside me.

No more cages, no more walls. And no more living without her.

"Nathan, what's going on?" she asked, her voice low and mumbled.

I pulled back and looked into her eyes. "You don't remember?"

She shook her head, then winced in pain.

"You were in a very bad accident…" I trailed off, my gaze traveling down her body.

Her leg was all wrong, bent in an unnatural way and swollen. The sound of her breath was labored and uneven. Gauze covered her arm as well as her head, which was probably the source of all the blood she was talking about when she called.

Her face was swollen in a few places, bruises beginning to appear. I ran my hand softly down her cheek, which still caused her to flinch in pain.

"I'm so sorry. This wouldn't have happened if I…" The list was never ending. If I hadn't been attracted to her. If I hadn't taken her. If I hadn't…

"If you *what*?" she spat, her anger surprising me. "Hadn't left me? Broken me? Left me a shell of the paper thin person I already was before you? If that's even possible."

Fuck.

I did all of that.

"All of those. I can't tell you how sorry I am." I could never say it enough, but I could make some of it up with my actions. I would show her.

"You didn't do this physical damage to me. What you did was far worse."

The guilt that weighed me down threatened to consume me. "Please, Lila, please!"

"Please, what?" she yelled.

Please be mine again.

"Please, I'll tell you everything, anything you want to know if you… Can we start over? I need you so much."

She was so angry, so hurt, that I couldn't blame her for lashing out at me. I only asked for a chance, but I could have fucked things up bad enough she wouldn't be willing.

"Why? Why did you leave me if you were going to beg for me back?"

My hands shook as we reached the tipping point. It was now, or she was never going to let me in again. I had to tell her what she never looked up.

"I'm so sorry I did this to you, to *us*. I was trying to protect you, and myself," I said.

"Protect you from what, exactly? What did you need protection from?" she asked.

I swallow hard, my chest so tight trying to keep it all in. "From losing you the same way I lost…my wife."

Her expression flickered, the anger ebbed away, but then bounced back. "And what were you protecting me from?"

"From the Marconi family."

I watched as her eyes widened, indicating she knew exactly who I was talking about. She knew what they could do. I should have told her sooner so she could make her own decision, but I was so adamant about not getting close to her, it didn't matter anyway.

But it did, because I'd found in her something I'd long been missing. Along with things I never had before.

"Why would you need to protect me from the Marconis?"

she asked, bracing herself.

I let out a shuddered breath. "Because if they found out about you, they would kill you like they did her."

She stared at me in shock. "Why did they want to hurt her?"

"They were trying to kill me," I admitted.

"Oh." Her lips formed a thin line.

"I can't let that happen to you," I said, trying to keep her listening, to understand.

Her eyes snapped up to me, and I saw anger flash across them. "So you let me go? Were you ever going to ask me what *I* wanted? Were you ever going to tell me and let *me* decide for myself to risk my life to stay with you or cut all ties? Do you feel anything for me?"

I grabbed her hand. "I feel *so much* for you. I tried to stop it. I knew it could happen with you—I sensed it from the beginning. The pull I feel to you is so strong. I tried to will myself *not* to develop these feelings for you, but you just won't fucking be denied!"

I couldn't escape her if I tried. Somehow, I was always meant to find her.

She shook her head. "I don't understand what the fuck you're saying."

"I'm saying Darren was right. I tried so hard to deny it, to deny *you*, but he saw it. He said I was being selfish by leaving you, that I did it because I didn't want to be hurt again, that I was a coward for it." And I was. Anything to avoid the pain of more loss. "He was right. He saw it from the moment he arrived at the hospital when you were unresponsive."

Her brow scrunched. "Dr. Morgenson? How do you know him, and what did he see?"

I shook my head, my heart racing in my chest. I'd tried to

say it without saying it, but she needed to hear the words. Three words that made her a target.

"Just fucking say whatever it is you're trying to say!" The exertion was too much for her, and she laid her head back down, face twisted in pain.

I stared at her, my mouth opening, then closing, as I tried to get them out. She had to know, had to hear, or there was no way she would let me get close again.

"He knew that I'm in love with you," I said, my voice just above a whisper.

Her eyes widened, locked on mine.

"I love you, Lila," I declared with more volume. "I'm so scared about what that means for you."

A bitter laugh erupted from her clenched teeth, and I flinched at the sound I'd put in her. "You love me? Then why did you leave me?"

"I'm sorry, I…"

"You love me? You're sorry? Do you somehow think that makes everything better?" she screamed.

I flinched. "No."

"Then what, Nathan? What the fuck do you want?" she asked as tears welled in her eyes.

"I…" I trailed off, not knowing the answer myself. I had no plan of action, no idea of what to do.

"Out." She pointed with her undamaged arm.

Ice ran through me. "Wait, Lila, please."

"I said get the fuck out!" she yelled.

Her eyes grew wide, and the beeping of the machines intensified.

I stepped toward her to help, but she turned and growled at me. "No! Out!"

She grabbed the water bottle next to her and threw it. The plastic slammed into my chest, the top popping off, and splashing ice-cold water all over me.

I stared at her in shock, both from the cold and from her reaction, before she screamed out in pain.

"Lila!" I stepped forward as two nurses also entered.

"Mr. Thorne, I need you to return to your room," the surly nurse who had chased me down the hall said with a tug on my arm. "They've got her, don't worry."

I couldn't tear my eyes away. She was in serious pain, and I could do nothing to help her.

Slowly I backed out. I felt numb as the nurse pulled me back down the hall. I gave no resistance because I had no strength of will or body left.

I could feel my family's eyes on me as I lay back down on the bed, the nurse plugging me back into the monitors.

"What are you going to do?" my father asked.

The total time I'd been awake since I received the call from Lila was less than an hour. Meaning, I'd had no time at all to even process what the future held.

"I'm going to get her back," I said. It was the one thing I knew. I couldn't live without her. The past weeks were torture on us both.

She'd lashed out at me, but I couldn't blame her, after everything I'd done, but I could make it up to her.

"Nate..." Darren started, but trailed off.

"Don't start with anything. I'm having a hard enough time trying to process it all."

"You fell in love, honey," Mom said. "It's okay."

"Is it? Or is she another tool for Marconi to destroy me with."

"We're all here for you," Erin said, squeezing my hand. "We're here for both of you."

I smiled at her and nodded.

"I never thought I could love again," I admitted. "And look how I've fucked it up."

No one said anything, which I took as a silent agreement. It was true anyway. Every move I made with Lila was a mistake on how I handled it. I should have agreed to more, to not let my fear cloud my mind of what my heart and my body already knew. Words that I said to her every day—she was mine.

And she was going to be mine forever.

I was determined to be with Lila, no matter what. Somehow, my panic attack served as a dose of clarity for what the beast already knew.

I loved Lila, and I was going to be with her in every way. My fear of the Marconi was still real and tangible, but I wasn't going to let it stop me from living any longer. Lila was life and love, and I wanted to be with her for the rest of days.

Forever with my sex goddess, my Honeybear, my love.

ACKNOWLEDGMENTS

Thank you to everyone that has read and loved Nathan and Lila's story. So many times I've heard that you wanted Nathan's point of view from Breach, but it wasn't until now that story could be told. He was too raw in my mind and I honestly didn't think he'd ever calm down enough to tell it, but he did. So for all of you that wanted more Nathan, this is for you. I hope it's everything you ever hoped for. I love you all for following me on this journey and for taking a chance on me and my stories.

Love,

K.I. Lynn

ABOUT THE AUTHOR

K.I. Lynn is the *USA Today* Bestselling Author from The Bend Anthology and the Amazon Bestsellers, Breach and Becoming Mrs Lockwood. She spent her life in the arts, everything from music to painting and ceramics, then to writing. Characters have always run around in her head, acting out their stories, but it wasn't until later in life she would put them to pen. It would turn out to be the one thing she was really passionate about.

Since she began posting stories online, she's garnered acclaim for her diverse stories and hard hitting writing style. Two stories and characters are never the same, her brain moving through different ideas faster than she can write them down as it also plots its quest for world domination…or cheese. Whichever is easier to obtain… Usually it's cheese.

Website—www.kilynnauthor.com

Facebook—www.facebook.com/kilynn.breach

Twitter—twitter.com/KI_Lynn_

Instagram—www.instagram.com/k.i.lynn

Get my Newsletter—http://bit.ly/1U9NSoC

MORE BOOKS FROM
K.I. LYNN

Welcome to the Cameo Hotel

I get what I want.

When I walked through the door of the Cameo Hotel I didn't expect such a beauty to be working the front desk.

The effect she has on me is intense, and I make her life a living hell because of it.

I love her spirit, her internal defiance when completing the most inane task I assign her. My two week stay has turned into unending, just to be near her.

She's under my every command if she wants to keep me happy.

There's one last thing I want.

Her.

Find out more here
books2read.com/WelcomeToTheCameoHotel

Becoming Mrs. Lockwood

Every girl has dreams of meeting Prince Charming, or at least
I know I did.

A fairy tale-like meeting of love at first site.
Real life and fairy tales are very different.

I'm just a small town Indiana girl that had a chance encounter
with one of Hollywood's golden boys. You may think you know
where this story goes—not even close.

Life is different. Marriage is hard. It's even worse when you're
strangers.

Find out more here:
books2read.com/BecomingMrsLockwood

Six

I had a one-night stand. It wasn't my first, but it would be my last.

A gun to the head.

A trained killer.

A deadly conspiracy.

Kidnapped and on the run, my life and death is in the hands of a sadist captor who happens to be my one-night stand. Armed with countless weapons, money, and new identities, the man I call Six drags me around the world.

The manhunt is on and Six is the next target. Can we find out who is killing off the Cleaners before they find us?

Two down, seven to go.

When it's all over he'll finish the job that dropped him into my life, and end it.

Stockholm Syndrome meets bucket list, and the question of what would you do to live before you died. The questions aren't always answered in black and white. Gray becomes the norm as my morals are tested.

Death is a tragedy, and I'll do anything to stay alive.

Are you ready for the last ride of your life? Six has a gun to your head—what would you do?

This isn't a love story.

It's a death story.

Find out more here: books2read.com/Six-KILynn
Check out the Trailer: youtu.be/fzpON3PadIA

The Executive

Business is king, and I have an empire to topple.

Ivy is my new assistant and a threat to me. She's my undoing. If ever I was to believe in a cosmic connection, it was the moment I met her.

For years I've had one goal--revenge. As CEO, I have crafted a strategic plan for business, but never a life beyond.

With one touch from her, the veil is lifted. Things are different, and every moment I'm near her, my world begins to change.

A wall of propriety keeps me from her. I need her as my pawn in this war, beside me in battle. Sharing the secrets of my enemies, and her desires in my bed. Her body to claim as mine.

Getting what I want has consequences.

Collateral damage is real.

In the game of crushing kings of men, I never planned on my heart being a sacrifice.

Find out more here:
books2read.com/TheExecutive

Cocksure

A life altering lie, ten years, and one wild night later, the game
has changed.

Niko

My life is great. I love my job, have awesome friends, and a great
family.

Women love me, even if they know it's just for a night.

I always thought love at first sight was bullshit. Then she came
storming into my life. She tore through my every rule, rocked
my world, and knocked me on my ass.

There's only one problem…she lied.+

Turns out my best friend's little sister isn't so little anymore.

Everly

I stole a night with my fantasy. Lied to him.

After ten years of not seeing each other, Niko doesn't even
recognize me.

So I take what I want from him, what I need from him. Without
worry. Without consequence.

What I didn't count on was the lingering need for him.

Once the truth is out, the game changes. There are consequences.

I should have known nothing in my life is ever simple.

My brother is going to kill his best friend and I have nine months
to figure out what I want.

 Find out more here: books2read.com/Cocksure-Lynn-Kelley

Need, Book 1

I was Kira's from the first moment I saw her. Maybe it was love at first sight, but I was only ten.

She became my best friend.

My crush.

The girl I can't live without.

But I have to.

She was almost mine, but my father took away my chance.

Now she lives across the hall from me. Instead of the title of girlfriend, she's now my stepsister.

But that doesn't stop how I feel, how I want her. Thankfully, I'm off to college two hundred miles away, but even that doesn't help.

She's under my skin, all around me, and I watch her morph from a sexy teenager to an irresistible woman.

I can't take it anymore, I need her.

Is it possible to ever be happy without the one person you *need*?

"I'm Brayden, baby. The man you've been dreaming about your whole life. And I'm about to fucking show you why."

Part 1 of a 3 part series.

Find out more here: books2read.com/NeedSeries